THE SALVATION MAN

JAMES CARVER

PROLOGUE

The bay was a constellation in miniature. Lights from the boats and fancy yachts were scattered like stars across the gentle water. It was the end of summer, and the village was settling down, like the air being let slowly out of a balloon. The tourists were trickling away, sunburnt, the scent of sunscreen in their noses and sand in their luggage.

For Detective Greg Paladino, sitting in his car in the Baron's Cove parking lot, the beauty of the bay at night had no appeal. His interest was in one particular boat. It was named the *April Rose* and had moored along the pier three days ago.

When Paladino had seen the crew of the *April Rose* coming and going, he suspected it might be a drug operation. And when he recognized a few of the crew as longtime members of the Pagans motorcycle gang, it had pretty much confirmed it for him. Now it was a waiting game. And tonight, he felt sure, was the night.

His cell lit up and pulsed on the console. It was his wife calling. For a moment he thought about answering but decided to let it ring through to voicemail. He wanted like crazy to talk to her. They had married a few months earlier and were still tingling with happiness about it, about being together, about making plans together. But tonight was getting interesting, and he didn't want to miss a thing. Because what Greg was hoping for now was the next link in the chain. The person or persons who took the contraband on the next leg of its journey. When they arrived he could put a tail on them so he'd know who was distributing the drugs inland.

He checked his watch. It was just after eleven. He drummed on the steering wheel and weighed how much longer he should wait. All night and morning? No. He had a life, a new bride at home. A big warm bed. He was conscientious, but he was no hero. He made a deal with himself that he'd give it till three in the morning, and then if nothing had occurred, he'd head home. But after a couple of hours ticked by without any activity, he started to toy with the idea of waiting it out all the way until dawn broke. Then, around half past two, something happened. A black sedan with tinted windows pulled up on the edge of the bay. A tall rake-thin guy in a black suit and an open-necked shirt got out and pulled an empty black duffel bag from the trunk. The guy took a look around, locked the car, and headed out along the jetty into the harbor.

It was deadly quiet, and the road along the bay was empty but for the very occasional passing vehicle. Once in a while, a car would roar at high speed along the front, most likely kids taking advantage of the late hour and the open road. But Greg Paladino wasn't here to hand out speeding tickets to local youths. He got out of his car and slowly walked across the road to get a better look at the sedan. He made a mental note of the license plate and then walked along the edge of the harbor wall, the gentle salt breeze on his face, squinting out into the bay.

The tall guy in the suit strode along the jetty swinging his empty bag by his side. He turned down a gangway, climbed onto the deck of the *April Rose*, then disappeared down below.

Greg weighed whether to radio for backup. Maybe he should wake Harrigan, the other Sag Harbor detective, and tell him to haul ass down here. But then he thought better of it. Harrigan wouldn't thank him for jumping the gun. Better to sit tight for a while.

He stood with a foot on the edge of the harbor wall, the water gently licking against the concrete a couple of feet below. He took out a small set of binoculars from his jacket, watching intently for the guy in the suit to reappear. His attention was lasered in on the boat, to the exclusion of everything else.

Greg was so preoccupied that he didn't hear the gull cry as it swooped overhead. He didn't hear the cry and curse of a drunk a block away. And he didn't hear the rev of a car half a mile down the road as it shifted from third up into fourth and then into fifth gear. He paid no attention to the climbing pitch of the engine as it strained to accelerate and bore down West Water Street, dismissing it as another speed-freak kid. He couldn't have known that the vehicle he hadn't seen approaching was stolen. That the driver of the vehicle had had two plans in mind when, only hours earlier, he drove it off the forecourt of a complex of vacation apartments in East Hampton. Plan A had been the pistol stowed under the driver's seat. But that plan had been ditched in favor of plan B, which the driver was executing now.

The driver pressed the pedal to the floor and jacked up the piece-of-crap Japanese radio that was blaring out a grindcore track full of rasping vocals, thrashing discordant guitars, and relentless beats. As the 2008 Toyota Land Cruiser approached the lonely figure of the detective looking out to sea, the driver couldn't believe his luck. He couldn't believe how Greg Paladino didn't think, until it was too late, until the last seconds of his life were ticking down, that the car tearing up the road was headed straight for him.

The front left wheel ricocheted off the curb onto the thin strip of sidewalk, and the grill caught its victim head-on, tossing him in the air, body and limbs rolling and flapping out of control. The driver turned the wheel hard and swung back down onto the blacktop. The sense of accomplishment the driver felt was immense. He'd been traveling at over sixty miles an hour and was as sure as he could be that no one would survive a head-on collision at that speed.

True, he hadn't seen where the body had landed, whether it had been tossed into the sea or onto the road, but he was damned sure he'd left a corpse and a widow behind.

ONE

Ten Months Later

"WHOA, slow it down, we'll overshoot." Detective Harrigan raised a hairy hand.

Officer Holly Paladino squinted and craned over the steering wheel. "I can't see an entrance. Why isn't this place on the goddamned satnav? How did anyone even find it, let alone break in?"

"It ain't Walmart for crying out loud."

"What the hell is it?"

"Far as I'm concerned, it's a huge pain in the ass. I said, slow it down, Paladino. You drive like this all the time?"

Paladino didn't answer. She was a good driver, but she felt nervous driving her boss around. Not just because it was her boss. More because it was Harrigan.

"There's a turn in there," said Harrigan, pointing to a dirt drive with a small lit-up sign planted by the roadside.

Paladino slowed so they could take a closer look at the sign.

"BioGenesis Industries," said Paladino. "That's the place."

They turned off, drove up a narrow track canopied by sycamore and mulberry trees, and came to a barrier. Paladino buzzed on the intercom and the barrier went up. The cruiser was let in without any questions. They parked in a well-lit courtyard between three large buildings that sprawled out in a U shape. The buildings, sleek and each a dozen stories high, looked like they'd been built recently and cost hadn't been an issue. As the two officers got out of their car, a security guard in a black uniform approached. Harrigan snorted out a laugh and shouted, "Jessop, you useless fat jerk."

"Hey, Curtis," replied the security guard sheepishly.

"You working here now?"

"Sure am. Head of security."

"No wonder you got broke into. Well, New York's finest's gain is BioGenesis's loss, I guess. Your pension not keeping the first and second wives happy?"

"You gotta do what you gotta do."

"Holly Paladino, this is Farley Jessop, one of the laziest, worst officers I ever worked with. Apart from you of course. We were in Montauk together."

"Hey, Holly." Farley reached out a hand, and they shook.

Harrigan took a moment to take in the hi-tech looking complex that was well hidden from the road and passing traffic.

"Some place you got here."

"Yeah, it's part of a big pharma multinational. Big bucks, Curtis. Big bucks."

"So what happened?"

"B and E in our research office. The alarm went off about midnight, and we found someone had tried to break in through a window. Nothing taken though. We searched the surrounding woodland. One of the guards thought he saw a guy running out into the road and getting into a sedan."

"Any description?"

"He said it was dark and couldn't be sure what he saw. But he said it looked like a big guy, six foot plus."

"You got any CCTV?"

"Yeah, we checked, but we didn't catch anything. The one covering the area where it happened was out of commission. Bad cables. The boss is furious about it. Especially as the whole place is new, the complex was only completed six months ago."

"Who's the boss?"

Just as Harrigan asked the question, the main door of the middle building opened and a slim, tall figure in a suit stepped into the courtyard. Farley looked around at the man walking toward them and then back at Harrigan.

"I think you're about to find out."

"Hello, Officers," said the man as he walked into the glare of the courtyard lights. "I'm Andrei Gromyko, the owner of BioGenesis." His tone was edgy, irritated. He had fine sandy hair, high cheekbones, an angular jaw, and pale green eyes behind round rimless glasses. Harrigan and Paladino introduced themselves, and Andrei turned to his head of security.

"I take it you've told the officers what happened here tonight?"

"Yes, yes I have, sir."

"You know," said Andrei, focusing his annoyance on Harrigan and Paladino, "that this is the second attempted break-in we've had? Two in as many months. Why aren't there patrols up this way? Where are all the police?"

Paladino noticed that Andrei Gromyko's accent, although American, had an edge to it. Every so often a vowel would give away an Eastern European sound.

"We're doing our best, sir," said Harrigan, in a conciliatory tone that surprised Paladino. "Unfortunately, there's a budget freeze at the sheriff's office and we're having to split this area between us and East Hampton PD."

"I don't care about the politics. I still pay the same taxes, Detective. I expect to be able to conduct my business in peace and security. I want this road patrolled more frequently. At least daily."

"That's a promise I can't make, I'm afraid, sir."

"Well, who can?"

"The chief of police and the mayor would need to make a—"

"For God's sake." Andrei shook his head and sighed. "Then I'll speak to them. And I'd ask you to pass my request up the line to your senior officer too. Good night."

He turned without waiting for a reply and headed back into the building.

"Well, screw him too," said Harrigan. "Is he a Russki or what?"

"Belarus. I think," replied Farley.

"Wherever he's from, I suppose at least I don't have to work for that dumbass. Like you do."

Paladino wanted badly to correct Harrigan and tell him that, as a police officer, he did in fact work for Andrei, but kept quiet.

"I better go back in and try and calm him down," said Farley anxiously.

"Good luck with that," replied Harrigan. "This guy thinks he can order a personal patrol? What next? He asks for his own personal police service? Moron."

"He's pretty good at getting what he wants, Curtis," said Farley. "And he has a point. There is a problem with too few patrols now the sheriff's office is getting cut back."

Harrigan stared at Farley long and hard, causing Farley to drop his gaze.

"Well, that's real interesting, Farley. I really want to hear your opinions on policing. Especially seeing as you had to leave the force due to various issues with your own unique performance failures."

"Oh, come on, Curtis..." began Farley.

"No, you come on, Farley," said Harrigan, stepping up close to the head of security. "You start giving me advice on my police force and I'll start giving advice to your boss on the extremely patchy nature of your service record. You got that?"

"Yeah, yeah... Sure, Curtis. Whatever you say."

"You bet whatever I say."

Back on the Turnpike, heading toward Sag Harbor village, Paladino drove in silence, only looking forward to getting back to the precinct and out of Harrigan's company. Truth was though, she wasn't that enthusiastic for any company but her own. Conversation took so much effort these past months. When she was around other people, she still felt isolated. Like she was underwater and other people's words and faces were distant and blurred.

Up ahead, a long, sleek limo with tinted windows was coming the other way. The limo's high beams lit up the two police officers momentarily and then plunged them back into the dark.

"That's the third limo I've seen tonight heading out of town. I wonder where they're all going to?"

"Who knows, Paladino? Who knows? This place is crawling with rich folk."

Harrigan yawned and stretched as much as he was able to in the confines of the cruiser. Then he scratched his belly and yawned again, and Paladino smelled the vapors of his last beer over the pungent notes of his cut-price aftershave—the last of his customary four or five beers he'd taken at the Bay Tavern before he'd come out on patrol with her.

As they hit the crossroads where the Turnpike hit Swamp Road, Paladino spotted a lone figure walking along the shoulder.

She slowed to take a better look and saw that the figure was male, well over six feet and big with it.

"Hey," said Paladino, braking and pointing across the intersection. "You see that guy over there? He could be a match for the break-in."

"Yeah," said Harrigan, leaning his bulk forward and peering over the dash. "Pull over."

Paladino flashed on the light bar and swung to a stop about ten yards ahead of the man. The two officers exchanged glances, and Harrigan checked his watch.

"Two o'clock in the morning," he said. "Funny goddamned time to be taking a walk down the Turnpike."

The officers got out of the car and waited as the figure approached them. Paladino could see now that he was around six three or four, broadly built, and had a bag slung over his shoulder. He was unshaven, had thick black hair that was pushed back from his temples and a little wild, and he wore a black jacket and pants and a white collar. A priest's collar.

"What the hell is this?" muttered Harrigan. "We got a priest walking about at two in the morning."

"Officers." The man had stopped short of Harrigan and Paladino. "Can I help?"

"You got any ID?" asked Harrigan bluntly.

"Sure." The priest dropped his bag, pulled out a wallet, and handed over his driver's license. Harrigan looked it over.

"Father Gabriel Devlin," said Harrigan, looking Devlin up and down, and handed the ID back. As he did, another vehicle passed through the deserted crossroads. A limousine. Paladino watched it go by.

"You've seen them too?" said the priest.

"Huh?" replied Paladino.

"The limos. They seem to be out in force tonight and headed in the same direction. Somewhere outside the village."

"It's a rich town," said Paladino flatly. "Especially in summer."

"Can you tell me where you've been tonight?" asked Harrigan.

"I was dropped off by an acquaintance a way back and was headed for Sag Harbor."

"Who's the acquaintance?"

"A truck driver I met in Montauk who was heading west."

"What's your business in Sag Harbor?"

"Looking up an old friend."

"Who?"

"Father Vijay Aranha at St. Michael's Church. Is there a problem, Officer?"

"We had a break-in nearby. Got a description that matches you."

"Well, it ain't me. I haven't been breaking in anywhere."

"You got any witnesses to say otherwise?"

The priest paused for a moment. "I guess not. But I don't go around making sure I have witnesses just in case I get stopped by the police."

There was a silence as the two men regarded each other. Paladino could see Harrigan sizing up this guy. Wondering whether to press his buttons or not. The lull was broken by the police radio crackling into life in the cruiser and the monotonous, nasal whine of dispatch.

"Update on the Turnpike break-in. Description given of male leaving property is over six foot and bald. I repeat...suspect is bald."

The priest gave the slightest of smiles. "You wanna check if I'm wearing a hairpiece, Officer?"

"No," said Harrigan. "I want you to get in the back of the car so you aren't wasting police time walking the backroads of the Hamptons in the middle of the night for no good reason. I want to make sure you get to wherever it is you're going."

Harrigan opened the rear door, but Devlin didn't move.

"It isn't a crime to walk around at night, is it?"

"This is my town. It's a quiet place, and I like it that way. Get in the car or I'll take you down the station."

"For what exactly?"

"Who is it you're staying with in Sag Harbor?" asked Paladino, looking to defuse things. "We can give you a lift there. If you like."

Harrigan shot Paladino a hard stare.

"Well, now, if you put it that way, Officer, I'd be much obliged."

IT TOOK HALF a dozen presses on the doorbell to get a response, but eventually Devlin heard shambling feet coming down the stairs and saw a silhouette through the frosted glass pane. The door opened to reveal Father Vijay Aranha, a small, potbellied man with a thick mop of gray-and-black hair standing at the door to the St. Michael's rectory. His hair was messed up, a couple of tufts stuck up from the crown, and he wore a robe and slippers.

"Gabe...?" said Aranha. "It's three thirty in the morning. I mean, I knew you weren't sure when you were going to arrive, but this is crazy..."

He looked over Devlin's shoulder and spotted Detective Harrigan looking out of the open window of the patrol car.

"What are the police doing here?"

"That's the reason I came this late. I was going to wait till the morning to come over, but they picked me up walking into Sag Harbor and insisted on dropping me off."

Aranha looked Devlin up and down, and he was suddenly

aware of his shabby appearance: unshaven, unkempt, and a little ragged from lack of sleep. The last time he'd showered was a couple of nights ago when he'd been staying in a dingy motel. A place that could still charge two hundred bucks a night because it was the height of the season.

"I know, I know, Vijay, I've looked better. The detective wants to know I've got somewhere to stay for the night. That's why he's hanging around."

"Very conscientious, I must say." Aranha smiled and waved at Harrigan and shouted, "It's all okay, Detective. I know Father Devlin very well."

This seemed to satisfy Harrigan, who gave a nod and a friendly wave. The patrol car started up, and he took off down the empty street.

"You know him?" asked Devlin.

"The detective? Only to say hello to. This is all you have?" Aranha was eyeing Devlin's bag.

Devlin shrugged. "I guess I should have planned better."

Aranha shook his head and tutted. "What on earth has happened to you, Gabe? You look a mess. You get picked up in the middle of the night in the middle of nowhere like a hobo. And the things I've heard, rumors that you left your church suddenly, disappeared. I've even heard you had a breakdown, were committed to a sanatorium, all sorts."

"Well, you know how priests gossip."

Aranha didn't look satisfied with Devlin's glib reply and impatiently ushered him in. He led Devlin along the hallway and into the kitchen. Devlin sat at the kitchen table, and Aranha set about making a pot of tea.

Father Aranha placed the cups of tea on the table and took a gulp.

"It's wonderful to see you, Gabe."

"You too, Vijay."

"When was the last time we saw each other? Five years ago?"

"Yeah. Must be."

"How did we let so much time pass?"

"Life, I guess."

"Well, we shouldn't have left it so long." Aranha stared down into his cup. "After all, if it wasn't for you, I probably wouldn't be here now. You talked me back into the priesthood when I thought I wasn't up to it. You were the one who took the time to talk me through my doubts and out the other side. The right side. I can't thank you too many times."

"I only did what a priest should."

"No. You did it in a way other priests wouldn't have been capable of. You live through your spirit in a way few others do, or can. And the faith you helped me hold on to has kept me afloat."

Aranha's lips twitched into a faint smile, but a pain seemed to pass behind his eyes.

"Are you okay, Vijay? Is everything okay with you?"

"Fine. Just fine. Now, what about you? What's going on with you?"

Aranha was watching Devlin carefully for his reply. He leaned his elbows on the table and clasped his hands.

"I'm curious. Why are you here in Sag Harbor of all places, Gabe?"

Devlin sighed, not knowing how to answer Aranha's question, not knowing where to begin, or even whether to begin at all. "I'm not sure you'd believe me if I told you."

"Try me."

Devlin could feel his defenses begin to weaken under his friend's gaze. He felt a sudden need to let everything out, to not have to hold the fantastic events of the last few months in his head anymore, to not have to be alone with the burden that he carried.

"Okay then. I will."

And so Devlin told Aranha everything. From the call he'd got from his friend Ed saying he was in trouble to the race to find Ed's killers and the killers of the young farmhands in Ohio right through to the discovery of the organ transplant business and the standoff with Clay Logan at the ranch. By the time Devlin had finished recounting his recent past, Aranha was wide-eyed and slack-jawed. Then the questions came, Aranha asking the hows and whys of it all. Finally, Aranha seemed as satisfied as he was ever going to be with a story like Devlin had to tell.

"Dear God, Gabe. That's extraordinary. What you've been through... But it still doesn't explain why you're here."

"Believe it or not, the reason I'm here may be even harder for you to understand."

"I really can't imagine how."

"Well then, you'd better brace yourself." Devlin took a breath and said a quick and silent prayer to himself. What he was about to say would likely shake the foundation of the two men's friendship. "Not long ago, before I got to Ohio, I tracked down the man who murdered Jane, and our child she was carrying. He'd been released from prison, and I...I killed him."

Aranha became still, so still Devlin wasn't even sure if he was breathing. The kitchen itself seemed to freeze in time in the wake of Devlin's admission.

"And I refused to repent his death," continued Devlin. He wasn't going to sugarcoat this; it was after all the core of his story, his rebirth, and purpose. "He, the man who murdered my wife, Felix Lemus, would appear in my dreams every night asking if I was ready to repent his murder. And each time I said no. As punishment for my sin, he said I would be cursed, outcast into the wilderness, and that wherever I went evil would rise to meet me. He named me 'Azazel' after the outcast demon. And he showed me a symbol, a symbol that I subsequently found on the body of Clay Logan, on a pillbox he was carrying, and that led me to Montauk and then to Sag Harbor... I know, Vijay—I'm at least sane enough to know that this sounds like the ravings of a madman..."

Aranha nodded solemnly. "It's okay, Gabe. I believe you."

Devlin felt moved almost to tears that his friend had taken his words as truth, and a great catharsis, a lightening of the immense load he'd been carrying for so long.

"Thank you. You have no idea how much that means to me."

"But," Aranha began, his features hardening, "I obviously can't agree with what you did. The taking of a man's life, even if he did murder your wife, is the most serious matter there is in the eyes of the law and God."

"I made my choice. I will need to live with it. I believe that I'm being punished for it. But, to be clear, I don't regret it and never will."

"I honestly don't know how to feel about that. It's not something that I can accept, morally, whether you feel you are being punished or not." Aranha took a drink from his cup, placed it on the table, and ran a finger around the rim. "What now? What will you do? How will you live with what you've done? With this...curse?"

"I have to atone. That's what I believe anyway. I will not ever repent the murder of my wife's killer, so I will live as an outcast, following the path that I believe is being laid down for me. And that's why I'm here. I'm going where the symbol leads me, the one that Felix Lemus showed me, and that I found on Clay Logan."

"That's an awful lot of faith to place in one little thing."

"Yeah, I can see how it looks that way."

"What does it look like, this symbol?"

Devlin reached into his pocket and pulled out the silver pillbox he'd taken from Clay Logan's body in Halton Springs. He gave it to Aranha, who studied it.

"I want to find where it's from. I think that's what's being asked of me. I tracked it down to a jeweler in Montauk, and all he could tell me was it was ordered from someone in Sag Harbor. But he didn't know who."

"How very mysterious..." Aranha had been twirling the tube in his fingers and paused when he spotted the design on the side, the snake wrapped around the bough.

"Have you seen the design before?"

"No." Aranha shook his head. "No, I haven't."

"It looked like you recognized it."

"No, Gabe. I've never seen it before. I was just taken by the design. It's a pretty little thing." He pushed the pillbox back across the table to Devlin as if it were nothing to do with him. "It's an extraordinary story, Gabe. And I do believe you even if I have the most serious reservations about your actions."

"Thank you." Devlin pocketed the pillbox. "Look, while I'm here I can help out, Vijay. Any way you want. I could take mass, or whatever's helpful."

Aranha hesitated for a moment. Clearing his throat, he looked directly at Devlin.

"Gabe, after what you've admitted to me, I don't think it's appropriate that you take mass."

Devlin felt a hot stab in his heart. "Yes, of course."

"I've known you for a long time, Gabe. I owe you a great deal, and it torments me to say this, but I don't feel I can even give you shelter here, knowing what you've done. It would be... sinful. Really, I should call the police right away, that's what I should do."

"If that's what you feel you should do, then yes, you should."

Aranha clenched a fist and looked up at the ceiling despairingly.

"Why, Gabe? Why did you tell me all of this? Put me in this impossible position?"

"Because you're my friend. And because I'm not ashamed of what I've done. What I had to do. What I will have to do."

"That is the problem, not the answer. Shame is not a bad thing. It's what drives a man to repent, drives him back to God." Aranha shut his eyes and shook his head slowly. "I won't go to the police, God forgive me. I can't bring myself to do that to you. You had your wife and child taken from you—I can't even imagine that order of pain. But...but you must find somewhere else to stay while you're here. You may stay until you have a place to go to. That's as much as I can offer and more than I should."

"I understand. I'll start looking for a place first thing."

The two men stayed up a little longer. But silences loomed and eventually they both admitted that tiredness had defeated them. Aranha showed Devlin up to the loft above the rectory where he would sleep.

TWO

Devlin awoke abruptly with a knot in his stomach. A dreaded sense of something just out of reach. For a moment he didn't recognize the room he'd woken up in. Then he remembered the truck journey back from Montauk, the ride in the cop car to St. Michael's, and the painful conversation with his old friend.

He looked around the room and studied it in the morning light. It had one bedroom with an iron-frame bed, a tiny, basic kitchen, and a bathroom with a shower that mostly ran tepid water. The walls were white and bare, the only decoration a heavy wooden cross hung above the head of the bed.

It was not long after first light. Devlin pulled back the sheets, pivoted out of bed, and parted the drapes to view the rooftops of the town and the vast tract of deep blue sky above. The air from the open window had a salt tang to it, and the heat was already beating down.

On the top of the nightstand were his crucifix, his rosary, a half-smoked cigar stubbed out in a saucer, and the silver pillbox. Devlin picked up the pillbox and twirled it in his hands, studying the motif of the snake and the tree on the side. He was no expert in these things, but to his eyes at least the craftsmanship was exceptional. The body of the snake was a striking ultra-marine color and ever so slightly raised up from the surface; it had been executed intricately and with a perfect line. The eyes were minuscule almond-shaped pieces of black jet and had been expertly inlaid and surrounded by a gold outline that was thinner than a hair. The tree that the snake entwined was a willowy jade silhouette. He read the inscription: *Montauk Jewelers. East Hampton.* Along with the hallmark, it was the only information the pillbox had yielded. Using that information, he'd tracked down the Montauk jeweler, but the only clue the septuagenarian storekeeper could provide was a scrap of paper from an old order book, damaged by floodwater and mostly illegible. On the scrap of paper, only two words were readable: *Sag Harbor.*

Devlin opened his left hand and studied his palm. The wound Packer had given him back in Halton Springs was now a bright red stain with a ridge of rough flesh where the skin had knitted back together. When he flexed it, there was still an ache, but despite the unsightly scar, it had healed better than he'd ever expected, and the aches that had riddled his body after the events in Ohio seemed to have lifted with remarkable speed.

Devlin lit the cigar stub and felt his chest bake up. Then he went into the kitchen to make coffee, and after it had percolated, he let it stand while he knelt by the unmade bed and prayed the Office of Readings and the Morning Prayer.

Before he had left Devlin to get some sleep, Father Aranha, conscientious as ever, had given Devlin the four-volume Breviary with the correct pages ribboned. Maybe it was out of hospitality but more likely it was because Aranha feared for Devlin's mortal soul after hearing what he'd done. He played last night's conversation through again and felt the heavy sadness of a friendship altered and likely damaged beyond repair. Devlin could only hold out the slimmest hope that maybe in time Father Aranha would see things the way he saw them.

After prayers, Devlin showered, shaved, and put on his clothes, then went down into the main part of the house. He found Father Aranha in the kitchen cooking bacon and eggs.

"Breakfast?" Aranha asked, though the offer came without a smile.

"Sure."

Devlin set the table while the bacon popped and hissed on the stove. Aranha dished out the food, and they prayed and tucked in. After only a few mouthfuls, Aranha's cell began to ring in his pocket. He dropped his knife and fork and thrust his hand into his pocket and pulled out the cell, holding the screen up close so he could study the number. Devlin watched his friend's face darken with tension as he registered the number and decided not to answer and waited for the call to ring off. Then, he placed his cell down next to his plate and looked up at Devlin, giving him a brief, forced smile as if to reassure him all was well. He picked his cutlery up again and resumed eating.

"Everything okay, Vijay?"

"Absolutely. Just got the routine with the bishop today which is always testing."

"You know, about last night. Whatever's been said, whatever happens, I'll always be here to help in any way you need. Always."

"I don't need any help, Gabe," said Aranha curtly. "I'm absolutely fine."

AFTER BREAKFAST, Devlin went to the nine-o'clock mass which Aranha took. There was a healthy turnout. Even taking into account it was the height of the season, it was a congregation most priests would envy. And not only was it a large congregation, it was a wealthy congregation too. Lots of folk in crisp shirts, expensive shoes, and designer dresses. Devlin bet that Father Aranha didn't have much of a problem fundraising in this neck of the woods.

When it came to communion, Devlin didn't approach the altar. It would not be right to place Father Aranha in such an impossible position.

As Aranha wound up the mass, Devlin wondered if, under that sober and precise performance, there was something else going on with Father Aranha. He sensed a nervousness, a vulnerability. Devlin wasn't sure whether it was his imagination, but throughout the mass, Aranha's eyes flitted from one congregant to another, searching the crowd, as if on the lookout for someone in particular.

After mass, and after Aranha had mingled with the congregation, they walked back to the rectory in silence. While Aranha changed out of his vestments, Devlin wandered into the study and perused the bible on his desk. It was open at the book of Psalms. One Psalm in particular had been asterisked with a light pencil. Devlin read the first line aloud to himself.

"Behold, You desired that truth be in the hidden places, and in the concealed part You teach me wisdom."

Devlin turned to see Aranha standing in the doorway, listening.

"Psalm 51," said Devlin.

"Yes, the years pass and I keep returning to it." Aranha paused, looked thoughtful for a moment, and said, "Do you think truth is in the hidden places, Gabe?"

"I do."

"Why?"

"Because if the truth were easy to apprehend, then you and I would be out of a job."

Aranha laughed out loud and seemed surprised by his own

laughter, and it suddenly struck Devlin that Aranha might not have laughed in a long time.

Aranha pointed to the bible. "It's a valued possession. King James. Given to me by my late mother. Whichever page it's opened at is where my mind last was. Or is. What are your plans for today?"

"I'm going to take look around the village today and find somewhere else to stay."

"Places are very expensive here, I'm afraid."

"I bet."

Aranha bowed his head in the doorway, avoiding Devlin's eyes. "I'm sorry, Gabe, but you must know that after what you told me last night, what you did, I don't feel I have any alternative."

"I do."

Together they walked out into the lot behind the church where people were streaming in and out of the church hall. Those coming out of the hall were carrying full grocery bags.

"You got a food pantry here?" asked Devlin.

"Absolutely. As you can see, it's well attended. I have a team of volunteers who practically run it for me."

"It's a contradiction, isn't it? You having such a well-heeled congregation and then this food pantry being so busy?"

"The way I see it, I do what I can to make the one pay for the other. Bring a little more balance to the world."

"Sure, I guess I didn't..."

Devlin didn't get to finish his sentence because at that exact moment he saw the sign he'd been searching for, the one he'd seen in his dream, that had been imprinted on Clay's pillbox, the sign he'd almost lost faith in. And it was swinging from the neck of a young Latina girl, not older than fifteen, who had come riding off the street and toward the church hall.

THREE

The kid was skinny and short. She had an uneven fringe and long, dark brown tangled hair that rose up on the still summer air and rested and bunched on her shoulders. She'd picked up a few things at the food pantry that she'd stuffed into a saddlebag and was in the middle of making her errand for the day. Cycling at breakneck speed, she beat down on the pedals, moving between cars like a breeze until the traffic began to slow into a solid jam. She braked and turned her bike from the road onto the sidewalk. Gliding at a steadier pace, she wound through crowds of tourists milling aimlessly about, dazed and softened by the long heat of the day.

Mostly people didn't notice her. She was fifteen, but she looked younger in her hooded top, bootcut jeans, and no makeup. Her confidence, purpose, and a hardness she shouldn't yet possess carried her along, in and out of the world of grown-ups.

A burst of siren broke the easy rhythm of the street, and a red flash split the dusk light on the storefronts. The girl's eyes flicked back and forth, light and quick, scanning the drag. Farther up Main Street, she saw the crowds parting on the crosswalk, revealing the blue-and-white livery of a Sag Harbor police car. The cruiser bullied its way through the gridlock and moved slowly in her direction.

Seeing the police car caused the kid to stop hard so that people walking toward her and following behind had to sidestep around and shuffle past. She threw a look over her shoulder, but there wasn't time to backtrack. The cop car had begun to speed up. A line of parked cars gave the girl cover and thirty seconds or so thinking time. She hesitated a fraction longer, then scooted down an alleyway between a pizza place and a bakery, following a high limewash wall with green netting tied along the top. At the end of the alley, the wall doglegged around into a parking lot. The kid checked there was no one about, no staff taking a smoke break out the back of the pizza kitchens. Then she got off the bike, swung it on top of a metal dumpster backed against the limewash wall, and lifted herself up so she stood on top of the wall. A stench of rotting meat and vegetables hung heavy above the dumpster in the warm, still air. Swatting away flies, she looked over the netting and saw the other side was a shorter drop into another parking lot. She lifted the bike over the netting and let it down as far as her arms could reach, dropping it the last couple of feet onto the concrete. The bike bounced on its tires a few times and fell on its side. Holding the netting down, she swung one leg over and then the other and jumped. She landed in a crouch, sprung up, righted her bike, and got back on the saddle, speeding into Church Street, a quiet back road, one way and narrow.

She cycled along Church Street, which was parallel to Main Street, in the same direction she'd been going before the cop car had turned up. Casting glances from side to side and backward as she went, she felt a tiny victory swell in her. The victory of someone who's beaten the system. Beaten the man.

Just as she got to the corner of Church Street and Sage

Street, a black convertible Volkswagen Polo with the roof down rode out in front of her and slammed to a stop. She recognized the car and the occupants instantly. Her victory evaporating fast, she muttered a curse, braked and swung the front wheel around, and headed back the way she came. A shout came from behind her, but her instincts had taken over and she was already working the pedals as hard as she could, having to build speed again, her heart knocking fast against her small chest. She heard a car door slam shut, followed by the sound of heavy, fast beats of sneakers against hot, soft-in-the-heat asphalt. The beats got faster and faster and closer and closer. Not far ahead, she could see the entrance to the alleyway that led back into Main Street. As she got ready to swerve hard to the left, a terrific force hammered into her back, taking her off her bike and down onto the blacktop. By instinct, she managed to get her arms in the way of the ground before it collided with her face and lay panting and defeated, trapped under a larger body that reeked of leather, stale sweat, and Tommy Hilfiger cologne. Hot bursts of breath spread over the back of her neck and filled her with revulsion.

"You thought you'd outrun me? I don't think so."

She was rolled over onto her back, her arms pinned down on the road by two large hands. The face of a teenage boy, seventeen or eighteen, leered down at her. He was square-jawed and blond-haired. Lean and strong with a deep midsummer tan. He sniffed and swallowed and licked his lips. There was a sheen of sweat on his face, and his jaw was clenched hard. Something narcotic, coke or speed, was surging through him. A strand of spit began to descend slowly from his pursed, full lips. She moved her face from side to side and shrieked. The saliva landed on her cheek, and she shook and squirmed furiously. The boy laughed. From behind him came another howl of laughter which the girl recognized as belonging to the boy's friend.

"You going up to Suffolk Street, little girl?" said the boy.

"Get off me."

"We've been watching you. We know that's where you're going. We know that's where you get the good stuff. We want you to get us some."

"Leave me alone."

"You thought you could keep it all to yourself? No, no, no. You're just a tiny fish in a town full of sharks, baby. So tell us, how do we get in on the action?"

The girl stopped squirming. She could feel the disgusting sensation of warm spit rolling off her cheek and across her ear. She needed to get away from this boy. She needed to get out of his clutches as fast as she could.

"You'll have to go up and see Harris yourself," she said. "I can put in a good word if you like..."

This seemed to mollify the boy, and his grip loosened a little. "Okay...yeah... Do that... What do we say to him?"

"Say Tinky sent you."

"Tinky?"

"That's what they call me there."

The boy chuckled. "Okay, Tinky. You have a word with Harris ASAP."

"I will...but you need to let me go... Let me go, you jerk."

"Now, now. That's no way to talk to your elders and betters. Maybe we should take you with us in the car. Drive out to Two Holes of Water and throw you in the river. No one would know, would they? No matter how long you were gone."

"I'd know," said a new voice that was low and rumbling and caused the boy to startle and look up.

"What the hell...?" Ahead of him, standing in the road, was a tall, broad man in a faded blue sweatshirt, black linen pants, and canvas sneakers. He had a cross hung around his neck. The boy glanced over his shoulder at his friend, who was looking a little freaked-out that he hadn't seen the man arrive—it was like he'd dropped out of the sky. The girl struggled, but the boy hardened his grip again, causing the girl to yell out in pain. Then the boy looked back at the man again, this weathered, beaten-looking man in thrift store clothes.

"This is nothing to do with you," said the boy. "Walk away now before me and my friend here beat the living crap out of you, old man."

But Devlin didn't go anywhere. He stayed still. Unnaturally still.

"Let the girl go," he said. "You're hurting her."

The boy shook his head, laughed, sniffed, and swallowed. "This is your last warning. You'd better get lost right now."

"Let's skip the warnings. Get off the girl."

The boy looked back at his friend again, who shook his bleach-blond surfer locks and laughed. Then he got up on his feet, sniffing and clenching.

"You dumb loser," sneered the boy. Standing up to his full height, he was about six two, two hundred pounds, and brimming with all the swagger of someone who had stimulants and youth powering through his veins. The girl, released from the boy's grasp, scrambled away, but the boy swung a hand out and caught the back of her head, sending her flying back onto the ground.

"It's all coming back to you," said Devlin. "All the pain you make. It's all coming back to you."

"It's coming to you first." The boy rushed at Devlin, all two hundred pounds of spite and craziness, but a large, hard, rock-like object hammered into his neck and sent him spluttering back, choking and panting frantically for breath. Through watering eyes, the boy saw the man lowering his outstretched fist. The same fist that, like the man himself, seemed to have come out of nowhere. For a split second, the boy thought his windpipe had collapsed until air finally rushed back into his lungs, and he heaved a stripe of puke onto his front.

The boy's friend had stayed out of the fray, had watched it all play out and silently made his own decision not to try his luck.

"Walk away," said Devlin. "Trust me. I've done a lot more of this than you."

The boy's stooped shoulders lifted and fell as he fought off nausea and the pain in his throat. The drugs had turned on him —all of a sudden he was shivering and afraid. Shivering on a hot evening in late July.

"I gotta go anyway," said the boy, unsteadily getting back on his feet and scraping around for his dignity. "But I'll find you again and I'll kill you—I swear I'll rip you up. I promise you."

The two boys backed off, then turned to walk back to their car, shooting each other recriminating looks.

The girl had stood up and was holding her bike close to her side. She looked at Devlin and frowned.

"I know you," she said. "I saw you at the food pantry. Are you following me?"

"No."

She wasn't convinced. "I don't need someone to watch over me."

"I wasn't watching over you. I happened to be passing."

"I can look after myself, you know. I know those guys— they're idiots, but they're harmless."

"Sure. That's what I thought. Harmless."

There was a silence, and the girl realized that Devlin wasn't looking at her face anymore. For a second she thought maybe he was a creep, after the usual thing creeps his age were after. Then she realized he was looking at the pendant she wore around her neck. The girl clasped her hand around the pendant and held it against her chest protectively.

"Where did you get that necklace?" asked Devlin

"None of your business."

"Did someone give it to you?"

"Yeah. That's right. Someone gave it to me."

"Who gave it to you?"

"You wanna know who gave this to me?"

"Yeah, I do."

"Someone called Mr. none-of-your-damn-business, that's who."

Another pause. Devlin was still gazing at the pendant wrapped in the girl's hand.

"What does the symbol mean?" he asked.

The girl cupped the pendant in her palm and studied the design engraved on it. In truth, she hadn't really thought about what the symbol hanging from the chain meant. She just thought it looked cool and weird, mystical and pretty, a deep-blue-colored snake with black-and-gold eyes wound around a green tree.

"No idea," she said and shrugged. "Just a nice pattern... I gotta go. See ya at the pantry." She got back on the saddle and began to roll the bike's front wheel around.

"Yeah. See you..." replied Devlin. "If you ever need any help with those guys again, just let me know."

The girl stopped and screwed up her young face into a sharp frown. "Shouldn't you be telling me to go to the police or my social worker or something?"

"I could do, but I'd say they're the people you spend your time avoiding. Just let me know and I'll fix it. Okay?"

"What's your name?"

"Father Devlin."

"Like I said, I don't need someone to watch over me, Father Devlin."

THE GIRL CYCLED BACK along Church Street, the same way she was heading before the cop car turned up, before the two boys rode up, before the priest appeared. The sun had nearly hidden itself away, but it was still warm and the last patches of yellow-and-red light in the sky were beautiful. She felt like the night held her in its hands, protecting her in a way no human ever had. She hooked a right down into Union Street and then a left onto Madison, riding south past Oakland Cemetery and along to where the road became a dirt track. On one side of the track were headstones set into the flat, dry grass: slanting headstones, fallen headstones, broken headstones, headstones worn blank with time. On the other side were entrances to drives that led up to large, expensive properties owned by the very rich. The very rich and very shy, their great houses kept well out of sight from the road- side and hidden by long dense rows of high brick walls, bushes, and trees. Tasteful fortresses. In their own way, the rich were as hidden from sight here as the dead that lived opposite them.

She carried on for another ten minutes till she was on the quiet outskirts of the village, cycling along Town Line Road, up by the really high-end real estate.

The girl stopped by a dirt track turnoff. A few yards up the track, tucked away from the road and secluded by trees, was a white gate, the entrance to a long driveway. The girl threw a look back to check the road was clear, dismounted, and quickly pulled the pendant chain over her head and tucked it away in her jean pocket. Then she pushed the white gate open and wheeled her bike up the driveway.

The approach to the house was about a quarter of a mile

long with acres of lush, well-watered grass on either side. Up at the other end of the drive was a tall, wide house, its windows spilling golden light out onto cars that were parked in a fanned-out formation on a graveled semicircle. In the center of the semicircle was a trickling fountain that stood in a circle of paving stones, English country house style. The house itself was long, tall, and wide, constructed out of a soft brownstone. Ivy had been allowed to roam free over the dark brickwork and around the sash windows. The house always took the girl's breath away; she had never dreamed she could get into this world. Get to be around people who lived in a place like this. Turned out all you needed was a lot of hustle and no heart.

A slim, gaunt man with a heavy shadow of stubble stood by a double oak door. Like all the visitors who came up the drive, he'd seen the girl coming from a way off, the intended consequence of the estate's layout. The man lifted the flap of his jacket, unhooked a radio from his belt, and spoke to someone inside the house.

The girl got to the oak door and stood in front of the gaunt man, waiting, her bike resting against her side. No words were spoken. The man didn't acknowledge the girl, and she didn't acknowledge him. Finally, one of the oak doors opened, revealing a short chubby man in a dark blue three-piece suit. No matter how many times the girl saw Harris, she was still taken aback by how ugly he was. His thick, slack lips, his thin brown hair that had been spread across his crown, and his large, gummy brown eyes. Unsightly moles stuck out from his round shiny cheeks. Yet there was an old-world elegance in the way he spoke, dressed, and moved. A gentleness of manners that offset and softened his appearance, that almost made him attractive.

"You're late, little lady," said Harris.

"I ran into some trouble, Mr. Harris."

"No doubt." Harris nodded toward the gaunt man. "Leave the bike with Mosley."

The girl handed the bike over to Mosley, and Harris moved back, extending a hand in an impatient come-this-way gesture. The girl stepped over the threshold and into the hallway. The heavy door thunked shut behind her.

Inside the hallway, the house was as warm and golden as the light from the windows outside had promised. It was a fairy-tale house, a house made from someone's dreams. Her dreams. The carpets were deep and soft, so soft that wherever she stood she could just lie down, snuggle up, and drift off. There was a grand double staircase and big bedrooms on every floor with ornate fireplaces and high ceilings. From the rooms adjacent came the sound of chatter and laughter, the clink of glasses, cutlery, and plates, and a piano somewhere playing a bluesy melody.

"Get everything you need from the kitchen," said Harris. "And start your duties as quickly as possible."

"Okay."

Harris took a cigarette case from his inside jacket pocket and lit up a filterless cigarette. The girl saw that there was a gold inscription around the base of the cigarette. Words in some strange language. Harris, picking bits of tobacco out from his fleshy lips, noticed the girl's curiosity.

"They're Turkish, he said. "I get them shipped in."

Rich people weren't satisfied until everything they did showed off that they were rich, thought the girl. She'd do the same one day when she was rich too.

"Well, run along," said Harris. "Your customers await."

The girl seemed to freeze for a moment, undecided about whether to speak.

"Well, what are you waiting for? Chop, chop."

"You remember you said you might be looking for some

more...talent, Mr. Harris?" She was pretty sure that was the word he used. *Talent.*

Harris's big, bloodshot eyes widened. "Why, that's right, I did." He gave a short laugh. "You have someone in mind?" He said it as if the idea were as incredible as time travel.

"Two people, actually. Two boys."

"Where are they from?"

"Queens, but they live out of their car and a camp they got set up at Ligonee Creek, near Brick Kiln Road."

"I see. How old?"

"Seventeen or eighteen, I think."

"And you're confident they're suitable?"

"Yes."

"What do they look like, these boys?"

"Blond... good-looking too. Like models."

Harris chuckled. "Like models indeed? Oh, well, in that case, tell them to come up to the house and ask for me... Now run along."

And the girl did run along, with a little spark in her heart, a little thrill that she would enhance her reputation no end if Harris liked the boys. She knew the boys were going to be so excited to be getting what they wanted. And she also knew something else, something she hardly admitted to herself. That what people wanted and what people got in this house were very different things.

The girl waited for Harris to rejoin the party, and instead of going to the kitchen as instructed, she skipped up the grand staircase, climbing right to the very top floor that was accessed by a single, narrow spiral staircase. At the top of the staircase was a battered wooden door which she pushed open. She stepped into a large room, octagonal in shape with wood-paneled walls. In the center of the room was a couch, and in front of the couch was a low, long table. In the center of the table was a marble chess set. Surrounding the couch and table, on the cabinets and shelves that lined the walls, were old and exotic objects, antiques from past centuries, that fascinated the girl. The room was straight out of a museum, an ancient oddity, from the strange octagonal shape to the wooden paneling to the curios that had been placed on the shelves. She had heard Harris refer to it as the turret room which only increased its mystery.

At the back of the room, below a high oval window, stood a tall glass-paneled cabinet. On display in the cabinet was a stuffed owl whose feathers had begun to mildew and a pair of buzzards in similarly frayed and aged conditions. Hung high on the wall looking down on the girl was a moose head. And on the right of the room were a series of shelves that held large leather-bound encyclopedias and other volumes that were bookended by identical black marble busts of a fat, pompous-looking man.

It seemed to the girl that this room was full of eyes. Dead eyes, looking at her. The thought sent a shiver through her. Even so, on the rare occasions she got to be in this room, her curiosity won out against her dread, and right at that moment she was fascinated by the marble busts. She crept closer to the bookshelves and read the gold inscription on the block of one of the busts. The name "Audley Jacob Harris" had been carved into the marble and overlaid with gold leaf. That must be Harris's old man, thought the girl. Or grandfather, or even great-grandfather. Whoever he was, he looked nothing like Harris. The man immortalized in marble looked stern, fierce, and grave, all at once. Oliver Harris had never looked like any one of those things.

Though the room was packed with odds and ends, it was little used by Harris himself. Ever since the girl had worked for Harris, the room had been set aside for one particular guest, a special guest the girl had not yet met. Luggage that had been sent on ahead of this special guest, who the girl knew was due to return later that night, stood unpacked by the door.

The girl took a look behind her, through the door to the top of the stairs, to check all was clear. Then she crept across the room to the table. She took the necklace from her pocket, knelt by the table, and pulled out a drawer that contained many other necklaces, bracelets, and a couple of watches. She placed the necklace back on the pile of jewelry, where she had found and first admired it. She could tell it was very expensive. The gold chain was heavy, and the pendant had the name "Cartier" inscribed in small letters beneath the picture of the snake wrapped around the tree. The picture the priest had been so interested in. The nosy jerk. It was a pity she had to give it back. Even though the chain was short and made for a man, it hung so nicely, so prettily, on her slim neck. But the owner was returning tonight, and she would be putting her position in peril by keeping hold of it. She rummaged around in the drawer, pulling out other pieces to inspect, but they were too manly, too chunky to consider borrowing in the future, so she pushed the drawer shut and headed back downstairs to begin her preparations for the night's events.

FOUR

"Stand up straight and look alive, Paladino. For God's sake." Paladino briefly wondered what it was she'd done in a previous life to be out on duty with Harrigan again. She figured she had to have been something like a serial killer.

They were calling on Senator Helen Lawson, who had reported a break-in. As they stood on the porch of a handsome but small cottage with impeccably kept grounds, Paladino noticed her boss didn't smell of stale sweat and booze. Maybe she detected a faint whiff of body odor now and again, but on the whole Harrigan had really scrubbed up.

The senator appeared at the door looking like she'd braced herself for their visit. A smile flashed across her face and then vanished pretty much for good.

"Sorry to disturb you, ma'am," said Harrigan. "My name's Detective Harrigan, and this is Officer Paladino. We're here about the..."

"Yes, the break-in. I know. Come in."

Paladino could feel waves of indignation coming off Harrigan beside her as he bit his lip and hid his irritation at being cut off.

They followed the senator into her living room which was furnished with a floral-print couch and armchairs and smelled of polish and fresh flowers.

The three sat and no refreshments were offered.

"To be honest," the senator began, "I don't know that it was worth you coming over. Whoever broke in didn't take anything..."

"Nothing is missing?" asked Harrigan.

"Nothing," replied the senator firmly, and the fingers of her left hand fluttered on the arm of her chair.

"How did they get into the house?"

"Through the back door. I wasn't here at the time—I was up in DC working late. It was my gardener who discovered the break-in and reported it. They broke the glass and forced the handle from the inside. But they don't seem to have had a chance to take anything. Something must have disturbed them. What it was, I have no idea."

"I don't see an alarm system here," said Paladino.

"I'm having one installed tomorrow as it happens. I kept meaning to but never got around to it. I didn't use to stay here more than a couple of months a year, you see. But since my husband died, I find I'm down here a lot more."

"Sorry for your loss," said Holly with more feeling than she intended.

"Thank you, Officer..."

"Paladino. Officer Paladino, ma'am. I lost my husband too, last year."

"Oh, that's dreadful. I'm so sorry."

"Thank you. It was...is... But you know that..."

"I certainly do."

There was a moment when the two women might have gone down a different path and opened up about what they both had in common. But then Harrigan trod all over the moment and spoke.

"Can I take a look at the door?"

"I've had it fixed. But if that's useful, then yes."

"I'll just take a look. You never know."

"All right."

The three decamped to the cramped kitchen where Harrigan looked at a brand-new door that had never been broken into and pretended it had satisfied some kind of investigative instinct.

"You're absolutely sure there's nothing missing?" asked Paladino.

The senator took a moment and then said again, firmly, "I'm sure."

"There has been a spate of burglaries in the area," said Harrigan, rubbing the back of his neck.

"So I understand."

"But I want to assure you that we're pulling patrols off the village and harbor to address that."

"I know that with the sheriff's office in dispute you must be stretched."

"We're okay, ma'am. We're okay." Paladino watched with fascination as her gnarly bully of a boss clumsily attempted to smarm his way around the senator.

"Can we go out this way?" asked Harrigan. "Through the kitchen door? We can look at the route they might have taken approaching the house."

"Of course."

"Thanks. We can see our own way out. Thanks again, Senator Lawton."

Harrigan and Paladino walked out into the backyard and scouted around both sides of the house with Harrigan making out like he was Sherlock Holmes, scanning the area for any signs of disturbance and clues.

Once they'd got into the cruiser and Paladino was driving them away from the senator's residence, he returned to his normal self.

"Goddamned stuck-up... That's why I don't vote."

"You don't vote?"

"Nope. Doesn't change a goddamn thing. Last person I voted for was Chuck Baldwin. The only person I'd vote for these days is me," said Harrigan, shifting in his seat and rear-ranging his pants. Paladino, though, wasn't really listening to her boss anymore.

"You think it's odd? The way she was? Like something was making her uptight?"

"Nope. Think she's like that with the staff. And that's what we are to her. The staff."

FIVE

It was around eleven when Devlin got back to his lodgings. He came up the back way to get to the loft, climbing the metal stairs up to the balcony and into the cramped, dark kitchen, feeling along the wall for the light switch. Once the light was on, he filled up the tarnished percolator on the countertop with water and coffee granules and placed it on the stove. Then he picked up one of a dozen matches that were scattered over the counter and flicked it against a flint strip torn from a matchbox that was tacked to the wall. He lit the stove and stood watching the pot as it began to heat and gurgle. Then he poured out the small amount of thick black liquid into an espresso cup.

Devlin went through to the bedroom and switched the main light on. He sat on the bed and pulled out the small silver pillbox from his pocket and studied it like he'd studied it so many times before. He ran his fingertips over the simple line etching of a tree and a serpent wrapped around its trunk and boughs, and his mind flashed back to the girl and her pendant with the same symbol. It was without question the same symbol that Lemus had burned into his hand in his dream and the same symbol he'd found on Clay's pillbox. And it was the same, in every detail: the colors, the shape, and the high standard of workmanship. What were the chances that the girl would be wearing a piece of jewelry with the exact same design? That he would randomly run into her in a town he'd only just arrived in?

He studied the object more closely, bringing it as close to his eyes as he could without his focus blurring, willing it to throw up one more clue as to why he'd been led here. But there was nothing more to glean from it.

Devlin pulled back the drapes and opened the window by his bed that looked onto the balcony. Leaning on the windowsill, he sipped his coffee and finished off the stub of a cigar he'd rescued from the ashtray on his nightstand. From the bedroom window, Devlin could see right across the town and out to the thin blue strip of the sea. Occasional noises flared up from somewhere among the lines of houses and roads—an engine revving, a shout from the street, a bark from a backyard—but mainly it was quiet. Quiet and humid. He stood at the window for a good twenty minutes, and twice in that time he saw them again, the limousines. Riding by and headed north, away from the bay. The cop was right, thought Devlin. Rich town. Rich part of the world.

The calm of the night and the peace it brought Devlin was suddenly broken by a pain in his hand, a pulsing pain that came from the wound in his palm causing Devlin to breathe in sharply.

Rubbing his hand, Devlin looked out again at the night sky and saw a comet shooting down from the heavens. White with a long vapor trail, it flashed across the dark blue. And at that moment, with the comet in the sky and his hand still aching, Devlin had the most extraordinary feeling. The feeling of something coming from far away, something strange headed for the shores that he could see from his window. Headed for him. It was as if, for a fleeting moment, a piece of the future came into focus. Maybe that's how time was, thought Devlin, solid and certain in the present moment but fading in the other directions, backward and forward. Like a painting where the center is clear and detailed but fades quickly toward the edges. But if you were lucky, for the briefest moment, you might be able to glimpse a clue, or even just a feeling, about what was to come.

His cell buzzed in his pocket, and he saw that he had a missed call and voicemail from Father Aranha. Devlin thought about going to see if Aranha was up, but given the late hour and the tension between the two men, he decided against it. He put his cell on the nightstand, resolving to call Aranha back in the morning.

Devlin stubbed his cigar out in his cup and, after prayers, got ready for bed.

Even with the window open, the heat pressed down on him. In the sweltering bedroom with a shot of caffeine and nicotine buzzing round his system, sleep should have been nearly impossible. Yet it did come, quickly, descending on Devlin like a spell, smuggling his soul away quietly into slumber without resistance.

In the confusion of his unconscious, Devlin fell in and out of dreams, dreams in which Jane, his wife, appeared to him. In which he vividly relived her murder and his vengeful murder of her killer, Felix Lemus. Dreams about serpents hiding in trees, dreams where he found himself back in the places of his itinerant, chaotic childhood. Then, abruptly, Devlin found himself sitting up in his bed. It was still night, but something wasn't right. There had been a loud bang, from somewhere in the rectory, Devlin was certain of it.

· · ·

DEVLIN THREW ON A T-SHIRT, pants, and slipped on his sneakers. He opened the door and crept down the unlit stairs to the entrance hall. It was dark, but there was some light coming from the other end of the hall, from the open door to Father Aranha's study where he could hear Aranha's radio playing classical music. Devlin sniffed the air. Overlaying the smell of furniture polish and air freshener was a distinctly smoky flavor like a firework had just been let off. With a rising sense of dread, Devlin moved carefully along the main hallway to the back of the house, toward the light coming from the study. As he got nearer to the study, the smell of fireworks got stronger.

He gently pushed the study door open to reveal the room in full. On the side of the room farthest from Devlin, slumped over his desk, was Aranha's body. Under his mop of gray-black hair, a thick disc-shaped pool of red liquid was seeping across the wooden surface and dripping onto the navy carpet. The wall and the framed pictures above the desk were sprayed with blood, dark and wet.

Devlin stood over the body. There was no point feeling for a pulse; it was plain that death had been instant. Despite the thick thatch of hair, he could see at least two sites that looked like bullet wound entry points. Aranha's right arm was dangling down by his side, the left arm sprawled out over the desk. Lying half in his left hand and half on the desk was his cell phone.

Shock and grief hit Devlin at once, paralyzing him.

He stood motionless.

Then he felt a gentle breath of air touch his cheek. The floor-length drapes drawn across the french windows briefly fluttered on a breeze coming from outside. In an instant, Devlin was on his feet and pulling the drapes apart. The french windows were open, and Devlin stepped out into the hot night.

Outside, in the backyard directly below Devlin's balcony was a small, walled garden and beyond that a parking lot.

Devlin ran through the garden and into the parking lot where he came to a stop. The empty lot was bordered on one side by the church hall and on the other by the road. There wasn't a soul about. Devlin was about to turn back when he saw the security light on the front of the church hall flicker on. Something or someone must have set it off. Without hesitating, he took off across the parking lot, toward the church hall entrance where the white light lit up the blacktop. As he rounded the side of the church hall, he spotted a movement across the street. A figure had climbed to the top of a stone wall and was sliding behind it, out of view.

Devlin flew across the road, and with a swiftness at odds with his bulk, he latched on to the top of the wall. Planting his feet on a narrow stone ledge, he managed to lever his body over. His landing, however, was not so skilled or decorous, and he found himself entangled in a bush. As he thrashed to get clear of the branches and leaves, he heard a low growling. Devlin looked up and saw two yellow eyes peering out of the darkness. From behind the yellow eyes came a hoarse, croaking voice.

"He's called Duke, and if you so much as move an eyelash, he'll rip your damn throat out."

The voice belonged to a thin, elderly man in his pajamas, who was standing behind Duke and pointing a shotgun at Devlin's head.

"My wife's called the police, so you just sit tight, you son of a bitch, until they arrive or I'll fill you with buckshot and Duke here will lick up the mess."

Devlin replied evenly and calmly, "I'm not trying to break into your house. My friend's just been shot and killed. The guy who did it came through your backyard. I was trying to chase him down."

The old guy with the shotgun considered Devlin's story for

a second, then tightened his grip on his gun. "Whatever. You just stay still as a stone and save your story for the law."

Devlin heard the dog growl again. He looked down the barrel of the shotgun that was only inches from his head and decided it was in everybody's best interests for him to wait it out for the cops.

SIX

"You again."

The voice was thick and gravelly, harsh and rasping. Devlin had been sitting on the back seat of a police cruiser, staring at the blue and red lights swimming over the front of St. Michael's Church. The voice snapped him out of his meditation, and he looked up to see the detective who'd picked him up on his first night in Sag Harbor.

"When I first laid eyes on you, I thought you were trouble," said Detective Harrigan. "And in the very short time you've been in my town, you've given me no reason to doubt that assessment and every reason to believe it. What the hell exactly happened here?"

"I told the other officer. Didn't she tell you?"

Harrigan rolled his broad, well-padded shoulders and gave Devlin a don't-mess-with-me kind of stare.

"I want you to tell me. Now."

Devlin looked around at the street lit up at night in all its red-and-blue glory, at the yellow police tape that haphazardly ringed the entrance to the rectory, at a couple of forensic people coming from around the back of the church holding evidence bags. Then he looked up at Harrigan's sweaty, droopy, irate face.

"I woke about one in the morning," he began, "because of a loud bang. I went down into the house to see what had happened and found Father Aranha dead at his desk. In his study. He'd been shot in the back of the head. Three times. I saw the doors to the backyard were open and went outside to see if I could catch the murderer. I saw a guy climbing a wall, so I took off after him and ended up looking down the barrel of a shotgun. And the murderer got away. That's the long version. The short version is my friend was murdered."

"What did the guy climbing the wall look like?"

"I didn't get a good enough look at him for any kind of description."

"Nothing at all?"

"Nothing."

"But he was definitely male?"

"Yeah."

"Hey, boss."

The call came from an officer standing behind Harrigan, the same officer who was with Harrigan when they picked Devlin up.

Harrigan turned away from Devlin and walked over to his colleague.

"What is it, Paladino?"

"CSU is nearly done. They found three shells but no sign of the gun the killer used. The rear windows weren't forced open. They could have been open already 'cause of the heat. The real headache is it looks like the whole area behind the church has no CCTV. The parking lot and most of the block aren't covered. A total blind spot."

"Crap." Harrigan looked over his shoulder at Devlin and back at Paladino. "What about him? What if there was no intruder?"

"The priest? You think he shot Aranha? For what reason?"

"No idea. But who the hell is this guy anyway? We pick him up on the Turnpike and two days later he's the only witness to a murder. And, on top of that, I don't like him."

"You don't like anyone."

"I especially don't like him." Harrigan hitched up his belt and planted his feet a little wider apart. "Suppose he is the murderer. Suppose they had a fight and he put three bullets in Aranha's head, then panicked and ran. But he got caught in the backyard by grandpa and his mutt."

Paladino shook her head. "None of that makes sense. Aranha was shot from behind. He was sitting down. How would that happen if they were arguing?"

"Because they had finished arguing, but this guy was still angry, so he put three bullets in the back of his friend's head."

"Okay. So, then what? He takes off. But not in a car. Not even down the sidewalk. He goes and jumps into a backyard straight into a bush. And in the time it takes him to get between here and the yard, he manages somehow to get rid of the gun, hiding it so completely that we can't find it anywhere."

Harrigan snorted up some phlegm and spat it out on the ground. "Maybe he straight-out panicked. Maybe we'll find the gun, but I'm keeping an open mind. 'Cause I got an instinct about this guy. Here's what's gonna happen. He's a person of interest anyway, so we take him down the station and make him go through the story again. Where we can focus his mind— Paladino? Hey! Are you listening to me?"

Paladino's attention had drifted, and she had been only half listening to Harrigan. Instead, she was looking hard at the priest.

"Yeah...yeah, I'm listening. You said take him down the station...I was just thinking..."

"What...what were you thinking?"

"We have done a GSR test on him, haven't we?"

Harrigan looked unsure for a split second, then blustered, "That's exactly what I was gonna do next. For crying out loud, Paladino, I'm not a moron." Harrigan snapped his fingers at a CSU officer and beckoned him over.

"Hey, you got a gunshot residue kit with you?"

The CSU officer nodded.

"Well, go get it and take some swabs from the guy in the back of the cruiser."

The CSU officer nodded and plodded off to his truck to fetch his kit, and Harrigan turned back to Paladino.

"Once that's done, we'll get him to the precinct. That'll put a fire under his ass."

Harrigan went to give instructions to a patrol officer who was standing guard by the perimeter, and Paladino found herself standing alone while everyone else was to-ing and fro-ing, busying themselves around the crime scene. She looked over at Devlin, who seemed to be consumed by thought, unaware she was looking directly at him. She began to study this guy sitting in the back of the car who had blown into town in the middle of the night. He was a formidable-looking guy, thought Paladino. Solid at the center and rough around the edges. He had deep-set eyes and a square, handsome face a little worn from time on the clock, and there was an aura about him, a magnetism. She suddenly found herself hooked on the absurd notion that she should go over and talk to this man. That she should tell him about her sadness that seemed to have no limits. Then Paladino heard her name being shouted and realized that, in the middle of a murder scene, she had become completely absorbed in some dumb fantasy. She pulled herself together, angry at herself for daydreaming on a homicide, and angry at the person who had decided to get himself killed and leave her alone forever.

SEVEN

Harrigan's face was jowly, his eyes were bagged, and the short, curly dark hair on his crown was thinning and sparse, fanned out to make a little go a long way. His coarse, dark features seemed to sag under the weight of who knew what inner battles. Devlin found it difficult not to stare at the detective, to wonder how it was that a man could look so beat up by life. He probably wasn't so old, thought Devlin, maybe in his midforties max. But however many years he'd had on the earth, they couldn't have been kind. It didn't help that Harrigan was carrying forty or even fifty more pounds than he should have been. But he was tall and big built, so that helped disguise his bulk.

They sat in an interview room, Devlin on one side, the two cops on the other. The desk was pushed close into the corner so Devlin had his back against the wall. Doubtless a tactic. Harrigan was scrolling through something on his cell, but Devlin couldn't tell if it was official or just his Facebook feed. He got the feeling that Harrigan's expression didn't change much whatever he was reading. Then he looked across the table at Paladino, who was patiently waiting for Harrigan to pull his face out of his cell phone.

Holly Paladino seemed to Devlin to be the opposite in all ways from Harrigan. There were faint lines around her eyes, but her skin was still taut and she kept herself in good shape. Her hair, cut short and side-parted, was still a natural ash blonde, and her eyes were quick and intelligent. Set out neatly in front of her were a pencil and a legal pad open at a fresh page.

Devlin looked at his hands that were placed in front of him on the table. They were still, steady. Despite everything he was calm. That was the gift and the curse of military training. The ability to live a step away from your emotions. Like it was all happening to someone else. He ought to be broken up about his friend. There ought to have been tears by now. But instead, there was only one emotion he could lay claim to: anger. It was an emotion that came so easy and coursed through him like the source of it was infinite. It ate at Devlin, how much anger he had. There shouldn't be so much of it in one man. Yet, alongside this fury was a total clearheadedness, an absolute sense of purpose. Devlin was going to find whoever killed Aranha and use that anger to turn them inside out.

His mouth tasted of the sweet, harsh tang of tobacco. He sipped at the water in the Styrofoam cup that had been placed in front of him and tried not to think about how much he wanted a smoke.

Harrigan put his cell down, hawked up some phlegm, swallowed it, and leaned back in his seat, like he was really settling in. His thumbs were parked in his Sam Browne, and his punch-bag face wore the tiniest hint of a smile.

"Father Devlin. When was the last time you saw Father Aranha alive?"

"Yesterday morning. About ten."

"Where did he go?"

"He had to go to the other church he looks after. St. Luke's."

"Where's that?"

"Northwest Harbor."

"He go with anyone?"

"No. He got a cab over there by himself."

"What cab company?" asked Paladino.

"I don't know. You'd need to check his cell phone."

Paladino scratched out a note on her pad.

"What about you?" said Harrigan. "Where were you between ten in the morning and the time of Father Aranha's death?"

This was where things could get sticky. The truth was he was tailing the girl with the chain until he lost her after the encounter with the two boys. He should have been looking for a place to stay after the fallout with Aranha, but using that as an alibi would be problematic in the circumstances.

"I went into town."

"That's it?"

"Yeah."

"What time you leave for town?"

"About ten thirty, I guess."

"You were in town all day? Doing what?"

"I hadn't seen the place, never been to Sag Harbor. So I was looking around. Doing the tourist thing. I only got here a few days ago, remember?"

"Oh, I remember."

"So I walked about. Got my bearings. Got a bite to eat and wandered back about eleven."

"You got any witnesses? Anyone who could testify to your whereabouts?"

Devlin thought for a moment. Thought about the girl with the pendant. "No."

"What happened when you got back to the rectory?"

"I got ready for bed and was asleep before midnight. I woke to the sound of gunshots, and that's when I went downstairs."

"You didn't see Father Aranha at the rectory?"

"No, I took the back way into the loft room."

"What did you talk about the last time you spoke to Father Aranha?"

"Catching up mostly. We hadn't seen each other in a long time, and we're old friends."

As Devlin spoke, he was suddenly hit by a realization. There was something else, something else he'd forgotten until now. Something he wasn't going to share with the cops.

"Are you telling us everything, Father Devlin?" The question came from Paladino, who seemed to latch on to some minute change in Devlin's expression.

"Yes," replied Devlin firmly. "Everything."

There was a silence, and Harrigan swapped looks with Paladino, who followed up with another question.

"You know anyone who might have had a reason to harm Father Aranha? Had he mentioned anyone he'd had a disagreement or trouble with? Anything playing on his mind?"

Devlin thought for a moment and shook his head. "No."

"Anyone in his congregation?"

Devlin thought again. "No, no one. But then I hadn't seen Vijay for about five years. And I don't know the congregation."

The room fell silent, and Harrigan lolled in his chair. Then he said, "Officer Paladino, could you get me a cup of coffee?"

Devlin could see what Harrigan was doing. He could see Paladino knew it too. A small man's way of exerting power in the room, getting his junior officer to fetch something he probably didn't even really want. And to get her out of the room. Paladino sucked it up and rose to her feet, taking her pad and pencil with her.

· · ·

OUTSIDE, Paladino ran into Maynard, a younger uniform cop in his twenties. Maynard wasn't like the other cops; he had a bit of an edge that Paladino liked. There was something a little punky about him that brought another vibe to the precinct. His shirtsleeves were rolled up to reveal a tangle of tattoos which he should, according to protocol, keep covered on duty, and his hair which he liked to keep long, touching his collar, was just within the NYPD Patrol Guide regulations.

Maynard was looking vexed, and the moment he saw Paladino, he rushed up to her.

"Holly. Thank God, you're out."

"What is it?"

"We need an extra hand out front. I'm in the middle of processing three DUIs, and we got Gerry Sutton going crazy too."

"Gerry Sutton?"

"Yeah, he says his wife's missing. Been gone two days. The guy's losing it. Could you just calm him down? Just till I got my DUIs processed?"

"Sure. No problem. I just gotta get Harrigan a coffee first."

"He's getting you to get him coffee? What a jerk."

"Yep, you know Curtis. Jerk of the century."

BACK INSIDE THE INTERVIEW ROOM, Devlin sensed the mood shift decisively with Paladino's exit and decided to try to bring things to a close.

"I don't need to stay here any longer. There's nothing else I can tell you about Father Aranha's murder. And every second you spend indulging your dislike of me, however justified you think it is, is time wasted while the murderer gets away."

Harrigan placed his hairy fists on the table and leaned in. "I don't give a damn what you think, and I certainly don't take any orders or advice from you. Far as I'm concerned, you're involved in what happened to Aranha, and if you're not, you're involved in something else I'm gonna take you down for. You turned up in my town like a turd that floated downstream, and I'm going to flush you out, you no-good son of a bitch. You should know that I have already made it my goddamned mission."

Devlin leaned forward and placed his elbows on the table. The two men were inches apart, and Devlin could smell beer and the stale sweat of a long shift wafting off Harrigan's uniform and sun-beaten skin.

"I am not going anywhere until I know who murdered Father Aranha. Nowhere. I will stay here as long as it takes. And there isn't a solitary thing you can do about it."

"Oh, there are plenty of things I can do about it."

There was a beat of silence, and Harrigan leaned back and crossed his arms over the mound of his stomach.

"You can't go back to the rectory 'cause it's a crime scene. And you won't be able to go back until I say it isn't a crime scene. Not for your belongings, such as they are, not for nothing. And if I see you sleeping on the streets, or any of my officers see you on the streets, I'll come down and personally straighten you out."

"Am I under arrest, Detective Harrigan?"

"I think you know the answer to that."

"Then I'm going."

Devlin rose, and so did Harrigan. Eye to eye.

"I'll walk you out," said Harrigan.

The two men walked back along the hallway and into the main office where there was a row of people waiting, sitting on a line of seats at the far end. A couple of cops sat at cubicle desks processing paperwork with members of the public seated opposite them. On the other side of the office, Paladino was caught in an intense conversation with a tall guy in a suit. He looked to be in his early forties, with auburn hair and pale skin. His eyes were red, and he was talking fast and gesticulating at Paladino about something that Devlin couldn't make out.

Harrigan stopped and turned to Devlin.

"Come with me."

He led Devlin through the desks, but instead of taking the route out through the main entrance, he took a shortcut through a hallway that led off from the main office. At the end of the hallway was a fire door with a push bar that Harrigan opened. Devlin followed Harrigan out into the windless night, and Harrigan shut the door behind him. The moment Devlin heard the fire door shut, he knew he'd made a mistake. He was standing in a small courtyard with a narrow entrance that led out into the police car lot, an enclosed area with one locked iron gate for an exit where there were no overlooking windows or CCTV cameras Devlin could see.

Devlin took a step back and turned quickly to put himself in the best position he could, but he wasn't fast enough for Harrigan, who'd been planning his move since they'd been in the interview room. The detective had already whipped out a baton and extended it with the flick of a wrist. By the time Devlin had turned, he'd already been struck once hard in the neck, and before he could steady himself, he felt a succession of hard blows around his ribs and hands. Devlin backed away, up against the wall, ready to come piling back in on the detective. Harrigan saw the threat coming and with his free hand drew out his pistol.

"That's what happens to people like you," said Harrigan. "People who treat me like a clown. Vagrant priests who wash up on my streets, who run away from crime scenes and then tell me they walked around Sag Harbor for ten hours without a single goddamned witness."

Devlin was standing and, despite the throbbing pain in his

neck, hands, and ribs, was not cowed. He would not give this man that victory. Not now. Not ever.

"We both know the truth, Detective," said Devlin.

"And what's that, Father?"

"That you're out of shape by forty pounds and driven by a fear of being found out for what you are: a bad cop. That only a small, weak man comes at another man from behind with a baton and a gun. And that if you try that trick that again I'll be ready, and I'll break you into pieces and spread you out over the floor."

Harrigan's face soured, wary now of Devlin, of the way he seemed immune to the beating he'd just been given. He pulled out a bunch of keys and semicircled around the priest to open the gate.

"You're free to go for now," said Harrigan and waved his pistol. "Now get lost."

Without a word, Devlin turned and went through the narrow exit from the courtyard and across the lot to the street.

Harrigan followed him out and watch Devlin go. Frustratingly, instead of the usual surge of pleasure these beatings gave Harrigan, he only felt relief that the priest had gone, and an emptiness.

———

DEVLIN'S upper body stung with pain where Harrigan's baton had struck him. It had taken all his rational mind's effort to hold him back from charging Harrigan and tearing him apart, gun or no gun. But Devlin also knew it was his own fault that he hadn't been more guarded, his own fault for underestimating the man's malice and recklessness. But the truth was he'd been eager to get away from the precinct and Harrigan because of the thing he'd remembered during the interview—the voice message from

Father Aranha he'd got when he'd arrived back at the loft the previous night.

When Devlin had got a couple of blocks away and put a safe amount of distance between him and the police station, he took out his cell and checked his voicemail. There was an automated voice telling Devlin he had one new message and then Vijay Aranha's voice, thin, hoarse, anxious.

"Gabe, I know things have been strained between us, but I need to talk to you. It's... There's something that's been weighing on my mind. Something I've done...and now I'm afraid...afraid that I'm going to pay for it... There's no one else I can turn to. Call me when you get back. Or when you get back, come and find me downstairs. I'll still be up..."

Aranha's voice was replaced by the automated voice reading out the call options. Devlin stared at his cell and then along the street that was slowly lightening in the early summer sun. He cursed himself for not picking up when Aranha had called, for not checking the voicemail. But he knew now that he could have had no idea of the kind of deep trouble Aranha had been in. And it had to have been deep trouble because that was the only kind you end up being murdered for.

EIGHT

A couple of the officers on shift and in the office at Sag Harbor PD had seen Harrigan walk the priest out through the fire door, and they knew instantly what was afoot. They knew that this was Harrigan's little trick, to take a suspect, or someone he just plain didn't like, out into the blind spot and give them a "wake-up call" as their boss put it. But these same officers were so afraid of Harrigan that when he came back into the office from the blind spot, they didn't dare swap knowing looks with their colleagues or acknowledge his return. They pretended to be so deeply involved in their work they didn't even look up. But they all knew the score.

Except for Paladino.

She had been so genuinely involved in her work that she had no idea the priest was being led out by Harrigan. Paladino's entire focus had been taken up by Gerry Sutton, the man standing in front of her now with pleading eyes. Paladino knew about Sutton the way she knew about most of the rich set that summered in Sag Harbor—through department gossip. The building was rife with rumors about these wealthy part-time citizens and what they got up to. Paladino knew that Sutton was a hedge fund manager who had made it good with a string of big deals that had paid out tens of millions. He kept a huge waterfront home in Sound View Drive and in previous years had been seen about town with beautiful young women on his arm. But it was common knowledge that only a few months ago he'd given up bachelorhood to tie the knot with Brandi Keeler, a beautician from Staten Island, who was some twenty years his junior and worked in a salon in East Hampton.

"So that's it? You're going to do nothing? Nothing at all," said an exasperated Sutton.

"We've got all the information we need from you, Mr. Sutton. But as your wife is an adult and there are no concerns about her vulnerability or evidence of involuntary disappearance, there's nothing further we can do right now."

"This is crazy! It's madness and it's incompetence. Why have a police department at all if you don't actually investigate cases?"

"We don't know that there is a case. It's been two days since Brandi went missing. We will keep in touch with her family and friends and monitor her bank accounts and social media, and if anything..."

As Paladino was talking, she could see Sutton looking over her shoulder, and she got a familiar feeling, a depressing sense of what was coming next.

"I wanna talk to another cop."

"Excuse me?"

"No disrespect, but I want another cop... Someone with more—"

"They won't tell you any different, Mr. Sutton."

"Maybe, maybe not. But I know these other guys. Officer Maynard, say, is he free? I'd feel more comfortable if..."

Paladino felt anger surge. She took a step closer to Sutton and squared up to him. Speaking slowly and evenly, though her pulse was racing and her temper was about to break, she said, "You don't get to choose which cop handles your case, or their gender, no matter who you are."

"I didn't mean—"

"It doesn't work that way, Mr. Sutton. You've reported your case, and I'll file the paperwork just like another cop would, male or female. Do you understand?"

Sutton's eyes flicked about nervously as he backed down from a confrontation. "Yes...yes. I understand."

"Good. Now, I'm going to file your paperwork, and we'll check in with Brandi's family and friends first thing."

"Right. Of course, I could easily use my own not inconsiderable resources to find Brandi. Maybe there's a private investigator who'll actually look into this..."

"As long as you stay within the law and don't get in the way of the police, you can do what you like, Mr. Sutton. Goodbye."

Paladino turned and left Sutton to make his own way out of the police station.

She exited the office and made for the break-out room to find a moment away from the job. On the way, she passed Harrigan's office. The lower half of the office wall was wood that had been painted white, and the upper half was glass. Through the glass she could see Harrigan had his back to her, his head pressed up against the outside window and a cell phone clamped to his ear. Paladino couldn't make out what he was saying, but he seemed to be in a fury about something. Paladino stopped and watched. As Harrigan spoke, he began to gently bang his head against the window, getting more exasperated as the conversation went on. Finally, he ended the call and threw the phone across the room where it hit the wall and broke into a couple of pieces. He cursed at the broken phone and looked up, saw Paladino, and raced over to the glass partition and pulled the blind down.

NINE

Devlin's mind was made up about where he was going next, whatever Harrigan had said. Back to the rectory. It was early morning, not much past dawn, and still quiet. A cop was standing in the front entrance, and the place was still cordoned off. But the forensics team had gone, and there were no police around the back of the property. The back stairs up to Devlin's loft was clear.

Devlin climbed the staircase and entered the kitchen. He walked through the loft out onto the landing and then descended the stairs to the ground floor, pausing a couple of times to listen out for any cops or CSIs. But the house was completely silent. Moving cautiously into the hall, he glanced toward the front door and saw through the opaque glass pane the silhouette of the cop outside standing guard. Then he walked along the hall and turned into the study.

The only light left on in the room was the desk lamp which illuminated the dark oval-shaped stain where Father Aranha's head had lain. Devlin scanned the room, his eye following the trail of yellow tags left by the forensics team, and then his gaze returned to the desk. He noticed that the top edge of the oval bloodstain stopped in a straight line where Aranha's laptop must have been. Place on the side of the desk was a pile of books and a memo pad, all stained with blood. Devlin stood over the desk and bent down, looking closely at the notepad. The top sheet was blank, but he saw that the blood had collected and dried into faint grooves. Grooves made from a note on a previous page that had been ripped off but that had left a palimpsest that had now been revealed by Aranha's own blood. Some of the letters were incomplete, but Devlin was able to decipher a fragment of writing, three words that said, "For all have..."

Devlin was suddenly aware of voices outside the front door. He ripped off the piece of paper and placed it in his pocket. Then, as fast as he could and as quietly as he could, he retraced his steps back along the hall, up the stairs to the top landing. Down below the front door opened and there were footsteps along the hallway. Devlin walked through the loft, out onto the balcony and, closing the door behind him gently, walked back down the staircase and across the lot out onto the street.

He came out onto Division Street and was walking toward the harbor, thinking about where he might stay while the rectory was off-limits, when a white Volkswagen Beetle pulled up ahead of him.

Devlin drew level with the car and saw officer Paladino in the driver's seat.

"Hey..." said Paladino.

"Hi."

"You need a ride anywhere?"

"Actually, what I need right now is a place to stay. What with the rectory being out of bounds. You got any ideas? It's the height of the tourist season, and I'm a little afraid for my wallet."

"If you don't know anyone, you're gonna be paying a small

fortune even for one night's stay... But...if you're not so choosy, then there are budget options. Still expensive though."

"How expensive?"

"I know a place in Southampton. Off the 27 and not a prime location. It'll still cost you a couple of hundred dollars. I can call and check if they have a spare room?"

Devlin winced at what Paladino called budget and briefly considered sleeping on the beach. But then he scratched that idea—maybe he'd keep that as an option further down the line, depending on the situation with the rectory.

"Sure. That's decent of you."

"Hold on."

Devlin waited on the sidewalk while Paladino made the call. After a short conversation, she rang off, leaned across the passenger seat, and pushed open the passenger door.

"It's on. They have a room if you got cash."

"I can get it."

"Hop in, I'll give you a ride out there."

"You sure? You look like you just finished your shift."

"I'm sure. Get in. It'll make me feel good to do a good turn for a priest. Do you think it'll count in my favor?"

"Without a shadow of a doubt."

Paladino laughed, and Devlin eased into the seat, still stinging from Harrigan's baton.

"You okay?" asked Paladino.

Devlin thought about telling Paladino about her boss's off-the-books methods but instead brushed it off and said, "Fine. I'm fine."

Paladino shifted the car into drive, and they pulled out. She drove up Division Street and stopped by an ATM so Devlin could get cash.

THEY HEADED WEST OUT of the village past long rows of trees and neat hedgerows behind which were large houses spread out and set back from the road in big open green spaces. They took a road that followed the coast, and from time to time Devlin could see the glittering blue expanse of Noyac Bay.

"You ever been to the Hamptons before?" asked Paladino.

"I've been out this way for conferences. I came out to Hicksville one time. But I don't know it well. Have you lived here all your life?"

"No. I came out here a few years back."

"For the job?"

"For the job and a man."

"You like it here?"

"Yeah... Well...I did..."

"What changed?"

Paladino let her gaze stray momentarily from the road out to a flash of blue as the bay came into view. Then she focused back on the road.

"The man died," she said matter-of-factly. "A few months back."

"I'm so sorry."

Despite her best intentions, she found her voice breaking and her eyes misting over. And then she cursed herself for even bringing it up. What was she thinking? She hardly knew this priest. This man who, according to her boss at least, was a person of interest in a murder investigation.

"I do understand what it's like," said Devlin. "How it is to lose someone close. I lost my wife. So I know the pain and the loneliness. How overwhelming it is."

Silence. More trees whipped past, more greenery basking under the clear blue of the sky as another glorious summer day got underway. The road broadened out as they joined the Southampton Bypass.

"When did you lose your wife?" asked Paladino.

"Nine years ago. Before I became a priest."

"Is that why you became a priest?"

"Partly."

"And it helped?"

"Yeah. But there are other, less dramatic ways of coping with grief, you'll be pleased to know."

"I am."

"I didn't know your husband. But from what I know of you, I think that he must have been a good man."

"He was. A damned good man." Paladino gripped the wheel hard. "Can you answer a question for me, Father Devlin?"

"I can try."

"Can you tell me why the good ones are taken and the bad ones aren't?"

There was a beat while Devlin considered the question. "I guess people have to be free to choose whether to do good or bad things. Or they aren't real choices that mean anything. That stands whether there's a God or not. I don't know why God let my wife be taken from me. But I believe what Paul said, that 'the sufferings of this present time are not to be compared with the glory which shall be revealed in us.'"

"Well, that glory had better be pretty damn glorious if it's going to make up for all the present suffering."

"It will get better. Life will start to be worth living again. How did you meet your husband?"

"I was training to be a cop, and he came down to run a couple of sessions on our course. I asked him a few questions at the end of class, we went for coffee, and that was the start. He was an easy man to fall in love with. I liked him so much I went for the first job that came up in Sag Harbor to be with him. He was a detective here." Paladino fell silent for a moment, then added, "That's how he died. On duty. Some son of a bitch mowed him down in a car."

"Did they find who did it?"

"No. They didn't."

She glanced at Devlin and back at the road.

"Greg...my husband. He had a funeral at the Methodist church. But the thing is, I really don't know if there's a God. And I sure believe less in him since Greg died."

"Grief can push you away from God. It pushed me away. But he'll wait for you to return if and when you're ready to."

Paladino shook her head. "But why should I believe in God at all? Isn't it just a bit...incredible? The idea of some supernatural being?"

"Yeah. It's incredible. But then aren't all the answers to the big mysteries in life incredible? Whichever answers you believe in?"

"What do you mean?"

"So, for instance, are we alone in the universe, or are there aliens out there? Whichever you believe, it's incredible. Either we are alone in this entire universe, or there are other intelligent life-forms. Both answers are extraordinary. Do you believe the universe is finite or infinite? Either you believe the universe goes on forever, or it was created and has boundaries beyond which lies nothing, whatever nothing is. Both answers are stunning and I think impossible to comprehend. And, if you believe in God, yes, that is extraordinary. But if there is no God, well, the fact that we have evolved from nothing into this miraculous, conscious life-form, that's extraordinary too. When it comes to the answers to the great questions of life and death and existence, whatever you believe is going to be incredible."

They had pulled off the bypass and driven down smaller roads until they got to a turnoff that had tired wooden signs pointing to a Hamptons Resort Motel.

Paladino took the turnoff and drove them into a parking lot. Scattered around the lot were wooden buildings comprising of rows of motel rooms. Lawn chairs and low tables had been placed outside each motel room on the porch to give the idea that they might be areas where guests could sit out at night. But Devlin doubted anyone sat out on the porch, which overlooked the parking lot, for any other reason than to have a smoke.

From the outside, he already knew what the rooms would look like. Worn, shabby, and chipped. Mold on the shower curtains, a toilet and tub in need of a proper scrub clean, and missing light bulbs.

He turned to Paladino and smiled. "It's perfect. Thank you."

"You're welcome. Thanks for the talk."

"Anytime."

Devlin stuck out a hand, and with an almost comic formality, they both shook.

And that was when it happened. One of the most extraordinary sensations that Paladino had ever experienced. The moment palm touched palm, for the first time in a year, Paladino felt like she'd taken a real breath. A clean, free breath that didn't snag on the hurt inside her as she took it. That didn't turn into molten pain on its way down. It was her first breath free from misery. And it was miraculous, miraculous because it meant there was hope. Because if she could feel like this just once, then maybe she could feel like it again.

Momentarily overcome by this wave of emotion, she hadn't noticed that Devlin had already opened the car door and got out, seemingly oblivious to the effect he'd somehow had on her.

Paladino tried to shake herself back into the present and watched Devlin walk toward the office.

"My God," she muttered in astonishment. "Do all priests do

that...?" She shook her head again. "Think I'm losing my goddamned mind..."

Then she cranked her window all the way down and called after Devlin.

"Look, I know it doesn't look great, but it's okay. The clerk is called Jake. He doesn't talk much, but he's a good guy."

"It'll be fine. Hey, I don't suppose you'd have any leverage in getting me back into my place at the rectory? I know it's a crime scene right now, but I got the distinct impression Harrigan was happy to keep me out of there for as long as he could just to spite me."

"I'll see what I can do."

Then Paladino drove off, still reeling, wondering exactly what had just taken place, and Devlin headed toward the motel office, a small white shack sitting by the entrance to the motel grounds.

Inside the office, a large guy with a Yankees hat, a Def Leppard T-shirt, long graying hair, and several visible piercings greeted Devlin and exchanged a set of keys for two hundred and ten bucks.

Devlin was tired, but he didn't have time to waste catching up on all his lost sleep. He set the alarm on his cell phone for two hours' time, lay out on the bed, and immediately passed into a deep sleep.

The sleep was deep and saturated with images of shooting stars arriving out of the sky and landing on the shores of Sag Harbor. When the alarm went off, despite the stings over his upper body and the general feeling of exhaustion, he got up, cold showered and shaved, said his prayers, and ordered a cab to take him back to Sag Harbor. Because now Devlin was a man on a mission. Or, to be more accurate, two missions.

TEN

The kid zipped across Long Island Avenue and let the bike freewheel down West Water Street between cars parked up on the seafront and tour coaches lined up along the other side. She took a right over a patch of gravel and left dry land proper, her wheels bumping and rattling across sunbaked slats of wood as she whizzed down the slight incline of a narrow, rickety pier, the calm bay water washing gently underneath.

Sleek white yachts were moored on either side of the jetty, and the kid stopped halfway down by an elegant sixty-five-footer, longer than a bus, that was white with dark-tinted cockpit windows. The name *April Rose* was stenciled in a flowing font on the stern.

A man wearing Oakley sunglasses and dressed in a loose white linen shirt and cream shorts had been sitting on the fighting chair, swiveling back and forth. When he saw the kid, he got up and went to the edge of the deck.

The girl shouted over a "morning," but as usual, the guy didn't answer.

The girl dismounted and wheeled her bike along the gangway. When she reached the deck, she handed it to the man, who took the bike around the side of the boat while the girl disappeared down into the master cabin.

While the girl waited, she cast a critical eye over the fittings and fixtures. Everything beneath deck, she noted, was some different shade of brown. Dark brown teak paneling, brown wooden blinds, a light brown vinyl L-shaped couch, and matching light brown curtains and carpets. It was all designed for old people, the girl thought. People who didn't like surprises. Who liked comfort and continuity and their furnishings conservative. Some old rock music that sounded like it was from the eighties, played by guys who probably had long hair and who wore vests and leather trousers, blared out of wall-mounted speakers.

The girl spread herself out on the sun-warmed couch. Through the tinted windows, she could see out over the bay; gulls were diving, a couple of jet skiers zipped across the blue swell, and farther out the white shapes of other yachts were dotted around. Maybe one day, thought the girl, she'd have a boat. Or maybe not. As far as she could see, boats were full of fat old people.

After a long wait, the man came back in, still wearing his Oakleys. The kid noticed that the arms of his sunglasses were tied to a cord so they could hang off his neck when he wasn't wearing them, the one sure way to make sunglasses look really lame.

The man was bald, and what hair he had was clippered down to dark stubble. Short and stout, his belly sagged over his cargo shorts. Decades of constant sun had turned him nearly as brown as the wood paneling in the galley.

"Here," he said and handed the girl a folded piece of paper. The girl took it and slipped it into the back pocket of her jeans. She remained seated on the couch and looked up expectantly.

"Right..." The man sighed, took a fold of bills out of his wallet, and handed them to the girl, who counted them out.

"Much obliged to you," said the girl.

"Any messages for me?" asked the man.

"No. No messages. My boss is happy with how things are."

The man didn't look like he was satisfied with the answer.

"Happy? I don't think he's got any damn right to be happy."

"Why?" asked the girl, but the question was ignored.

"You can go now. Got things to do... Go on—get."

The man followed the girl back onto the deck, and he went and got her bike. He wheeled it out from the side and handed it back to her.

Back on her bike, the girl pedaled along the wooden slats toward land, thrilled with the satisfying bulge of twenties wedged in her jean pocket. The sea spray blessed her arms and face as she bulleted back onto dry land, giving a short, high musical giggle. At times it seemed to the girl that taking money off adults was like taking candy from a baby.

As the girl swung back through West Water Street, she saw a familiar figure, and her heart sank. The figure was broad and dark, sitting on a bench by the grass meridian strip that divided the harbor roadway from Long Island Avenue.

She slowed as she rode by Devlin, watching him carefully. He had a smoking cigar pinched between his thumb and forefinger.

"Hi," Devlin called over.

The girl came to a gradual stop a few yards from where Devlin was sitting.

"What you doing here?" asked the girl suspiciously.

"Just out admiring the view."

"Are...are you following me?"

Devlin gave a short, deep laugh. "No. I come down here a

lot. Get breakfast at the cafe over there before it fills up and then take a walk along the harbor."

The girl didn't look convinced. "You must have a lot of time on your hands."

"I make time."

"Well, that's real interesting. I got to go..."

The girl raked the pedal up with the heel of her foot, ready to push off.

"Where's the necklace you were wearing?" asked Devlin.

The question caused the girl to sit back on her saddle. She looked a little startled. "Excuse me?"

"The necklace with the pendant—the one you were wearing the last time I saw you, the one with the tree and the snake etched on it."

"You know, you're starting to creep me out. Are you obsessed with that necklace or something?"

"You know, I sort of am."

The girl's eyes narrowed. "Do you think I stole it? Is that it? 'Cause if that's what you think, I didn't. The person it belonged to let me borrow it awhile."

"Hey." Devlin put up his hands. "It's okay. I didn't think you stole it."

"Then why are you so interested in it?"

"I collect antique jewelry."

The girl's expression changed from guilty to appalled. "You do what?"

"Antique jewelry." Devlin clamped his cigar between his teeth and rooted around in his pockets. He brought out the pillbox and showed it to the girl.

She leaned forward to study it, and her eyes lit up in surprise. "Hey, it's the same design."

"That's right, Sherlock. Exactly the same. Here's the thing— this here is a real unique piece. Or so I thought. Then I saw yours and I realized it wasn't so unique. So that's why I'm so intrigued by that necklace you had. I think they were made by the same person and somehow got split up. And that's why I'm very interested in where it's from."

"How interested?"

Devlin paused for a moment, then pulled out his wallet. He opened it up and thumbed out a twenty.

The girl took it and said, "You said you were intrigued. Intrigued is more than a twenty."

"Forty and that's my final offer," said Devlin. "If it ain't enough, I'll find out some other way."

The girl immediately opened up her hand, and Devlin handed over another bill.

"So? Spill the beans already," said Devlin.

"You gotta promise you won't say who told you?" replied the girl.

"I promise."

The girl didn't look convinced.

"I'm a priest. If I don't keep my promises, I go to hell."

"Gimme a break."

"I swear to you. I won't say. You want me to go get a bible to swear on?"

The girl thought about it for a moment. "That's a nice cross you've got."

Devlin glanced down at the pearl-and-gold crucifix hanging from his neck. "Thanks. That's antique too."

"Swear on your cross."

Devlin clasped the cross with his right hand. "I swear I won't tell a soul. So help me God."

That seemed to satisfy the girl. "I got it from the place I work. A house on Suffolk Street."

"Which house?"

The girl chewed her bottom lip pensively. "You just collect old jewelry, right? You're not a cop?"

"I'm a priest. I collect old jewelry. I'm just a really boring old man."

"Okay. A house on Suffolk Street where I work. Cleaning, but that's it. I'm not telling you anything else. In any case, I don't actually know who owns the necklace," she said a little too quickly. "I just found it lying around in one of the rooms, and then I put it back."

Any other questions Devlin had were cut short by the moan of a siren and the sound of a car pulling over.

Devlin turned to see Harrigan coming to a stop in his cruiser.

The girl didn't wait around. As soon as the cop car arrived on the scene, she was gone. As she rode into the distance, he paid particular attention to the bike itself, a silver, brand-new, very expensive-looking mountain bike. The brand of the bike was Kingdom which Devlin was willing to bet was high quality. He looked at how, despite the mint condition of the bike, the frame of the bike sat low and the tires looked a little flat.

"Morning." Harrigan had got out of his car and was standing over Devlin wearing aviator shades with his thumbs tucked into his belt. "I hope you had a nice rest last night wherever it was you slept."

Devlin didn't bother answering.

"Who's the girl?" asked Harrigan.

"She comes to the food pantry in the church."

"She local?"

"No idea."

There was a silence, the sound of gulls, someone laying on their horn in the street behind, and the whoosh of surf picking up across the harbor.

"Is there anything else you wanted, Detective?"

"Yeah. I want you to get the hell out of my town."

"I'm not going anywhere."

"Then you can expect this special attention every day. I'll be looking for you, watching you. Riding up and checking in on you. Until you do something wrong. And the crazy thing is, in the end, I find everyone I give special treatment to does something wrong. And then you'll be back in the police station and I'll make sure you get a real good beating the second time round."

Devlin looked up, squinting at Harrigan. "There won't be a second time around. Trust me."

"We'll see." Then Harrigan turned, walked back to his car, and drove slowly by Devlin before speeding off.

Devlin waited for about five minutes, smoking down his cigar and surveying the harbor. Waiting till he was sure as he could be that Harrigan had gone. Then he stood, threw his cigar away, crossed the harbor front, and walked out along the jetty. He stopped by the boat the girl had boarded, the *April Rose*, and saw the bald guy wearing sunglasses coming up on the desk from a hatch along the side of the cockpit. The bald guy walked onto the stern deck, wiping his hands with an oily rag, and spotted Devlin leaning on the gangway rails.

"Can I help you?" asked the bald guy abruptly.

"Maybe you can. I'm looking for a yacht. I'm supposed to be blessing it, you see. I know you're thinking, they bless boats now? They sure do. I've been asked to bless all sorts of things. Even a motorbike once. This boat is called... Oh, wait now...the *Spirit of the Wind* or something like that. Do you know where that is?"

"No, I don't," said the bald guy flatly, and he turned and went below deck down the main stairway.

Devlin waited a minute or two, then stepped onto the yacht. He didn't have much knowledge of yachts or boats generally, but this one seemed to him to be midrange. A cruiser. Nothing really fancy but still worth a bundle of dough.

In the middle of the deck was a fighting chair, and on the starboard side a line of fishing rods hung along the hull, their handles slotted into plastic tubes that were attached to the side. On the same side, tucked into the corner, was a long plastic crate that had spare rods, reels, and a long gaff with a hook placed on top of it.

For a moment Devlin just stood, still, feeling the motion of the sea rocking the boat gently, the faint breeze and the unforgiving heat of the sun burning away at him. Then he scooted around the side of the cockpit, walking along the wraparound deck to the hatch the man had first appeared from. The lid of the hatch was up, and the opening was about three feet square with a narrow wooden ladder leading down from it. Beside the hatch lay some tools: a wrench, a set of hex keys, and a screwdriver. Devlin levered himself down through the hatch and onto the ladder and climbed below.

Beneath deck, he found himself in a cramped aft cabin with bunks on either side. The space was lit by overhead lighting and daylight that came through small slits in the port wall between the bottom and top bunks. Clear plastic sheets littered the bunks and floor. Between the bunks, the sheets had been pushed aside to make a narrow path that led to the bulkhead. One of the panels in the bulkhead had been prized off to allow access to the plastic water tank that was housed behind it. Lying on the floor below the open panel were a white plastic cap and a utility knife.

Devlin leaned through the space where the panel had been so he could get a closer look at the tank and its contents. The tank was half-full, and below the surface of the water were dozens of long, very thin white tubes stacked together. Devlin reached in and picked up one of the tubes to get a closer look. It contained white powder that had been shrink-wrapped into long cylinders.

Devlin heard the sound of approaching footsteps up above and then the creak of the ladder behind him. He turned to see a pair of deck shoes and hairy legs stepping down the ladder into the cabin. Devlin reached up and grabbed an ankle, yanking it downward so hard and fast that the owner's hands lost their grip on the rung and their bulk came tumbling down and backward into the narrow space. A bald head ricocheted off the wooden side rail of one of the bunks before coming to rest at Devlin's feet. Without waiting to check if the man was going to come around, Devlin grabbed his collar, lifted his head a few inches off the floor, and knocked him back down with a sharp jab to the temple.

"That's for getting a child to run your poison."

Devlin stepped over the dazed body and climbed out of the pokey cabin up into the bright daylight, the slight breeze, and the sound of gulls. As he walked back over the deck, he considered calling 911 and tipping off the cops. But there were two factors that held him back. First, he wanted to protect the girl who had become involved in something beyond her years and understanding, and second, he had a strong sense there was more to uncover, like who it was the girl was taking the drugs to.

There was a lot about this setup he didn't know and needed to unravel.

What he did know, though, was that the symbol on the pillbox had led him to the boat and a drug operation, and he felt certain it would lead to much, much more.

ELEVEN

Washington, DC

SENATOR HELEN LAWTON was strung out on no sleep, lots of coffee, and one little thing eating away in a corner of her mind and that wouldn't let go of her.

She was sitting in her hideaway office, her second office she kept in the Senate office buildings. It was unmarked and a short walk from the Senate floor. Probably once used as a broom closet, it was where Lawton, as head of the Senate Select Intelligence Committee, held her most confidential meetings.

There was a knock on the door.

"Come in."

A short, squarely built man in a suit entered, and Lawton almost smiled at the figure who shambled toward her. Mike O'Reilly, assistant secretary at the Bureau of Intelligence, had risen through the ranks of government from an entry-level job. He hadn't gone to an Ivy League college, didn't have the advantage of a network of social contacts, and his awkward, self-conscious body language and badly fitting suits still betrayed his lower-middle-class origins.

"How are you, Helen?" O'Reilly smiled broadly and took a seat.

"Oh, you know. Losing myself in work. Not healthy, but it's something."

"It's been a hell of a time for you, I know."

"It has. It really has. But Dale passed two years ago. I really should be getting to the other side of it soon. Shouldn't I?"

"I don't suppose that's how it works. I guess grief doesn't make scheduled stops. Sorry, that's a cheesy thing to say..."

"No, Mike, it's not... Well, it is, but I get your point."

O'Reilly leaned forward. "You been sleeping okay?"

"The bags show through the makeup, then."

"Not so anyone who didn't know you as well as I do would notice." O'Reilly tapped the desk playfully. "You're a busy woman, Helen, so I'll cut to the chase."

O'Reilly had been carrying a brown folder in his hand which he now placed on the table. "I know you were already given the relevant papers."

Lawton stiffened in her chair and nodded quickly. Something about this reaction made O'Reilly unsure.

"You did get the papers, didn't you?" he asked. "I had them sent by classified courier."

"I got the papers, Mike. I just have them in the main Senate office. In the safe."

"Sure. Okay. Well then, you'll have read them?"

"Yes. Yes, I have. But I still don't know what this is all about. All the papers said was that we had bagged a major Chinese intelligence asset. A professor...sorry, I forgot his name..."

"Zhou. Professor Feng Zhou."

"Professor Zhou. Apparently, he'd just walked into the consulate in Almaty and handed himself over. That the bureau's proposal was to give Zhou the asylum he'd requested. But there was no information whatsoever about what that asset had of value to offer us. Do we have that information now?"

O'Reilly puffed his cheeks. "No. Not exactly."

"What? Why not?"

"Zhou won't tell us what he's been working on till he's here, on the ground and safe. He wants to keep what he knows to himself. To make sure we keep our end of the deal."

"Oh, come on. Then he's probably bluffing us, Mike. He doesn't know anything."

"I'm not so sure."

"I have to be the one that calls out the big picture here. We have a very delicate relationship with China. The administration is pushing aggressively on a number of diplomatic and economic fronts, really pressing Beijing's buttons. What sense does it make strategically to put ourselves on the line for a guy who won't tell us why he's worth it?"

"Because there is evidence he might be worth it. Really worth it. First, Helen, you have to understand that when it comes to China, the reality is our intelligence is thin on the ground. It's just a reality we have to deal with—the China desk at the bureau has one of the hardest jobs in intelligence gathering. I mean, the first we heard about Chinese scientists modifying the DNA of human embryos was through rumors in the global scientific community. That tells you all you need to know about our shortcomings when it comes to Chinese state secrets. But with this guy, we do have something else, something that tells us he might be worth the gamble. And then some..."

"What do you have?"

"Project Jiù ēn."

"Project what?"

"Project Salvation. For the first time in decades, we have a contact in Beijing passing information to us. They're inside the

Ministry of Science and Technology. They're not senior, but sensitive documents do pass through their hands. One of these documents listed a half dozen of the ministry's most secret current projects and also the attached head of research. On that list was Project Salvation, and the name alongside it was Professor Feng Zhou. Helen, I really think that whatever he's working on is worth the risk. It's possible that there are areas of Chinese scientific research that are at least half a decade ahead of anything we're working on."

"Do we know anything about Zhou?"

"We know he trained in physics and micro-tech at the Xinjiang Technical Institute. But not much else. This is China we're dealing with; the level of secrecy is unlike any other country. "

"Mike, look, I trust your judgment, but I'll be selling this to a hostile committee."

"Sure, I know, but by the next official session of the committee, I should have more for you, fresh information that will make your job easier. As soon as that happens I'll pass it on to you. That's a promise. And I know you know this, Helen, but even so, I'm bound to remind you that none of this information can be shared with another living soul outside of the senate committee. There are state and private actors who would kill to get hold of Zhou and his research."

"I understand."

O'Reilly stood.

"Thanks, Mike."

"Not at all. Now you need to get some rest, a vacation maybe. Look after yourself, Helen."

O'Reilly left, and Lawton gazed into the middle distance in silence with that one little thing gnawing away at her a little faster and a little deeper now.

TWELVE

Harrigan's eyes were a millimeter away from shutting completely. Through thin slits he watched the six trustees, sitting in a line behind a long desk at the end of the room, looking like hazy blobs, black spots getting farther and farther away. He was in the last place on earth he wanted to be, a village meeting. But he'd done the chief of police a favor by covering this one for him and expected unspecified future favors in return.

It was eight o'clock at night, and the village hall was full with the local citizenry all up in arms about zoning laws and some gazillionaire rock star who'd made a pile in the seventies building a McMansion in Bay Street. Harrigan had heard the rock star was a drummer from some long-hair outfit, but when he'd asked someone who the band was, he didn't recognize the name.

As Harrigan dozed in and out of full consciousness, he listened to a small, bald guy in a loose-fitting sweater and shirt who was standing at the lectern giving forth on something or other. The small bald guy was an architect and had a thin, droning voice that matched his body. He seemed to Harrigan to have been talking for an age, so much so that the people in the room who only fifteen minutes ago had been promising another civil war were practically asleep. The architect whined on for another few minutes till everybody had practically lost the will to live, and then the board of trustees offered an opinion which caused fresh uproar and which was quelled by one of the trustees calling the room to order and moving on to the next item of business on the agenda.

Harrigan shook himself awake and sat upright. This part of the meeting required him to pay attention. It was why he'd been required to show up. The treasurer, a well-fed guy with a thick gray beard, dressed in a green cable-knit sweater and baggy brown corduroy pants, was sitting in the middle of the trustees. He stood up and cleared his throat.

"I've been asked by the chief of police to give an update on the situation with the sheriff's department. So far there hasn't been any movement toward a compromise, but there is a meeting next Tuesday between the Suffolk County Executive and the sheriff's office to reopen negotiations. So, we will continue to cooperate with our colleagues in neighboring juris-dictions to cover the shortfall in law enforcement provided by the sheriff's office." The trustee looked about the room. "I believe we had a representative from Sag Harbor PD here?"

Harrigan got to his feet.

"That's me. Detective Harrigan."

"Have you anything to add, Detective Harrigan?" asked the trustee.

"No. No. It's like you say. Same as the last update you got. We're covering the extra territory just fine for the moment. As long as it's temporary, we got it covered."

The treasurer looked like he was expecting Harrigan to say

something else, but Harrigan looked back at him blankly like a man whose work had been done.

"Very good," said the treasurer eventually. "Anyone else wish to speak on this matter?"

There was a silence, and Harrigan dutifully waited it out until he felt he'd given it enough time and started to lower himself back into his seat.

"Actually, I would like to say something." A faintly accented voice came from the back of the room, and Harrigan just about prevented himself from giving out an audible groan as, deprived of the comfort of his chair, he straightened back up to full height. His knees twinged, and for the third time that day he remembered his doctor's warnings about his rising weight.

A sea of heads turned to see where the voice was coming from. Standing behind the last row was a tall, elegant-looking man, blond and in his forties. He wore a beige linen suit and white cotton shirt. His hair was sandy, and his eyes were a pale green. Harrigan immediately recognized him as the guy whose business had been broken into a couple of days back, the break-in he and Paladino had attended.

The trustee squinted to make the new speaker out. "Could I ask your name?"

"Andrei Gromyko. I am a businessman. My offices are along the Sag Harbor Turnpike, and we have had two break-ins. Two. In the last month. One of them was even attended by Detective Harrigan. And I know of other residents here who have also suffered a spate of burglaries, including the senator's residence."

There was a hum of agreement, and a couple of hands shot up accompanied by shouts of "me too" and "it's getting out of control."

"As you can see," continued Gromyko, "there is a real situation here. We don't feel protected or safe, and I think the police force is stretched too much. So they cannot cover the areas outside the village. They cannot do their job."

Gromyko's comments were followed by other residents getting to their feet and protesting that they too lived out along the Turnpike or farther out and were not being properly served by police patrols. The treasurer allowed the commotion to run its course, and when the voices had subsided, he looked hopefully over at Harrigan, who was still standing.

"Detective Harrigan? Is there anything you and your officers can do to reassure the people here?"

"Well, not really. I can't clone my officers. Not yet anyway. And the budget we have won't cover any more shifts being laid on. That's the only way I see it working. We get more money to cover extra patrols. Even then we may have to switch our focus from the town center graveyard shifts to...you know...crack down on the break-ins further south."

The treasurer nodded and leaned down to consult with the lady beside him, who wore round glasses and had her dark hair lashed back into a ponytail. The lady listened, nodded, whispered back at the treasurer. Then the treasurer looked over at Harrigan.

"What about if we released extra funds to cover more patrols? At least until we know the outcome of Tuesday's meeting with the sheriff's office?"

Harrigan nodded and did his best to hide the little glow of victory he felt in his belly. More shifts, more overtime, more money. Everybody happy. "Sure. That would be a real help. Absolutely."

"In that case," said the treasurer, "I'll look at what's available, and we can finalize the extra number of patrols, say, tomorrow, with the chief of police?"

"Sounds like a great plan...Mr....Treasurer."

Harrigan thought he heard a faint titter in response to his

awkward formality, and then there was a clap of hands which turned into applause, and at last Harrigan could sit down. He'd done his job, and the mayor would finally be off his back. Happy days.

The meeting finally wound its way to an end, and people started to get up from their chairs and file away. Harrigan decided to wait for the bottleneck to ease, anxious to avoid being ambushed on the way out by some earnest citizen with a pressing question about village policing. But, as it turned out, this strategy also made him a sitting duck. Andrei Gromyko sat down beside Harrigan, and the detective had to make an effort to hide his hostile reaction. Jeez, he thought, hadn't he done enough? It was after nine in the evening, and he would hardly have any time to squeeze in a few at the Bay Tavern. No salary was worth this.

"Detective."

"Mr. Gromyko."

"I wanted to thank you for helping us get to a solution here tonight."

"No problem."

Harrigan avoided eye contact with Gromyko but allowed himself a brief glance at the man sitting beside him. Gromyko was leaner and more sinewy than he remembered him being when they had met at the BioGenesis labs. He was relaxed and effortless in his movement, incredibly comfortable in his own skin, like a pro athlete at the height of their achievements. The hall lights seemed to make his fine blond hair glow golden and give his green eyes and delicately chiseled face an otherworldly quality. It was like Harrigan could see his aura, if he believed in that crap.

"Well, I had better be going," said Harrigan, leaning forward in his chair. "Paperwork to file. Back to the grindstone."

Gromyko placed a hand on Harrigan's shoulder, and

Harrigan had the most curious feeling—his will seemed to melt away. Inexplicably, like a tame dog, he submitted to Gromyko and remained seated.

"You should know that I have the ear of your superiors, Detective. That I am very close with the mayor. He is really indebted to me for the contributions I have made to this community. So if there is anything I can do for you in return, anything, all you have to do is let me know."

"Sure."

Gromyko put his arm over the back of Harrigan's chair and moved closer to Harrigan, creating an intimacy that made Harrigan's innards shrivel up.

"I can do so much for a man like you, Detective. I know you've been under tremendous pressure, what with your...issues."

"What issues?"

"Your last few quarterly evaluations have been very poor, and you've been referred to the performance monitoring unit..."

"How...?"

"But I can change that. I'm the sort of man who you are lucky to have run into, to have done a favor for. I have connections and can make life so much better for a man like you. Just get in touch anytime."

Again, Harrigan felt powerless to talk, reason, or argue his way out of this encounter and merely nodded his head faithfully.

"I look forward to hearing from you."

Andrei patted Harrigan on the knee and rose gracefully from his chair, all the while looking down at Harrigan, smiling munificently.

Harrigan watched Gromyko leave and felt somehow that, in a way he couldn't quite articulate, or explain exactly how, his integrity had been compromised. For someone who had spent his life attacking and doubling down, protecting himself at everyone else's expense, he'd finally met a man who had taken something from him. Though how that had happened and what he had taken, he couldn't rightly say.

THIRTEEN

"Hello. Can I help you?"

"Mr. Harris?"

"Yes?"

"My name's Noah, and this is Marcus. Tinky told us to come up to the house... Did Tinky mention us? She said she would."

"I don't... Wait..." Harris stepped over the sill out onto the porch and into the direct sunshine. He was wearing a red tracksuit with white stripes and chunky white Nike Airs, box-fresh without a mark on them. His tracksuit top was unzipped to below his flabby chest. He shaded his eyes and looked up at both boys, who towered over him, then smiled and nodded. "Oh... yes...the boys from Queens. Yes, I told her that you should come up to the house."

"That's right," said Noah. The boys shared a quick look between them, to get some mutual reassurance while Harris studied the two of them in turn.

They were both handsome, thought Harris. The one called Marcus had a surfer look, frayed jeans, baggy T-shirt, shaggy beach-bum hair. Muscular but not overly so. But Noah—Noah made Harris catch his breath. He was a rarity. He could be a model. Flawless complexion, great bone structure. Tall and rangy with that pure beauty you only possess for a few fleeting years. He was right in the sweet spot of perfection. His friend wasn't bad, not bad at all, but Noah had real potential.

"Yes, yes. Come in," said Harris. "I think I have something for you two young men."

Harris opened the door, and the two boys stepped into the hall, looking around in undisguised wonder. The door closed and Harris arced around in front of them, looking them up and down.

"Now, what are your preferences?" asked Harris with a glint in his eye.

The boys swapped uncertain looks, and Noah said, "How do you mean, 'preferences'?"

"PlayStation or Xbox?" asked Harris, smiling broadly.

The boys chuckled and shared another look.

"PlayStation, I guess," said Marcus.

"Good. Follow me."

Harris led them up to a games room on the first floor. There was a pool table, some arcade games, a bar, a big Smeg refrigerator, and a long, soft leather couch facing a huge flat-screen bolted to the wall. Games consoles sat in a pine cabinet below the TV, and on either side were racks of games.

"I hope it's to your liking?"

The boys nodded in unison.

"I had it set up for my nephews when their mother used to come visit. Is it okay if I leave you here for a moment?" asked Harris. "There's everything you need. If you want a drink, help yourself to the bar, and if you need to eat, help yourself to the food in the fridge. There are also other goodies in the pot by the window. Special kinds of goodies." Harris pointed to a red clay pot on the carpet. "I'll be back in a while. Forgive me, but I have some errands to run. Then we can discuss business."

Harris disappeared. Noah shrugged, and the two boys grinned at each other. They both looked at the clay pot.

"Best see what the goodies are," said Noah, and he sauntered over to the pot and picked off the top and peered inside.

"Dude...!"

Noah picked out a Ziplock bag of grass, opened it, pinched some in his fingers, and held it up to his nose. "Smells so damn fresh..." Then he dipped his hand back into the pot and pulled out a small plastic bag packed with white powder. He peeled it open, wetted a finger, and took a little dab which he placed on his tongue. It only took a couple of seconds before he felt the tingle and numbness he was hoping for. He licked and smacked his lips.

"Dude..." said Noah triumphantly. "Fire up the PlayStation and let's get toasted."

FOURTEEN

The light outside had softened as the summer day slowly began to lose its grip. The two boys were slouched into their clothes and sunk into the couch. The game pads glued to their hands clicked along like Morse code with a precision and alertness that was absent from their stoned, hollow eyes. A thin line of snot hung from Marcus's nose. He gave a short, loud snort and wiped it away with the back of this hand. He swallowed and, slack-jawed, mumbled, "Where did that guy Harris go? How long have we been here?"

"Hours, man," Noah replied blankly. He eyed the nearly empty clay pot. Everything in it had been smoked and snorted apart from a few buds of grass that lay scattered at the bottom. "I'll roll one up for the road, but then we should split. We've had our fun."

Noah dropped his game pad and reached for the skins and grass that were perched on the arm of the couch. As he was filling the narrow paper trench curled between his fingers, Harris appeared in the doorway.

"Gentlemen. I am so, so sorry—my errands took much longer than I anticipated."

The two boys looked up at him with vacant eyes and grunted back. Noah kept rolling and said, "We're thinking we might split, Mr. Harris."

"Oh, I do hope not."

"Yeah, we got to get back I'm afraid." Noah licked the lip of the Rizla paper and sealed the joint up. "But thank you for your hospitality. Just making one for the road." Noah waved the long spliff in the air and planted it behind his ear.

"That would be an awful shame," said Harris. "I'd hate for you to miss out on the opportunity to make some money."

"Money?" said Noah, suddenly marginally more alert. "How much?"

"Lots. That's how much. I have a party tonight, and what my guests love more than anything is the company of young, beautiful people."

The boys nodded their heads and looked askance at each other.

"So we...what? Just...hang out?" asked Marcus.

"Yes. You can do. You can absolutely sit around looking handsome. That would be dandy. But there are other even more lucrative possibilities for two young men like yourselves. The happier you are able to make my guests, the more I and they will feel able to pay you."

"So...you want us to sleep with them?" asked Marcus.

"It entirely depends. Some folk just want to talk, some folk just want company and maybe a little affection. But some...some will see you and will want more." Harris shrugged and smiled. "But you only do what you feel comfortable with. My guests are exceptionally wealthy people. Exceptionally wealthy. If you make these sorts of people happy, you can make yourselves a lot, I mean *a lot* of money. Like I say, it's entirely up to you. What you're comfortable with." Harris pulled out his wallet and slid

two fifties from it. "This is just for starters, my dears." He gave
one to each of the two boys. "Why don't you two take a shower
and get yourselves ready?" Harris glanced toward the empty red
pot. "There's plenty more where that came from too."

FIFTEEN

Noah slumped down on the edge of the bed. He had a towel wrapped around his waist, and behind him, his clothes were bundled in a heap in the middle of the comforter. Harris had shown him up to a bedroom with a private bathroom. It was decked out in old-style furniture like it was a classy hotel looking to attract rich businesspeople, executives, that sort of thing. Noah and Marcus had both been given separate bedrooms to get ready in. From downstairs and along the halls Noah could hear the hubbub of guests arriving and talking and the sound of a piano playing a laid-back swing number.

All the weed and coke from his afternoon session had started to go funny on Noah. The sweet feeling of the two drugs working their way through his body had long since faded away. Now he felt hollow and weird, vulnerable and edgy. He really didn't want to be here anymore, here in this weird house where reality got turned away at the door, and money and drugs just appeared right out of nowhere. Screw the money, he thought. He was getting out. He'd just reached over for his shorts when the door handle turned, and Harris poked his head around.

"Oh, I'm sorry," said Harris. "I didn't mean to intrude, but

THE SALVATION MAN   99

the party's really getting going now. We've got some people downstairs who are dying to meet you."

"Uh, yeah," replied Noah. "About that. I think I'm gonna hit the road. I'm not feeling so well."

"Oh," said Harris, looking hurt. "I'm sorry." He stepped into the room and shut the door behind him. Noah noticed he'd changed out of his sweatpants into a velvet dinner jacket and cravat. His hair had been plastered back, and a filterless cigarette burned in his chubby brown fingers. The sweet smell of tobacco mingled with a heavy citrus waft of Harris's aftershave.

Harris sat by Noah on the bed and hummed a little tune to himself. Then he dipped his hand into his jacket and pulled out a wad of notes.

"Here."

Noah took the money and flicked through the bills. It was more money in one place than Noah had ever seen.

"There's about fifteen hundred dollars there, Noah. And that's for doing nothing else than coming downstairs and greeting the lovely people who are only here to admire you. That's it." Harris tapped Noah's knee in an avuncular manner. "You know, I have an idea. I think we should get you something to perk you up. Something a little different to grass and coke. Something more amenable. Soothing. You wait there and I'll get some room service."

Harris left, and Noah heard him calling out down the hallway while he flicked through the bundle of cash sitting in his hand. Then the door opened, and the girl appeared, holding a small fold-up leather case.

"Hi," she said.

"What are you doing here?"

"I'm room service. That's one of the jobs I do here for Mr.

Harris." She looked at the bills in Noah's hand. "So, I guess he liked you? That's good."

"I guess. Not sure the feeling is mutual."

"Oh, you'll get to like Mr. Harris." She smiled and said brightly, "And he's ordered you something nice."

"What?"

The girl sat down beside Noah, in the place Harris had been sitting, quietly thrilled to be introducing this handsome, grown-up-to-her boy something new, something really grown-up. She placed the case on her lap and zipped it open, then laid it out on her knees. Inside the case were pouches containing separate items. A glass tube, some foil, and a row of needles poking out of different compartments.

"Junk?" asked Noah.

"Not just junk," said the girl. "This is anything but. It's top quality, the very best. What I've got in here costs more than a new family car."

"You sound like a salesman."

"It's the opposite. I'm not selling nothing to no one. It's free. That's the beauty."

The girl pulled out a folded sheet of foil from one of the pouches inside the case and pried it open, gently laying it out on the case. From the other pouches, she pulled out a paper bag of white powder with "Hellboy" stamped in thick orange letters on the front and a thin silver spoon and a miniature vial of clear liquid. The last item she laid beside her on the bed. With a care and steadiness that fascinated Noah, she scooped the powder onto the foil. Then she added two drops of the liquid onto the powder.

"Now we sit and wait a minute," said the girl, who was neatly folding and rolling another square of foil into a narrow tube. The music had changed downstairs to a jazzier, up-tempo tune, and the mix of voices had turned up a notch. Noah was starting to enjoy the precision and thoroughness of this little ceremony. It had calmed him down. Focused his mind down to something small, quiet, and intricate, exorcising the afterburn of the earlier session with Marcus.

"I'll heat up the foil," said the girl.

"I know how to do smack..."

"Okay. Sorry. I didn't mean to... Have you done it before?"

"Well...no... No, I haven't...actually done it...but I know how to...do it..."

"Sure. Well, I think this is the best way for the first time. It's a little wasteful to burn such good powder, but what the hell. We aren't paying."

The girl handed the foil pipe to Noah and held the foil sheet out in front of him, heating the underside of it with a lighter she wafted back and forth. Wisps of white smoke began to rise up as the powder bubbled and cooked. Noah put the pipe between his lips and chased the smoke up and down the foil.

The hit was instant. So was the nausea. The girl seemed to know it before he did and put her tools aside and grabbed the wastepaper basket from beside the nightstand. Noah's body convulsed, and he puked into the trash can. But it was only a brief pit stop on the way up because peculiar things were already happening to Noah. His body felt like it was turning into pure energy, into a bright flame, an angel. The sense of well-being was unbelievable. He simply hadn't known that you could feel this good. Hadn't even suspected. He was in love with how he felt. He decided instantly that he would go on feeling like this whenever he could, however he could. Nothing else mattered. If you could feel this wonderful, why would anything else be important?

"Jeez," He shivered and lifted his head up, his eyes half-closed and his heart banging.

"Good? Huh?" he heard the girl say from somewhere else in the room.

Then Harris appeared. Or maybe he'd been standing there all the time, but Noah had only just noticed him.

"I see Tinky's little present agrees with you. You must come and meet a friend, Noah. He's absolutely dying to say hello. And there's more of this too. If you want."

What happened next was like a dream, but the warmest dream Noah had ever had. He was in a bathrobe walking with Harris up the staircase. Harris had his hand the crook of Noah's arm. And all Noah could think was, if there's more dope where we're headed to, sign me up.

He asked Harris where they were going, and Harris replied merrily, "To meet important, clever, and fascinating people who are anxious to meet you."

THE GIRL MADE another visit to a bedroom to fix a couple of guests up and then walked down the hall, back to one of the staircases that led down to the first floor. On her way, she saw a tall, young woman, extremely pretty, in a low-cut ball gown with a large bust, a small waist, and good legs tottering toward her on black-and-gold stilettos. She was sloshed and lost. From behind the girl, Harris's voice called. He had come back down from the upper floor but without Noah.

"Brandi," he called.

The sloshed woman in the low-cut dress looked over and saw that it was Harris calling her. "Get lost," she shrieked. "Not you. I don't want anything to do with you, Harris." And she teetered away, back downstairs.

.   .   .

THE SALVATION MAN   103

MARCUS HAD BEEN VISITED by the girl too. And he had taken to her medication every bit as well as Noah. Not long after the girl had left, a woman in her late fifties, glamorous and in good condition for her age, had knocked on the door and entered. She'd closed the door behind her and leaned up against it, one hand on the door handle, the other wafting around a cigarette in a holder. She ran her eyes over Marcus, who was sitting on the edge of the bed, over his face and body. She made no attempt to hide what it was about Marcus she was appraising. Her gaze was frank and confident. Assessing what she was getting. The drugs had made Marcus docile. He let everything just wash over him.

The woman walked over and sat beside him. Up this close, he could see the work she'd had done. It was good work. You had to be this close up to see it. As close up as they were now. Close enough for her to run her free hand where she wanted on Marcus's body. Then she stopped, leaned over to open the nightstand drawer, pulled out a thick fold of bills, and placed it on top of the nightstand.

"That's for you. Oliver told me all about you, so I reserved you." She drew on her cigarette and said, "Does that bother you?"

Marcus eyed the fat stack of notes and replied, "No. Doesn't bother me, ma'am."

The woman laughed, a throaty smoker's laugh. "Ma'am," she said. "Okay, farm boy. Ma'am it is."

There was another knock at the door, and the woman said, "Come in, Roger."

An elderly man dressed in a dinner jacket entered. He didn't look so good. Overweight, wrinkled, and liver-spotted with a crooked back. If he'd had work done it had been wasted, every cent of it.

"This is my husband," said the woman. "He reserved you too."

Marcus looked at the money on the nightstand again. This time it didn't look quite so fat.

HARRIS HAD FOLLOWED Brandi Sutton down into the throng of the party on the ground floor but lost her in the crowds. Then he heard a commotion coming from one of the rooms off the entrance hall, a coarse, nasally voice rising above the music and civilized party chatter. He made his way with a heavy heart to where the high, shrill squeak was coming from. He knew who the voice belonged to. And he felt responsible for the whole sorry situation.

Brandi Sutton stood by the drinks table at the far end of the room.

"Yeah, here's to all of you, you frickin' snobs!"

The other guests were doing a reasonably good job of ignoring her, but the strain of their pretense was beginning to show.

"I get it. No one wants to talk to me. I'm just someone with the wrong accent and no class. But I know what goes on here... so you don't get to judge me..."

"Mrs. Sutton, please. You must stop." Harris had appeared at her side, whispering urgently to her.

"Oh, look who it is...it's the pimp in chief... Of all the people here, you are the most pathetic..."

"Please, Mrs. Sutton...this is doing nobody any good, least of all yourself..."

"You want me to stop?"

"Ardently."

"Then let me see him."

"I'm afraid that's impossible..."

Brandi Sutton turned away from Harris and swung her drink in a wild arc. "Let me tell you few things about good old Mr. Harris here..."

"Okay..." Harris had gripped her bare arm. "Okay... Let me see what I can do..."

Brandi's head whipped around, and her sozzled, big, blue eyes locked onto Harris's.

"Good. Then get your greasy hands off of me and take me to him."

"One moment." Harris took a step away and pulled out his cell. He speed-dialed and mumbled a sentence into the phone that Brandi didn't catch. Then he put the cell away and turned back toward Brandi.

"I'll need to go and see if he's free."

"Tell him that he'd better make himself free."

Brandi said it like a threat, and it made Harris feel a little queasy. He trotted off, out into the hall and up the stairs, where he found a huge, shaven-headed man waiting. The man loomed over Harris. He had a long dip running down the top of his skull where the stubble no longer grew. His nose had been broken and smashed and reset so many times that it was nearly smeared over the middle of his face. Scars radiated around his small eyes and down his gnarled, sunken cheeks.

"Markham..." wheezed Harris, recovering from the dash up the stairs.

"What's up?"

"Brandi Sutton. That's what. She's causing a scene. Demanding to see Randall Boyd. I knew she was trouble. I knew she was bad news. And he's as bad. He can't help himself. Where is he?"

"He's with three of the girls."

"Well? What are we going to do?"

Markham sighed, and his massive frame rose and fell.

"I'll go see him. Maybe we can get him to calm her down."

"Thank you," said Harris with genuine feeling. "I need to see to some other guests." Then, having handed over the mess to Markham, he turned and made his way back to the party downstairs.

Markham watched Harris prance away and, for a moment, considered what would be the best course of action. He was under strict orders to keep Mayor Boyd happy, so it was all way more delicate than he liked. Then he made his decision and marched off along the hallway, his ungainly frame yawing from side to side. He passed a line of rooms that were occupied by guests and came to the last door. He put his ear to the door and listened for a moment to the excited giggling coming from behind it, then raised a meaty fist and knocked twice. His knock got an instant reply.

"What?" The voice from the other side of the door was harsh and angry.

"It's Markham."

"I'm busy."

"It's urgent. Can't wait."

There was a pause. A curse. Some muttering. The sound of a body getting out of bed and stomping to the door. The door opened to reveal a short, fleshy, pugilistic-looking man. Dark hair, deep, deep suntan, and a shadow of stubble. His face was shiny from exertion, and he wreaked of aftershave.

"Mr. Boyd," said Markham. "We have a bit of a situation."

"Yeah? Me too. So what?

"It's Brandi Sutton."

"What about her?"

"She's demanding to see you and won't take no for an answer."

"So what? What do I care? It's nothing to do with me."

"You invited her over. You gave her the idea—"

"I gave her no goddamn ideas. She knew the deal. I wish to God I never got involved with her. I wish she'd go back to that putz of a husband. It ain't my fault she got obsessed with me, and I ain't seeing her. Okay? I have no obligation to see her."

"It'd just help the evening go smoothly if you had a word with her. That's all. Give her five minutes tops to calm her down."

"No. She's crazy, and there's nothing I can do. Markham, I pay a lot of money to make these evenings happen. I expect you to sort this out. So go sort it out. Especially if you want me to play nice with you. I did a lot of favors for you guys, and this ain't how you treat me back."

Boyd shut the door, and Markham felt rage rising like a tide of magma. But he rode the anger and set his mind to what to do next.

When he returned to the top of the stairs, looking back up at him from the foot of the staircase was his problem, Brandi Sutton.

"Well, well," said Brandi. "If it isn't Lurch himself. Where's Boyd? Harris promised I could see him."

Markham nodded and beckoned Brandi up the stairs, away from the crowds that filled the hallway below. She complied, and as she ascended the stairs, he had time to take a good look at her. He could see all too clearly why Gerry Sutton and Boyd Randall had been so attracted to her. She was stunning. Dark flawless skin, thick brown hair, bright blue eyes, and a figure that would make men stop in the street.

"What's the frickin' deal?" Brandi demanded.

Sadly, reflected Markham, her beauty really was skin-deep.

"He can't see you."

"Can't or won't?"

"He can't see you."

"I see." Brandi looked at Markham. Her big round eyes

dwelled on his face, his smashed nose and scarred brow. He thought he saw a flicker of pity. But then he decided it was highly unlikely that either of them had ever truly experienced that emotion.

Brandi leaned in conspiratorially and whispered, "Okay, here's what's going to happen. You're going to take me to that son of a bitch, or I'm going to the *New York Post* and giving them an exclusive. I'm going to tell them what happens here all the way out in the woods. I'm gonna tell them that Mayor Randall Boyd is screwing around behind his wife's back. I'll give them names of the people I've seen up here and the dates they were here. I'll blow this show sky high. You got me?"

Markham nodded slowly and replied. "I got you."

"So, what's it gonna be?"

Markham sighed again, and his huge upper body rose and fell. "Come with me," said Markham, beginning to climb the stairs.

"That's the spirit," replied Brandi, following Markham. "Where is our honorable mayor?"

"He's in the top room."

"The top room?"

"Yeah, the turret room."

"I don't think I've been there."

"Very few people have. It's out of bounds to the guests. Except of course for our most special guests. Boyd's up there, waiting for you."

SIXTEEN

By three in the morning, most of the guests had found their way to one of the bedrooms or decided that the night for them had ended and gone home. A few loitered in the dining room and drawing rooms, talking and drinking the very last of the small hours away.

In the kitchen, Harris had taken off his jacket and sat himself down in an old winged armchair that was upholstered in a faded checked fabric that had begun to split in a couple of places. It was nestled in the corner by the kitchen door so he could see out past the pool onto the long back lawn that stretched out into shadow and forest. He rubbed his sad wet eyes, took off his Oxford shoes, handcrafted and resoled too many times to count, and massaged his aching feet.

He heard quick, light steps echoing along the hallway and knew their owner instantly; the dainty rhythm was so soothing and familiar. The girl's face appeared around the kitchen door, and Harris's heart began to flutter with excitement.

"Tinkerbell. A sight for very sore eyes. Come in."

The girl tip tapped over the tiled floor and knelt gracefully by Harris's socked feet. She placed her case on the floor and opened it out.

Harris picked up his cigarette case and lighter that had been lying by him on the countertop and lit up a smoke.

"My little angel," he almost sang. "My precious Tinkerbell. Bringer of all that is good and wholesome. Bringer of light. Come and set the world right."

Harris perched the cigarette in his thick lips, undid his cufflinks, slipped them in his pocket, and folded his shirtsleeve up above the elbow. Then he laid his naked arm along the side rest, and with a sigh he sunk back into the chair, taking a long, deep suck of thick, sweet smoke. He closed his eyes.

"It is a dark world, my dear," he said in diction that belonged to a classical actor. "We must endure the pull and push of temptation and enmity of others. Sartre once said, 'Hell is other people.' I say, why limit it to other people? We are small and flawed creatures at the mercy of bigger, flawed creatures...at the mercy of fallen beasts..."

The words stopped as he felt the girl's needle shoot warmth into his arm. Now he was alive, on the terms he wanted to be alive. The ghastly, nearly unendurable nature of the human condition couldn't get to him now; the world no longer had him by the throat. He had deliverance. His angel had brought him to his God.

Her work done, the girl packed her tools away in her case and sat back on her heels. She would stay a while like she always did to listen to the old man's free flow of words. His memories, his rants, his imploring, his rationalizations.

He began to rail about the staff, he railed about his mother, about the Democrats and the Republicans. Finally, he tailed off. His chest rose and fell slowly, and he smacked his lips. Then he was off once more, describing some other episode in his life. The girl gathered up her instruments, folded her case closed, and tiptoed away.

SEVENTEEN

Morning—bright, hard, nauseous morning. His neck and the side of his face hurt. Then the rest of his body felt bad too. He felt sick and dirty. He could smell chlorine and hear pipes creaking. His eyes opened and he pulled his face up off wooden boards. Then he got his hands under and pushed himself into a sitting position, rubbing his sore face and neck. He was by an indoor pool, dressed, but he had no memory of how he came to be dressed. Though he did have other memories. Memories of what had happened the night before. Memories that he quickly buried away.

Noah put his hands around his knees and squeezed, then shivered. Sharp morning sun poured in through the floor-to-ceiling windows onto the surface of the pool, and the walls rippled with the reflected light. He felt a vibration in his pocket and pulled out his cell. Marcus was calling. Noah answered and heard Marcus's voice. He sounded ridiculously upbeat.

"Yo! Dude...what's going on? Where are you?"

"I'm by the pool."

"Well, get your ass out here. I'm standing round the front. What a night, man. What. A. Night."

Noah made his way through the kitchen and the dining room out into the front hall. There wasn't anyone up and around yet. Not even staff. No one had started to clean up, to clear away the empty bottles, glasses, and plates of half-eaten food that were still lying around. As he rounded the corner into the hall, he nearly bumped into Harris, who was no longer in evening wear or cologned up to the eyeballs with oiled-down hair. He looked a fright, hollow-eyed and about ten years older than he had the day before. He eyed Noah warily.

"Morning," said Harris.

Noah grunted and pushed past Harris.

"I gather you were handsomely rewarded for your work last night, Noah."

Noah didn't answer.

"If you ever wanted to come back again...?"

Noah turned away, angrily thinking that nothing could ever reward him for what he had sold last night. Nothing. He opened the front door and then stopped. An idea had hit him, and he turned back to Harris.

"I want more money."

"Excuse me?"

"I want more money."

"What on earth for?"

"For what happened last night. For me not going straight to the police and telling them what happens here."

"What happens here? People enjoying themselves at a party. Enjoying each other's company. The last time I checked this was still a free country."

"Not to take dope it isn't. Not the kilos your guests must be getting through."

Harris shook his head wearily. "Noah. Don't be silly. Even if you did go to the police, you think they'd believe you? A homeless teenager?"

Noah closed in on Harris, close enough for Harris to get uncomfortable.

"These days, Mr. Harris, the police tend to believe people like me more than they do people like you..."

"Look, you had a good time last night and were very well paid for it. You were paid more money than—"

"I want more. I want more or I'll walk from here straight to the police station and tell them everything and make up more stuff if I need to. Stuff about you, Mr. Harris."

"This is blackmail. It's criminal—"

"So, come to the police station with me and we'll both tell our stories together."

Harris hesitated, and then he caved. "How much do you want?"

"How much can you lay your hands on?"

"Wait there."

Harris toddled off huffing and puffing and returned a few minutes later with a wedge of bills which he handed over to Noah.

"Thank you, Oliver."

"There will be no more invites to the parties here for you, Noah. You are no longer welcome. This is disgraceful behavior. There will be no more handouts for you. Do you understand?"

"Oh, I understand, Oliver. I understand, perfectly."

After Noah left, Harris hovered in the hall, fretting about what had happened. He turned to see Markham standing in the doorway.

"Markham..." Harris spluttered. "Good morning..."

"He'll be back."

"What...?"

"The kid. He'll be back for more money. Who is he? He wasn't bussed in from the city like the others."

"I found him."

"You found him? Where?"

"Tinky recommended him to me."

"Tinky...? The girl? Are you out of your dumb mind? Why didn't you run it by me? You know that you leave that part of things to me. Always. You're too soft. You can't manage a kid like that. He'll walk all over you."

"I just wanted to bring a little class. And he went down a storm with the guests."

"You made a mess, Oliver. A mess I have to clean up. The kids I bring in, they have people who control them. And they have me too. It's a hard, ugly business, Oliver, and it's not for you. And now I'm gonna have to clear up the mess you made. The way I did with Brandi."

"What do you mean, 'clear up'?"

Markham walked over to Harris and placed a hand on his shoulder. "You don't need to know the details. You just need to enjoy the glory, Oliver. You get to be the belle of the ball. And you get an awful lot of money for hosting our parties. But someone has to tie up the loose ends after the party's ended, Oliver. Dry away the tears, clean up the spilled drinks, and bring the night to an end. And that's where I come in. Life can't be all parties, Oliver... Listen, there's a bit of business the boss wants you to do for us. Another guy he wants you to make contact with."

Markham pulled out a folded piece of paper from his pocket and handed it to Harris. "Just like the last guy. We got a very promising lead on him. The place he hangs out, times he likes to hang out there. It's out of town. Means a trip to DC."

"I see. Same as usual?"

"Yeah, same as usual. Say hello, charm him like only you can, tell him about the very exclusive setup we got out here. From what we know about him, he's a good bet. Just hang the bait in front of him and he'll bite. We'll send you business class, as usual. Put you up in a five-star place. And, if you're successful, you'll get a bonus. Some more money for repairs, to throw at this money pit of a mansion. Or you can take on some more staff, restock the wine cellar. Okay, Oliver?"

"Sure. Sure."

Markham patted Harris on the shoulder. "We got a great thing going on here, Oliver. Thank you." Markham turned to go, then stopped and turned back to Harris. "Oh, what was that kid's name?"

"Excuse me?"

"The kid who stung you for cash just now."

"Oh, er, Noah. I don't know his second name, I'm afraid."

"Where does he live?"

"I believe he lives in a tent at Ligonee Creek...near Brick Kiln Road. With his friend, Marcus."

"Okay. Good. So, remember, you don't ever invite people we don't approve of to the parties. Got it?"

"But it's my house, Markham. I should be free in my own house."

"That's not the deal. If you want us to keep you and this house afloat, to keep you living the way you want to live, you abide by our rules. Okay?"

Not wanting for a reply, Markham disappeared into the house, leaving Harris to open the folded note.

EIGHTEEN

Holly Paladino had managed to get eight hours' straight sleep. Which was a good thing. But the downside was that when she woke up, she had a tight half an hour to shower, dress, and grab a piece of toast before she had to leave for the precinct. When she got into the office, she had no time to check her emails or do any housekeeping and went straight into roll call.

As soon as she entered the room she knew something wasn't right. It was too silent. The other four patrol cops in the room were way too serious. Instead of being slumped in their seats and making light banter, they were sitting up to attention. Paladino looked over to the lectern, and in the place of the sergeant, she saw Harrigan standing there like he was General Patton. Sitting down by his side was Mayor Randall Boyd.

Paladino sat down, and Officer Maynard leaned across, giving off a waft of cigarettes and more surprisingly patchouli oil, and whispered, "You look like you didn't get the memo."

"I sure the hell didn't," she replied. "Where's the sergeant and why is the mayor here?"

But Maynard's reply was cut off as Harrigan began to speak.

"Okay. Now we have a full house, let's kick things off.

Before we get down to the regular stuff, it won't have escaped your notice that we have a very special visitor. Mayor Boyd Randall has come to say a few words to us. Mayor..."

Harrigan stepped back and Randall stood up, placing his tanned manicured hands and chubby gold-ringed fingers onto the lectern. Even at the height of summer, he wore his tight, blue three-piece suit which was a hell of a snug fit against his short, stocky frame. A silver clip that matched his cufflinks kept his blue silk tie in place. His thick black hair was carefully combed back into a small mane, and even though he must have shaved this morning, he still had his customary five-o'clock shadow.

Randall surveyed the four cops, gave a brief cough, and began to speak. He exuded arrogance, and when he spoke he made it clear he wasn't expecting questions. He was giving the facts, not an explanation.

"I'm here to give an update on the situation we have with the sheriff's office. Unfortunately, there's still no sign of a compromise being reached over the budget freeze, and the sheriff's department and the Suffolk County Benevolent Association are playing hardball. So, for the foreseeable future, Sag Harbor PD will have to go on splitting the areas between here and the East Hampton boundaries with East Hampton PD. I know it's not ideal, but there's nothing that can be done about it. We've given as much as we can in the way of compromise, but we're up against a brick wall. However—" At this point Randall pointed a finger to underline the seriousness of his intent. "—I promise you we will find a way through. But right now, my priority is you guys. I believe in our police department one thousand percent. And because of this, and because of the extra you're having to give, myself and Detective Harrigan have got the village trustees to sign off an emergency fund for extra overtime at a higher rate. So," said Randall with a big white-toothed grin, "the sheriff's loss is your win."

An appreciative murmur went around the room, and Harrigan began clapping and the other cops joined in.

Mayor Randall was about to take a step back when, despite the fact he hadn't invited any questions, he saw Paladino's hand raised. Detective Harrigan was already on his feet looking to round things off quickly and snapped at Paladino.

"What is it, Officer? We got to be getting our asses out onto the streets."

"It's just that I'm puzzled," said Paladino. "Why are we spending all this money on police overtime when the whole point is to cut the sheriff's budget? If we have enough money to pay us extra time at a better rate, why aren't we putting that money into the county sheriff's pot?"

Mayor Randall wiped a hand down his face as if to say "why am I having to answer this?" and replied, "Yeah, it might look that way to you from the outside, but I can tell you it's way more complicated due to the different funding structures that support the two different departments. How I wish it was as simple as your question makes it sound."

Randall looked around the room, smiled, and winked. "But I think any questions all you fellas have will be answered when you open your paychecks at the end of the month."

The other three cops and Harrigan laughed, but Paladino didn't; she still couldn't see why it wasn't such a straightforward question.

"But," she said, cutting through the laughter, "it's the height of the season, and we won't be able to cover the town and the harbor like we should."

"So you might miss out on half a dozen DUIs and a handful of kids out joyriding is all," said Harrigan. "Our manpower will be much better spent down around the village borders and beyond 'cause that's precisely the area we've had a whole spate of break-ins. Including, if you hadn't already forgotten, the senator's place."

"That's the truth," said Mayor Randall. "I've had the senator chewing me out about it and a number of residents calling my office complaining."

Harrigan waved his finger at Paladino. "And you ought to know, Paladino. You were with me attending a B and E just a few days ago. Now, the mayor's a very busy man, so let's do the BOLO alerts and get out on the road, doing what we do best, keeping the people of Sag Harbor safe."

"Amen to that," said the mayor, and the two men shook hands and clapped backs like they were best buddies from all the way back.

The roll call broke up and the officers signed out their weapons and made their way to their cruisers.

Paladino was riding by herself that night. She checked her vehicle for dings and dents, got in, and started the engine. She drove out of the lot, intending to turn left down Division Street for a sweep around the front before heading south toward the village borders. But her headlights picked out a familiar figure sitting on the wall by the side of the narrow street. Paladino immediately recognized the figure as Father Devlin and pulled over.

"You waiting for anyone in particular?" asked the detective.

"Yeah. I was waiting for you."

"Well, you better get in."

Devlin opened the door and slipped into the passenger seat, and Paladino set off.

"What's got you hanging around street corners in the middle of the night, Father?"

"I think you know what. What's the latest on Father Aranha?"

"Well, the good news is I checked the situation with CSI, and they've packed up at the church. So you'll be fine to go back there. Just don't tell Harrigan I told you."

"That's a weight off my wallet."

They hit the end of Division Street, and Paladino hooked a left at the intersection into Bay Street; then, though she was supposed to head south toward the village borders, she cut across town and headed along Long Island Avenue onto West Water Street out by the bay. She slowed to a cruise by the harbor. It was late, it was quiet, and the lights from the multitude of bobbing boats in the bay twinkled back from out of the dark blue of the sea.

"What about the murder investigation?" asked Devlin.

"I don't get briefed on it; it's Harrigan's case. But I do know from a friend in Suffolk County that Homicide has been brought on board. To give Harrigan backup. More resources."

"Why do I have a feeling Harrigan isn't going to find anything?" said Devlin. "Get anywhere with it?"

"He's got a duty to investigate this. Murders happen once in a blue moon here. There will be enormous pressure on him to get the killer."

"Can I ask a question?"

"Depends on the question."

"Did Harrigan get anywhere near catching the guy who killed Greg?"

Paladino stiffened in her seat. She didn't answer. They traveled for a block and then another.

"I think Vijay had gotten himself involved in something. Something he wasn't supposed to be involved with."

"What?"

"I don't know. But the last couple of days before he was killed, he was caught up in something. It was like a black cloud was hanging over him. I had a missed call from him before he died. I only picked the message up afterward. He sounded upset."

"What did he say?"

"That he'd done something bad. Something he was going to pay for."

Devlin's head was turned by a passing vehicle.

"What's the deal with those things?" he asked.

"What things?"

"The limos. I see half a dozen of them some nights and other nights none at all. And they all seem to be headed out of the village somewhere."

"This place is a rich person's playground."

Paladino slowed and turned the car over to the side of the road. She switched off the engine. Devlin got out a cigar and rolled it between his finger and thumb.

"You're not smoking that thing in my car," said Paladino.

"No. I'm gonna smoke it while I take a walk." Devlin looked out one the harbor. "Pretty spot."

"Not for me. This is where Greg was killed."

Devlin turned to Paladino. "Right here?"

"That post there." Paladino pointed to a parking sign planted in the narrow sidewalk in front of the low harbor wall. "That's pretty much where he was standing when the car hit."

Paladino got out, rounded the car, and stood facing out to sea. Devlin got out too and stood by her. He could feel emotion radiating out of her. She sat on the harbor wall, her feet over the water, and Devlin followed suit. She didn't speak.

"You know, Holly," said Devlin gently. "Can I call you Holly?"

"Yeah..."

"I really don't think you're anywhere near okay about Greg. And I can't see it should be any other way."

Paladino's shoulders trembled, and a gasp came from deep

down inside her that she knew had been coming for some time but still surprised her. She started to weep uncontrollably.

Devlin put an arm around her, and she let herself fold into him. And, in the same way it had happened when they had shaken hands at the motel, the breaking waves of grief slinked away for a moment, washing back into the great body of water they had come from. For the first time since Greg died, Paladino let someone else make her feel safe. She cried and shivered and cried and shivered some more, until it was out of her. Then she sat upright, and she and Devlin looked out at the bay for a while.

"The answer was no, by the way," said Paladino.

"No to what?"

"Harrigan didn't get anywhere near solving Greg's case. In fact, from what I know, he got precisely nowhere."

"I can help you," said Devlin. "With Greg. Look into who killed him. I was a detective with the Air Force."

Paladino looked at Devlin and smiled. "I bet you could. I don't know why, but I get the feeling you're the kind of guy who could just about do anything for anyone." She breathed in, deeply and evenly. "The problem is that I should have done something. Something more. I've been in some kind of suspended animation for nearly a year. I want to leave this town because it turned into a nightmare for me. But how can I leave when my husband's murderer is walking free?" She turned to Devlin. "I need to do something about Greg's death. The way you need to do something about Vijay's."

"What will you do?"

Paladino shrugged. "I really don't know. But I'll think of something. I have to. I have to do something to save myself. What will you do?"

"I'll think of something too."

"I've grieved Greg for a long time, and I'll grieve him for the rest of my life. That's a fact. But I need to find out what happened here. No one else. Otherwise, I'll have failed Greg. I just don't get it. Why do bad men win and good men suffer and die, Father?"

PALADINO SET OFF ON PATROL, and Devlin walked back toward the village center, smoking. Thinking. Thinking about Paladino's question: *Why do good men suffer?* All he knew was that all humans suffer, good and bad. We were born to suffer. Without suffering we could not have redemption. Devlin knew that all too well.

Was he, Gabe Devlin, a good man? He had done bad things. Killed the man who murdered his wife without remorse. His own friend, Father Aranha, believed he wasn't fit to take a mass. To be a priest.

No. He wasn't a good man. He was a bad man who was trying to do good things.

"We all have sinned," he said to himself and took a long toke on his cigar.

Then he stopped dead in his tracks.

"Of course..."

He pulled out Aranha's bloody note from his pocket. He read the three words again: "For all have..." And then he completed the line: "For all have sinned and come short of the glory of the Lord."

NINETEEN

Devlin checked his watch.

It was three in the morning. About the same time that he'd heard the shots that killed Father Aranha.

And he was in the same place.

Back at the rectory.

He was standing in the doorway to Aranha's study, surveying the murder scene with a focus that was almost trance-like. He went back over the voicemail that Aranha had left him. Remembered how confused and desperate he sounded. Aranha, Devlin knew, had been a private man, a man who had guarded his feelings. But even so, Devlin felt sure that if things had gone so badly wrong for Aranha that some evidence of that rupture would remain somewhere. There would be evidence of his sin, the particular way in which he had come short of God's glory.

Devlin would book a crime scene cleaning company first thing in the morning. But for now, the stains of blood were still present, still haunting the room, causing Devlin to shudder at the sudden violence of his good friend's death.

Then Devlin started searching, having no idea what it was he might be searching for. He trawled the desk drawers and checked behind the furniture, far more thoroughly than he'd been able to on the morning of Aranha's death. But there was nothing out of place, no evidence of anything troubling or concerning. He went up to Aranha's bedroom and searched through his possessions, through his clothing, but turned up nothing. He sat on the edge of the bed and took another look around the room. There wasn't much in the way of furniture in Aranha's bedroom, and Devlin got the feeling the heart of the house was the study. There were two nightstands on either side of the bed, and two closets were at the other end of the room, either side of an open fireplace. To Devlin's right was a large sash window beneath which was a desk with a crucifix and bible placed in the center. Above the fireplace was a picture of the Pope which dominated the room.

To Devlin, Father Aranha's bedroom felt like a safe refuge from the world. More than that even, a fortress against evil. He was about to get up when he saw little amounts of black charred fragments lying on the fire grate. The remains in the fireplace puzzled Devlin. It couldn't have been needed to be lit recently, not in the middle of July. Was it left over from last winter? But there were two heaters in the room, so would he have even needed a fire in winter? And, judging from the fastidiously clean state of the rest of the house, Devlin would have expected the grate to have been swept, not left for months.

He knelt in from of the fireplace and sifted carefully through the covering of ash and black flakes of material that looked like the charred remains of paper or card. Devlin pulled the grate and the fret out from the fireplace and then slid out the ash pan. The fragments in the ash pan were larger than the remnants on the grate, and as Devlin sifted through them, he began to see the outer edges of what looked like photographs. Devlin fetched a large piece of white paper from Aranha's study and arranged the tiny scraps of images that had survived the fire on the paper. Frustratingly, the images were too incomplete and too small to be able to tell what was in the original photographs. There were glimpses though: a hand, part of a leg, the side of a bed headboard. Glimpses of naked limbs. Devlin started to get a sinking feeling, a depressing sense of what it was his friend might have been involved in.

He folded the paper up into a pocket for the fragments he'd collected and returned to the study, the room that seemed to be the sanctum of a man whose intellectual qualities and predisposition to deep reflection drove him to solitude. This time Devlin's eye was caught by the family bible that he'd last seen lying open on Aranha's desk. It had been closed and moved to a small table by the french windows.

Devlin pulled out the bloodstained notepaper he'd retrieved from Aranha's desk and looked at it.

For all have sinned and come short of the Glory of God.

He picked the bible up and opened the pages at Romans 3:23, where the line was from. And there, slipped into the pages, were the remains of a card, a burned fragment that looked as if it had been retrieved from the bedroom fireplace. Only a sliver of the bottom half of the card survived and on was printed three words: The November Club.

"Vijay, what happened?" murmured Devlin.

But even as he asked the question, he suspected the answer.

Devlin sat in a deep armchair that was placed in the corner of the room, facing the french windows, and opened the bible on his lap. He began to read and pray, smoking all the while until he eventually drifted off into sleep just as the dawn chorus ended.

He was woken at ten by a call from the bishop's office letting him know that a Father Martinez would be taking over Aranha's duties at the church for the time being. They agreed to reopen the church for mass later in the week when the new priest would be free to take up his temporary charge. In the meantime, the day-to-day administrative stuff would be left to Devlin.

After the call, Devlin showered, shaved, prayed, and ate eggs and bacon washed down with strong black coffee. Then he thought about what church business needed attending to. The first thing was a delivery for the food pantry that Devlin had forgotten to cancel.

Devlin headed outside toward the church hall and heard the deep-throated roar of an engine. A yellow Lamborghini turned off the road and into the parking lot and came to a stop, slung across the blacktop, its chrome and windows twinkling in the midmorning sun.

Out of the Lamborghini stepped a man with red hair wearing pressed chinos and a polo shirt. He took off his sunglasses and waved at Devlin. Devlin recognized the man from the night before at the police station. He'd been talking to Paladino as Devlin was being led across the office by Harrigan.

"Hey, Father Devlin?" said the man as he advanced toward Devlin, holding out a hand. "Name's Sutton. Gerry Sutton."

They shook hands.

"I was so sorry to hear about Father Aranha," said Sutton. "It's just the most terrible thing."

Devlin nodded.

"I come to mass at St. Michael's," Sutton continued. "Not as often as I should, I'll admit." Sutton gave an apologetic smile. "I knew Father Aranha. I guess you knew him too?"

"I've known him since I trained to be a priest."

Sutton nodded sympathetically. "I'm sorry for your loss."

"Thank you."

There was an awkward pause. Then Sutton spoke with what seemed to Devlin to be forced friendliness.

"I got married here, in fact. A few months back. Just the most wonderful spring day, and Father Aranha married us."

"I see."

"In fact, I wanted to speak to you, Father, about that."

"About your wedding?"

"About my wife. Brandi. She went missing. A few days ago. And I wondered if you might be able to help?"

"How?"

Sutton smoothed back his hair with a hand and squinted into the distance, then back at Devlin. "I saw you down at the station a few nights back, and I got talking to one of the cops, who told me that you used to be a detective. That's right, isn't it?"

"Yes, in the Air Force."

"Well, thing is, the cops are doing nothing about my wife's disappearance. Squat. They're telling me they can't do anything because Brandi's an adult. And I'm getting more worried by the day. I haven't heard from her, which is completely out of character, and nobody knows where she is. I thought maybe you could use your experience to help find my wife."

Devlin shook his head. "No. I'm afraid not. I'm a priest now, not a detective."

"I can pay you. Top rate. I'm a rich man, Father Devlin. Very rich. Whatever you want. Name your price." Sutton slid a hand into his pocket and pulled out his wallet.

Devlin put up a hand. "No. No amount of money will change my mind. I'm just not in that line of work anymore."

It wasn't strictly true, of course, but though he'd only met Sutton moments ago, Devlin had taken against him.

Sutton slowly put his wallet away. "Right."

"But even if I were, I'd tell you what the police are telling you. That as hard as her going missing is for you, if there's no evidence she's in danger or vulnerable, as she's an independent adult they aren't in a position to do anything. It's not easy to hear, I know, and I'm sorry for that. But that's the situation."

"Yeah... Funny thing is, Father, everybody's sorry. But nobody's sorry enough to help me." Then Sutton put his sunglasses back on, turned, and strode back to his car. Devlin watched Sutton rev the engine hard and then speed out of the lot back onto the road and disappear into the distance.

TWENTY

Before she had even got to the pier, she knew something was up. She could see a figure standing on the prow of the *April Rose*. He never stood, thought the girl. He was always waiting in the fighting chair, swinging back and forth, catching an imaginary tuna, or whatever people caught in the sea. She turned onto the pier and cycled across the wooden slats, a feeling of foreboding slowing her to half her usual pace. As she came to a halt by the *April Rose*, she cautiously eyed the bald man with the sunglasses who had come to the foot of the gangway and now stood waiting with his hands on his hips. Up close she could see something had happened to his face. His head was bandaged, the skin around the right lens of his sunglasses was bruised and raised, and he had a split lip.

The girl dismounted, wondering whether to say anything. But the man spoke before she could make up her mind.

"It's off today," he said bluntly.

"What?"

"We need to move the pickup point. Tell your boss we're going to berth further round the bay."

"What happened to your face?" asked the girl, curiosity getting the better of her.

The man looked down at her like she was dirt. "Tell your boss there's going to be a new pickup point. We'll let him know where it is. But we won't be able to do business for another twenty-four hours. Till we get set up again."

"Why are you moving somewhere else?"

"Security."

"Do I get paid?"

The man ignored the question. Instead, he looked back along the pier and then back down at the girl. "Have you been followed?"

"What?"

The man didn't bother repeating the question and waited for an answer.

"No. No way," protested the girl, but the man didn't give the girl any clue as to whether he believed her or not.

"Tell your boss it's tomorrow for the next pickup," he said. "Same place, different location. We won't tell him where till an hour before. And the day after that, it'll be different again." Then the man turned and headed back up the gangway and took the stairs below deck.

The girl wheeled her bike around, got back on the saddle, and cycled back to shore. As she rode, she started to worry that she had been followed. But by who? The priest had been waiting for her yesterday when she came off the pier. But had he seen her get onto the yacht? Even if he had, he wouldn't know what was going on or what it was she was picking up. He was just a dumb priest who had a weird obsession with jewelry. But, despite the reassurances she was able to give herself, a knot of worry remained, lodged in her stomach. And that knot grew a whole lot bigger when she cycled over the grass meridian into Long Island Avenue and saw, diagonally opposite from her, a silver pickup parked at the entrance to the municipal parking lot. Sitting inside the pickup was the priest.

Her heart began to beat wildly, and she didn't know whether to cycle away or go and tell him to get lost. In the end, she wheeled over by the pickup and scowled at him.

"You are following me."

Devlin got out of the pickup and shut the door. "Yeah. I am."

"You creep. You've got no right—"

Devlin didn't wait for her to get indignant. "I know what you've been carrying in the bike. What the guy on the boat's filling your bike frame with."

"I don't know what you're talking about." The girl started to wheel her bike away.

"Walk away and I'll call the cops..."

The girl stopped and threw a look meant to be full of scorn back at Devlin, but all he could see was a frightened little girl.

"Unless you give me half an hour of your time."

"What for?"

"First of all, so I don't call the cops. Second of all, so you can hear what I've got to say. If you do that, then I promise I won't call the police."

The girl wheeled her bike full around, back toward Devlin.

"Ten minutes," she said angrily. "I got somewhere I have to be."

"Fifteen."

"I'll be timing it to the second."

"Fair enough."

THE LIGHT HAD SHIFTED to a mellow evening glow, and the sun that had blazed down all day like it had a score to settle was on its way out. Devlin and the girl sat up on stools at the window counter of a coffee and donuts place on Main Street. The girl had a donut covered in a brown slick and a cup of cola in front of her. Devlin was nursing a large cup of black coffee.

One of the staff suddenly clapped her hands and started dancing about, chasing and shooing a big yellow jacket around the shop. People started to laugh, and one of the customers warned her she'd just make it angry, but the insect made a dipping arc and fled through the doorway and up into the blue yonder. Then the whole place settled back down to a quiet hum, slow and easy under the spell of the summer evening.

The girl made a show of placing her cell phone on the counter between her and Devlin and pressing start on the timer. The cell phone was inside a case that was also a wallet, and in the compartments within the wallet Devlin could see a couple of ATM cards and the orange top of a New York State library card peeking out.

"You a big reader?" he asked, pointing to the library card.

"Yeah. I read."

"What are you reading now?"

"A biography on Eleanor Roosevelt." The girl said it defiantly, and Devlin wasn't sure whether she was being sarcastic or not.

"You know what Eleanor Roosevelt's nickname was when she was a kid?"

"Granny. On account of how grown-up she was."

"Kind of like you in some ways, don't you think?"

"You got twelve minutes left," said the girl, looking at the stopwatch ticking down on the cell screen.

"I'm not here to interrogate you."

"Then why are we here?"

Devlin rubbed an eyebrow with his thumb, thought for a moment, and said, "Where are you from?"

"Brooklyn," replied the girl.

"Why did you come to Sag Harbor?"

"For the sun."

"What you're doing is dangerous. It'll kill someone. You, most probably."

"No, it won't. I have rules. Rules I stick to."

"Like?"

"Like I don't touch the stuff I courier. Ever. Like I'm careful.

"

"Have the people who asked you to do what you're doing told you why they chose you?"

"They don't have to. It's obvious. It's 'cause I'm young and because I'm a girl. People won't suspect me."

"That's what they told you?"

"That's what I worked out. And I'm a juvenile, so chances are I'll get rehabilitation. Drug counseling. I can take that. It's a walk in the park."

"Did they tell you that? The people who own the drugs you're running?"

The girl didn't answer. She just took a big slurp from her straw and burped.

"If I were you," said Devlin, "I'd get yourself a different legal advisor. I know what you're hiding in your bike."

"You don't know."

"I do. I got into the yacht. The *April Rose*. I got a good look at what they got stashed there. What you're running is hard stuff, controlled substances, schedule one and two. You get caught with that and you'll get a custodial sentence, no question, for the kind of drugs and the amount of drugs you're carrying. How old are you?"

The girl didn't answer. She took a bite of her donut and pointed at her cell which was hitting the eight-minute mark.

"I'd say fifteen, but you look fourteen, at a guess," said

Devlin. "You do know that if your sentence carries over into your sixteenth year, then you'll be sent to an adult prison."

"If I get caught."

"Yeah. If. That's the one thing you've been right on since we got in here. You think your odds are good—I don't. After all, I worked out what you're doing pretty fast. So let me use the remaining time we have to tell you what happens if you do get caught. You'll go to juvenile hall. First day at juvenile hall will be the worst day of your life. You'll be cuffed and shackled on the way in, then strip-searched, showered, and given a jumpsuit and sneakers, without any laces. While you're waiting with the other kids to be led to an overcrowded dorm, or if you're really lucky a ten by ten with a five-inch square window, you'll look at the other kids there and you'll be wondering about them. Wondering, is she in for drugs? Or for violent assault? Or for murder? But you won't have much time to wonder because right out of the gate you'll need to learn all the rules by heart. The official rules and the unofficial rules. You have to memorize the official rules before you're allowed to spend your daily hour of downtime reading or watching TV. The unofficial rules you have to work out for yourself. And you better pray you work those rules out before you break them. But the main rule is, don't let anyone mess with you or they won't ever stop messing with you. Ever.

"In juvie, you don't see daylight, so you don't know what time it is. All you know is it's mealtime, downtime, time to get up, time to wash, time to go to sleep. And while you're in there, other kids your age will be going to prom night, starting college. But you won't do any of that. By the time you get out, you won't even know how to relate to normal kids. And I haven't even begun to touch on the really dark stuff."

The girl had stopped chewing and slurping. She squinted

her eyes and said, "How do you know so much about juvenile hall?"

"'Cause I spent a year in one."

"For what?"

"Stealing and assault. And I can tell you, it's a living hell. First night I was there, my roommate hanged himself. I was fourteen. About the same age as you. I will never forget that night for as long as I live."

The girl had forgotten about her food and drink. For the first time since she'd first met Devlin, she hadn't got a wiseass reply ready to go. She just stared at him.

"Looks like our time is up," said Devlin, pointing to the cell. He pulled out a pen from his jacket and scratched out his cell number on a napkin and handed it to the girl.

"I know you think you're immortal. I know you think you're smarter than everyone else. And who knows, you might turn out to be right. But if you ever need a way out, call me."

"I don't need a way out."

"If you do, call me."

The girl took the napkin, looked down at the timer, and pressed the stop button. It read eleven minutes and thirty seconds. Without a word she left the shop and got on her bike and didn't stop thinking about juvenile hall all the way to Suffolk Street.

DEVLIN FINISHED his coffee slowly and then ambled out of the shop. The moment his foot hit the sidewalk, a cruiser pulled slowly to a halt in front of him. The driver's window rolled down with an electrical whirr, revealing Harrigan wearing his aviator sunglasses.

"Afternoon."

"Afternoon," replied Devlin.

"I said I'd keep an eye on you."

"You sure did."

"When I say I'm gonna do something, I do it."

"Where have you got with Father Aranha's murder?"

"When there's news, you'll hear. But my eye is on you right now. As long as you're in my town, I'm watching you. I'm gonna make you so paranoid, and I'm gonna make bad things happen to you just by me willing it so."

Then Harrigan gave a couple of revs and took off down the street.

TWENTY-ONE

Riverdale, Suffolk County, New York

"HEY, CARL."

Carl Liberman didn't respond to his name being called immediately, He closed the window on his screen and turned lethargically to see who was addressing him. And then there was a split second in which Carl Liberman struggled to recognize the person standing in from of him. And after that, there was the moment when the penny dropped.

"What? You gotta be kidding me... Holly Paladino. It's gotta be ten years..."

Carl was up on his feet, and without either of them deciding it should happen, they embraced. Then they stood back from each other to take another look, to see how the passing years had treated each other.

"You look great, Holly."

"Thanks, Carl, you too."

"Yeah, one of these days I'll lose the thirty pounds three kids gave me."

"You look good."

"Well, we're a long way from the academy."

"We sure are. How's Debbie and the kids?"

"Good. Great. Debbie's got a part-time job as a counselor with Farmingdale College. And the kids...the kids are on the PlayStation."

As they spoke, a shared understanding overshadowed the exchange, that there had been a few months before they both graduated when something could have happened between them. Liberman was sweet on Paladino, and Paladino liked Liberman enough to think she could get sweeter on him, given time. But they went off in different directions, and truthfully, Paladino had stopped looking back and wondering how things could have been a long time ago.

But as they stood in the middle of the shabby cubicle farm that comprised the Suffolk County Homicide Bureau, Paladino could see that Liberman still carried some of the old torch for her.

Liberman gave a sympathetic look, and sadness filled his puffy brown eyes. "I was sorry as hell to hear about Greg. I'm so sorry, Holly."

"Thanks, Carl. And thanks for the card and the flowers."

"I wasn't able to get to the funeral because my mother-in-law took ill, and then she passed."

"Oh, Carl." Paladino reached out and for a couple of seconds held Liberman's hand. "I'm sorry to hear that."

Then they broke hands, and Liberman said, "You here to see anyone specific?"

"Actually, I'm here to see you, Carl."

"Oh. Okay. What can I do for you?"

"I wanted some information on a case I know you worked on."

There was a pause, and Liberman looked uncertain.

"Holly, did you make detective?"

"No. I'm still a patrol officer."

"Well, you should have done. But you know I'm not allowed to discuss cases without the permission of the lead local detective."

"This case is different."

"Which case is it?"

"It's my husband. It's Greg."

Now Liberman looked really uncertain. Pained.

"I think you're gonna put me in a really difficult position, Holly."

"I think I am. In fact, I know I am. But there's a very easy way out of it. You show me what you got on Greg's murder and I won't tell a soul."

"Haven't you talked to Harrigan about it? He's the Sag Harbor PD lead."

"He's told me very little. And I have no idea if that's because there is very little to tell or...because he's Harrigan and he's just not doing his job like he should. And I just don't trust him. But you, Carl, I trust you."

Liberman looked about the office nervously. It was busy with the sound of keyboards and cell phones and different conversations coming from different parts of the room.

"I don't know, Holly. I mean, I wasn't even part of the team."

"But you would have had an interest in it. Asked about it, heard about it. Because it was Greg. Because it was me."

Liberman rubbed the back of his neck and nodded.

"Sit down, Carl."

Liberman sat down, and Paladino took the empty chair by the side of his desk.

"I'm not just anyone."

"I know that, Holly. Jeez."

"You and I were very close once, and that meant a lot to me. Means a lot to me."

"Me too."

"And I know I'm coming to you about something that couldn't be more serious, couldn't mean more to me. And I know you won't refuse me. Because of who I am, who you are, and who Greg was."

Liberman mulled it over for a few seconds, looked at Paladino, and puffed his cheeks.

"Come with me." Liberman stood and led Paladino to a glass meeting room off to the side of the main office. Inside was a long, oval, hardwood meeting table, and a PC sat on a small desk in the corner. Once they were in and he'd closed the door, he pulled down the blinds and they both took a seat on either side of the table.

"Okay," said Carl, hands clasped on the tabletop. "What do you want to know?"

"What leads were the investigation in Greg's murder following, and where did it get with them?"

"From what I was told and overheard, they had about half a dozen suspects they followed up on. They found a burnt-out vehicle recovered on Widow Gavits Road that was used in the murder. But no eyewitnesses except someone who saw the vehicle, a Toyota Land Cruiser speeding along West Water Street at a time that matches the time of Greg's death. And the burnt-out wreck we found was a Toyota Land Cruiser with blue paintwork. We still got it impounded. But you probably knew all this?"

Paladino thought that maybe she did, but for months after Greg's death, she'd been in a no-man's-land of numbness and nearly insupportable pain. A lot of people had said a lot of things to her, but she had often been off somewhere else inside herself when they said them.

"Yeah," she replied. "Who were the suspects?"

"They were the guys Greg was surveilling, fringe members of the Pagans who had a route opened up to the Bahamas. But we couldn't tie them to the car, and Greg's investigation hadn't given us anything solid enough to act on."

"So, nothing?"

"I'm sorry, Holly."

"So what's Homicide doing on it now?"

"Now?"

"It's still working the case, isn't it?"

"Well, it's not officially closed. But we haven't got anyone working it. Not for about a month now."

"You're kidding?"

"Last I heard it was back with the local detective."

"Nobody told me they'd pulled Homicide off it. I mean, I had regular updates for a while, but no one told me that."

"Harrigan didn't tell you?"

"I've worked with him most days since I came back from compassionate leave, and he didn't mention it once."

Paladino got out of her chair with a sudden urgency.

"You going?" asked Carl.

"You bet. I'm going to see Harrigan. Right now. Thanks, Carl. You've been a huge help."

"Funny, it doesn't feel like I've helped at all."

Paladino hugged him. "You really have. Thank you."

She turned to leave but then froze halfway to the door, hit by a sudden thought.

She turned back to Liberman. "The Toyota. Which impound is it in?"

"The garage on Columbia Street. We didn't have capacity for it in Riverdale. We're all full up here."

"Wait...Columbia Street? Columbia Street, Sag Harbor?"

"Yeah."

TWENTY-TWO

Switches were being turned back on inside Holly Paladino, vital signs returning, and there was a new heat in her blood, a desire to put things right. It was early afternoon by the time she got to Sag Harbor. A slow crawl all the way on the 27 in a hot haze due to tourist traffic. Her first stop was the precinct where she was told Detective Harrigan was off shift and had gone home. So her next stop was the Bay Tavern right next door to the station. Harrigan's second home. Maybe even his first.

The Tavern wasn't anything more than a rectangular sand and sun-blasted wooden shack with a faded, weather-beaten sign outside. Inside it was long and narrow. Along the right-hand side was a bar that Harrigan was sitting up at, nursing a pint of Guinness and watching the Rockies v the Reds on the screen on the wall. Scattered around the place was a mix of tourists that had stopped by and yachties who had come up from the bay.

Paladino drew up a stool and planted herself right in front of Harrigan, ordering a shot of bourbon from the barkeep. Harrigan's heavy, bloodshot eyes slid down from the TV screen and registered Paladino.

"I wasn't looking for a drinking buddy," he drawled, and his eyes slid back up to the screen.

"I just went up to the Homicide Bureau in Riverhead."

Harrigan's eyes slid back down to Paladino and stayed there. "Oh yeah? That's an out-of-the-way place to be for a patrol officer."

"Not if it's to find out what happened with the investigation into your husband's murder." Paladino swigged back her bourbon, then put her hand up and ordered another.

Harrigan didn't say anything and carried on watching the game.

"And you know what I found out?"

Harrigan's eyes slid back down.

"Do tell."

"The county homicide investigation into Greg's murder was effectively suspended a month ago."

She said the words like they were spears she was shooting straight into Harrigan's bloated, unshaven face. Then she looked at him, watched closely for his reaction.

"Yeah, I know."

"You know? That's not the point. The point is I didn't know."

"Homicide didn't tell you when they pulled their men off the case?"

"No. They didn't..."

"Well, they were supposed to. That's what they told me. They said they'd arrange for a couple of their guys to go visit you and let you know."

"Why didn't you tell me?"

"They promised me they would. I was told they'd handle it." Harrigan put his beer down and turned to face Paladino. "Listen, I can see how crappy that is for you, but Homicide must have messed up."

Paladino couldn't make up her mind whether to believe her boss or straight out call him a liar. She straightened up on her stool.

"Why didn't you tell me? I see you most days. It never crossed your mind to tell the victim's wife something like that?"

Harrigan put up his hands and started to backpedal. "Okay. Sure. I can see I should have kept you informed. Sorry, I should have said something."

"You're sorry?"

"Yeah, I'm sorry, Holly. You're right, I shouldn't have trusted those jerks in Riverdale. I shoulda told you myself, and I'm sorry that I didn't."

Harrigan went for his beer, but Paladino swept it out of his reach.

"Hey—what the hell do you—?"

"That's not the end of it. Sorry isn't gonna magic this stuff away, Curtis. The next question is what have you done, Curtis? What leads have you been following since Greg's death? What leads are you working now you are the only detective working this case?"

"There are no live leads right now. Nothing came of the witness or the abandoned vehicle. Now, give me back my goddamn beer."

"So nothing's being done?"

"I can't magic evidence out of nowhere. There were no eyewitnesses. Nothing retrieved from the stolen vehicle. I wanted to catch whoever killed Greg as much as you. I mean, jeez, give me a break."

"Give you a break? Why? Have you lost your wife? Has the closest person to you been murdered? Is the murderer still free? Has all of that happened to you?"

Harrigan rolled his eyes and shook his head. "No. No, it hasn't."

Paladino wanted to hang on to her anger, but instead, unexpectedly and for the first time, she felt pity for Harrigan. He looked so pathetic and washed up sitting there in the gloom of the bar in the middle of the afternoon. She pushed Harrigan's beer back to him.

"You know, Curtis, I just wish you cared about what happened to Greg. That's all. When did you stop caring about being a cop? When did it all become just a big cynical game to you? When did you stop being a detective?"

"I'm still a detective and you're just a patrol cop, so you watch your goddamned mouth, Paladino."

"You're still a detective? Then how come most days you can't detect your way out of this dump of a bar? And how come my husband's murderer is still free? Why do bad men live and the good men die?"

Paladino turned and walked away, leaving Harrigan slumped on his stool, anxiously picking at the label of his beer bottle and cursing under his breath. Then he ordered another beer and a chaser.

PALADINO OPENED the door and felt the sun's flames on her face. Her heart was beating so fast. There really was no such thing as justice, she thought as she wandered back to her car.

Then her cell buzzed, and she fished it out of her pocket. The number looked familiar, and she answered.

"Officer Paladino?"

"Yeah?"

"It's Devlin. Can we meet? I've found something important. Something about Father Aranha."

"I guess...sure. When?"

"Now."

TWENTY-THREE

The coffee and donuts place on Bay Street was swarming with customers. Paladino joined the line for the counter and saw the priest had already got himself a large cup of coffee and was sitting at a table for two by the window. She nodded at him, and he nodded back, and then she stole curious glances at the priest while she waited in line, watching him turn a large unsmoked cigar in his hands and study it thoughtfully.

Paladino collected her smoothie and sat down opposite Devlin.

"So, what's the deal? Why the urgent need to meet?"

"You ever heard of a thing called the November Club?"

Paladino shook her head. "Nope. What is it?"

"I don't know, but I found this in Father Aranha's study."

Devlin slipped a hand into his jacket and pulled out a strip of card from his pocket.

Paladino read the print on the card. "It could be anything."

"I also found fragments of photos that had been burned in the fireplace at the rectory. In Vijay's bedroom. There wasn't much left of them, but from what there was it looked like they were photos of people having sex."

Paladino's eyes widened. "What kind of people?"

"I think Vijay was being blackmailed."

"What for?"

"Money... It's usually money, isn't it?

"Yeah. It's usually money."

"Looks like he didn't play along. Maybe he said he'd go to the police. Or tell someone. Blow the whole thing wide open. And that's why he got three bullets in his head."

"Did he say anything to you?"

"No. But he was trying to, in the voice message he left for me. The one I didn't pick up till after he was killed. He said he'd got into trouble. That he needed help. Needed to speak to me. But he didn't say anything specific."

"You know, strictly speaking, you should tell Harrigan. The remains of the photos are evidence."

"Yeah, I should. Are you going to make me give them to Harrigan?"

There was a pause. "No," said Paladino. "No, absolutely not. In fact, I suggest that if you want to find who killed your friend, you don't count on Harrigan for anything. He's the worst kind of cop. The kind that doesn't care. But I think you knew that from the first time you laid eyes on him."

"Yep. He's the rot at the center of Sag Harbor PD."

"Ain't that the truth." Paladino stirred her smooth with the straw, thought for a moment, and then said, "Why use photos for the blackmail?"

"Why not?"

"They didn't send him an email or a thumb drive. Just old-fashioned photos. Why so low-tech?"

"It could be because whoever tried to blackmail Vijay was hi-tech and they knew that all the ways of sending digital images would have digital fingerprints. These photos could be printed off anywhere."

"Maybe." Paladino glanced at her watch. "I gotta head off."

"You back on shift?"

"Not officially. Like you, I've come to realize that if I want to get to the bottom of what happened with Greg, I need to do it myself. And right now, I gotta see a guy about a car."

Paladino left, leaving Devlin alone, mulling over what he was going to do next. He finished his coffee and, deep in thought, strolled out to his car, an old, battered, silver Dodge that had belonged to Father Aranha. His thoughts, though, were thrown out of the window by the sight of a dark-haired girl mounting her bike and flying off down the road. Had she even been watching him? Watching him talking with Paladino? He ran to his Dodge, started it up, muscled his way across the traffic into the far lane, and took off after the girl.

At first, he thought he'd blown it and lost the girl, but as he turned right out of Division Street, he saw her a block ahead and sailing left into a side road. Devlin, not wanting to give himself away, took the next left turn into a street that ran parallel with the one the girl had taken and came to a stop at a set of red lights. Devlin swore under his breath and leaned forward with his foot poised on the gas, ready to take off. The lights changed, and he swerved right and caught sight of the girl zipping across the next junction along. Instead of taking a left turn and heading down the same street the girl had taken, he drove straight on till he hit Main Street, again trying to mirror her journey without being seen. As he got to the last set of lights on Main Street, he had a lucky break—the girl came out of a turning up ahead and crossed the strip, riding right across his path. He watched her cruise on a little further down Main Street and take the turn out to the coast road heading east.

Devlin followed suit and got onto the coast road. From here on he had a clear view of the road as it stretched out eastward by the sea and the girl cycling at speed along it. She whipped in and out of cars like she was immortal. But the clear, unbroken view of the coastal highway meant Devlin could hold back without losing sight of her.

After a couple of miles, she came off the road and took a steep, narrow footpath down to the bay below. Devlin carried on a little farther till he found a small turnout and pulled into it. He got out of the pickup and walked back along the coastal road and took another, wider path down to the sea, about a half a mile farther east from the one the girl had taken. This path was wide enough for a vehicle, marked out by low wood fencing on either side and wound down to the same bay.

Devlin stopped at the bottom of the path where it hit a narrow wooden walkway that ran along the beachfront. This small, naturally enclosed area was nearly deserted. Farther along the wooden walkway was a short pier, and moored against it was the *April Rose.*

Devlin couldn't see the girl or anyone else on board the yacht, so he waited and watched. After about half an hour, the bald guy with the sunglasses emerged from the side of the boat wheeling the girl's bike along beside him. Devlin noted with satisfaction the bandage around the bald man's head and the bruising around his left eye. The bald guy stood the girl's bike upright on its kickstand and disappeared down the hatch under the cockpit. Another five minutes passed, and the man appeared again, this time with the girl behind him. Devlin retreated behind the fencing and scrambled farther up the slope till he found a couple of dunes to hide behind. From this relatively secure vantage point, he watched as the girl rolled her bike down the gangway and set off back along the pier and then up the footpath toward the coastal road. The man watched her go from the deck and scanned the harbor. Then he headed back down below.

Devlin waited a little while longer, looking out into the bay, watching how the sea was beginning to chop up a little. The wind coming into the cove was catching on the surface of the water, building lines of swell farther out that broke and crested toward the shore.

Just as he was thinking about making a move, he heard the sound of an engine and tires descending down compacted sand and earth. He looked up to his right and saw a white van edging cautiously down the path Devlin had come down. It stopped a few feet short of where the path met the walkway, and two men, both in suits, got out. One was a tall, thin-as-a-rake guy with dark hair and stubble, and the other was a much bigger guy with a shaven head. The guy with the shaven head had heavy scars all over his face and cranium and a nose that looked like it had been broken to the point of destruction. The two men then opened the back of the van and slid out a long wooden crate about two and a half feet wide by six foot. From the way the two men struggled with the crate, Devlin could see it was heavy. Awkwardly, navigating the uneven surface of the walkway, they carried the crate between them to the boat, carrying it along the gangway, across the deck, and then, with even more difficulty, manipulating it down the narrow staircase below deck.

About fifteen more minutes passed until the two men appeared back on the deck, their suits crumpled, their ties loose, and their jackets open and flapping in the breeze. The bald guy with a bandage appeared briefly and exchanged a few words with the visitors before disappearing below deck. Then the two men in the suits disembarked the boat and walked back along the bay to the van. They closed the back doors and got in the van, and the tall, thin guy went about reversing the van back up the path, over-revving and spreading a stink of burning clutch across the front.

Eventually, the van reached the top of the rise and did a three-point turn back onto the coastal road.

More minutes passed. Devlin didn't move.

The bald guy came out onto the bobbing deck and walked around the side of the boat farthest from Devlin, disappearing from view. About five minutes later he appeared again and went back down into the main cabin. Devlin watched him go below deck and then sidled down to the harbor front, walked along the pier, and crossed the gangway to the *April Rose*. He got on deck and positioned himself opposite the main staircase and waited.

After a few minutes, Devlin heard the sounds of someone bumping around below and then the sound of footsteps creaking on the ladder. The steps were heavy and accompanied by short gasps. A stubbled crown appeared, coming up from the shadows, and then the bald guy's head emerged above deck, his eyes widening as he caught sight of Devlin looming over him, waiting for him.

"I told you to stop using kids to run your poison."

If the bald guy had a response, he didn't have the opportunity to voice it. Devlin's foot scythed across his temple, sending him back downstairs without touching a step on the way. He heard the bald guy hit the floor with a hard crack.

Devlin hoisted himself down into the passageway below, stepped over the unconscious body of the bald guy, and began looking around the cabin rooms.

The first thing Devlin noticed as he walked the length of the boat was the incredibly strong smell of fish that hung in the air. There were a number of smaller cabins off the passageway and the main cabin at the end which was paneled with dark wood and served as a living room. In the living room, set down on the floor, was the crate that had been brought aboard. The top had been prized off, and it was empty. Devin crouched to inspect the inside of the crate and saw that there were small lengths of fabric and strands of hair caught between the planks.

Devlin backtracked through the smaller cabins and turned

into a narrow kitchen by the foot of the ladder where the smell of fish was strongest. On the right were cabinets and a countertop. At the other end of the kitchen, pushed into the corner, was a chest freezer. Devlin would have left it alone and moved on were it not for the handbag that sat on the countertop next to the freezer. Devlin was not, it was fair to say, an expert on handbags, but even he recognized the branding on this one—a Louis Vuitton with gold clasps. He opened the bag, and through the stench of the fish, he caught a sweet waft of scent mixed with leather. Inside was a matching Louis Vuitton purse and a cell phone in a matching Louis Vuitton case. He opened up the purse and slid out a credit card. The name B M Sutton was embossed on it.

A white card had been tucked in behind the credit card, and Devlin picked it out. Embossed on it was the logo of a blue serpent with gold outlined black eyes entwined around the jade silhouette of a tree, and below it were the words "The November Club." It was the same card that Devlin had found in Father Aranha's bible. Devlin's mind flashed back to the moment Aranha had seen the symbol on the pillbox. He had recognized it.

Devlin put the card in his pocket and the purse on the countertop and turned his attention to the freezer. Lodged in the narrow gap under the freezer lid was a tiny pearl of red. He braced himself and pulled open the freezer.

Inside the freezer was crammed with fish. But in amongst the fish, Devlin spotted something else, something crescent-shaped and livid. A human ear, pale and blue. Devlin brushed away the fish and the ice to reveal the side of a face, the ruined, delicate, drained features of a young woman.

Devlin didn't have time to absorb the discovery of Brandi Sutton's body. A dull, sickening blow sent him hammering into the kitchen bulkhead. Before he had time to comprehend what was happening, he was reeling under a rain of random, vicious blows to his head and body. His face was forced downward into the slimy mound of fish and against the cold, hard body beneath.

Devlin's arms were useless to him pinned down in this position, but a backward dig with his heel connected good and hard with his attacker's shin and created a brief window of opportunity. The hold Devlin was in loosened only momentarily, but it was enough for Devlin to grasp the edge of the freezer and spring all his weight back, taking him and the assailant behind him down onto the narrow floor space. Sandwiched between the cupboards and the bulkhead, Devlin found himself on top of a thick-set, greasy-skinned guy wearing a black Metallica tank top, who was desperately grabbing and swinging at Devlin to get free. Devlin fended off the blows as he wrestled for stability and dominance. His hand clutched at the attacker's chest, and beneath the cotton material of the shirt, he felt a small metal-ring piercing. Devlin gripped at the material and the ring underneath and wrenched upward, ripping away the nipple piercing from his attacker's chest. Devlin's ears nearly split from the howl his attacker gave out. With unrelenting fury, Devlin began to hammer his fist into the twisted face beneath him. A berserk fury had taken hold of Devlin, and a dark anger flooded out like hot blood from somewhere deep within him. He drove blow after blow across his assailant's face until eventually the anger had decayed into shame and he realized the guy beneath had long passed out.

Devlin's heart banged like it was going to explode, and sweat and fish guts covered his face, jacket, and shirt. He rolled back onto his haunches, then hoisted himself to his feet.

Footsteps were coming along the passageway, and Devlin

stepped out to see the bald guy with new face wounds coming toward him holding a crowbar. But the bald guy wasn't a fighter, and a half-hearted swing of the bar missed its target. Devlin planted a jab in the bridge of his nose, felling him instantly.

TWENTY-FOUR

"There's nothing more to tell you."

"I don't believe you."

"I've been here for three hours. When can I go?"

"When I say so."

Harrigan stood in front of Devlin with the sun behind him. Devlin was smoking and leaning against a low fence along the narrow harbor front. He had used the tiny bathroom on the *April Rose* to wash away the residue of fish on his face and clothes as best he could. His hair was still wet and straggled over his forehead, and his jacket and shirt were damp. But even over the stink of fish, Devlin could still smell the booze on Harrigan's breath. He squinted at the detective, who was holding a notebook he hadn't got around to using yet. Behind Harrigan, the *April Rose* had already been turned into a crime scene with white-suited forensic officers buzzing in and out of the main hatch.

"Has Gerry Sutton been told about his wife?" asked Devlin.

"Yeah. He's been told. Right now, we're gonna go through what happened, again. From the top."

Devlin blew out some smoke and for a moment caught the

smell of dry wood, salt air, and seaweed before he was over-whelmed again by the stink of fish from his clothes.

"So," Harrigan drawled. "You just happened to be out walking, and you thought there was something suspicious about the boat, so you went to investigate? You saw two men drive a van down to the front and carry a long wooden box onto the boat which made you curious enough to want to board the boat and look around."

"That's about it."

"How the hell did you find yourself below deck opening a freezer with a dead body in it?"

"I went below deck and opened the freezer and found a dead body in it."

"Just like that?"

"Just like that. And that's when I was attacked, of course."

Harrigan slid his notebook away and folded his arms. "That's a load of crap. You got one more chance to tell me the truth, you smug son of a bitch. To tell me why you happened to board a boat filled full of narcotics and a dead body. And I want to know what you're hiding, and I want to know it now."

It was a fair question, but Devlin wasn't going to involve the girl. But Devlin also understood what the real meat was here. The other question hanging in the air. Why hadn't Harrigan been the one to bust a drug operation happening in his back-yard? Why had some out-of-town priest managed to do it but not the village detective? And they were questions the whole of Sag Harbor and beyond would be asking too. Harrigan was staring a whole lot of professional humiliation in the face. And that had to hurt.

"Or what, Detective?" replied Devlin.

"Or I take you back to the station and arrest you for obstruction of justice."

Devlin looked over Harrigan's shoulder and nodded in the

direction of the police officers standing guard by the gangway to the boat.

"You and I both know that isn't a realistic priority for you right now. What with you having every cop and forensic officer at your disposal combing a murder and drugs-trafficking crime scene. What's on that boat is going to keep you busy for months. And it's the height of the season. You really want to try and rope me into an obstruction charge on top of all this?"

Harrigan's sneer turned into a smile. "I get it, you're sore because I gave you a beating. Well, when I get you into custody again, I'm gonna beat you inside out. That's a promise."

A voice came sailing over the short stretch of water from the boat, and Harrigan turned around. A forensics guy had come on deck and had been trying to get Harrigan's attention. He looked over at the boat and back at Devlin. "I'm not done with you. Not by the longest goddamned way."

Devlin stood to his full height, sucked on his cigar, and blew it over Harrigan's face. "Well, I'm done with you. I've been in this place a matter of days, and I've found a body and a drug operation that was running right under your nose. How you can stand there and look me in the eye I have no godly idea."

Without waiting for a reply, Devlin blew out another jet of smoke and walked back down the path.

Up ahead he could see Maynard, the young patrol officer, stationed at the end of the path. As Devlin approached Maynard, he could see him speaking into his radio, no doubt communicating with his boss. Maynard stepped out in front of Devlin and puffed himself up.

"Detective Harrigan doesn't want you to leave the crime scene."

"I'm touched. But unless he's got a reason to arrest me, I'm free to go."

Devlin pushed past the young man and felt for him. He'd

probably get a roasting from his boss. But there was too much that needed to be done. Devlin hadn't told Harrigan about the photos, and he hadn't told him about the November Club card, so he had a hell of a head start on Harrigan's investigation and he intended to use it.

TWENTY-FIVE

Paladino had never seen the car that ran her husband down. At some point she'd been told by someone, she couldn't remember who, that the car had been some kind of Toyota, a 4x4. She'd been told this somewhere in that first never-ending period when she'd been wrecked and short-circuited by grief. She couldn't remember who told her, but she remembered being told that the car, stolen hours before from outside a house in East Hampton, had been chosen due to its size and weight—its husband-killing size and weight. At least that was the theory. But for a theory, it had a grim logic to it, too grim and logical to be untrue.

Hobie, the desk sergeant, rattled and jangled an absurdly big bunch of keys back and forth until the wide chain-link gates snapped free, and he pushed them open. Then he shut the gates behind them, and they walked across the lot.

The Sag Harbor impound lot was a small rectangular square filled with towed cars. Rows of mostly sedans and minivans and a couple of flatbed trucks. Paladino followed Hobie to a long white cinder block garage that ran the length of the lot. As he walked, his keys jangled against his expansive hip. At five foot ten and two hundred and thirty pounds, Paladino worried for Hobie's heart. Hobie raised the keys again with a flourish and opened a door that led into a side office with a desk, a PC, a police radio, and a desk phone. They walked through the side office into the main part of the garage where there were three other cars parked. In the far corner, alone by itself, was the Toyota. Most of the bodywork was twisted and buckled, scorched and warped, charred black and white. It looked like Paladino felt.

"You okay, Holly?" asked Hobie.

"I think so."

"You want me to get you something? Water? A coffee?"

"No. I'm okay." There was a pause. Outside there was the sound of the chain-link gate opening and a big vehicle entering.

"That'll be another tow," said Hobie. "But they won't come in here."

Paladino nodded. "Do you know anything about what happened to Greg?"

"Only what I was told. Nothing more than you, I don't think."

"Do you know what part of the car struck him?"

"Well, from what I heard the guys say at the time, it was head-on. Right in the center of the grille."

Paladino walked around to the front of the vehicle and touched the charred remains of the grille, hoping to feel something—a bolt of sensation, a remnant of the last surface that had had contact with her alive husband before he became her dead husband.

"It was dumped at the north end of Long Pond," said Hobie. "They found it on fire and managed to put it out. The fire didn't take so well, so the damage was contained to the bodywork. The inside is practically untouched. Dusted it for prints, of course, but it didn't turn up anyone part from the owner it was stolen from and their family. You might even be able to start it up."

"Right."

Paladino fell silent. Then she said, "Actually, I'm a little thirsty... Could you get me that water?"

"Oh, sure."

Hobie slouched off, his keys jangling on his hip. For a moment Paladino just looked at the car. Wondering if she should hate it. Wondering why she didn't hate it. But it was just a thing. The driver, on the other hand, she hated the driver plenty. Enough to live out twenty lifetimes of hatred.

Slowly, Paladino circled the car. Then she went around to the driver's side and wrenched the door so it came free and looked inside. The seats were worn leather, and the dashboard was completely intact. The glass on the dials and digital screens hadn't cracked from the heat of the fire. Paladino sat half in the car with her feet on the concrete looking over the interior for a minute or two. As she gazed around the car, she noticed that there were exposed wires by the steering wheel. She could see that the plastic housing around the ignition cylinder had been removed, and the power and starter wires had been cut in order to hot-wire the car. Then she remembered what Hobie had said about the car probably still being in good enough condition to start up. Paladino reached down to look at the wires. She got the exposed ends of the power leads and twined them together. As soon as they touched, the car's electrics blinked into life, lights started blinking, and the radio boomed into life, filling the car with twisting electric chords and screaming vocals. Then, as quickly as the electrics had started up, they died. The radio fell silent, and Paladino heard the jangle of keys coming for the back of the garage.

"Here you go," said Hobie, holding out a Styrofoam cup in front of him.

Paladino took the cup and downed it in one.

"I'm done here, Hobie, thanks."

"Has it been...helpful...? Coming here?"

"No. But I had to come."

TWENTY-SIX

In the dark, you had to slow to a crawl to see it. There were no road lights, and the moon wasn't much help either. A narrow dirt track under a canopy of leaves led onto a broader drive that opened out into a large apron of green and a white three-story complex of buildings with dark glass windows. Along one side of the buildings were four double garages, and dwarfing the garages was the house itself, a mid-twentieth-century piece of modernist architectural history. Clinical and minimal.

Devlin parked the battered, scraped-up Dodge in front of the house and wondered if just parking his banger of a truck there took a couple of thousand off the value of the place. Jutting out was a wide porch and steps up to the front door. Devlin stood on the porch, pressed the video-com button, and pictured Gerry Sutton somewhere in the house looking into a screen full of Devlin's face and making a decision. A minute passed, and then the lock on the door switched and the door slid open. Standing in the doorway, golden hall light spilling out from behind him, was the haunted figure of Gerry Sutton. Devlin didn't think he looked like he'd been crying. But he looked like he'd had his very soul sucked out of him.

"I'm so sorry about Brandi," said Devlin.

Sutton didn't answer. And for a moment Devlin thought the door was going to slam shut in his face.

Then Sutton spoke. It came out in a near whisper. "The police said you found Brandi."

"That's right…" Devlin began to reply, but Sutton had turned his back on him and was walking away with the door still open. So Devlin took it as an invitation, of sorts, and followed Sutton into a vast living room off the hallway. The floors and walls were polished marble, and the furniture was carefully chosen not to upset the minimal aesthetic. It had all the style and warmth of a high-class hotel.

Sutton stood in the middle of the room, his hair ruffled and his shirt untucked.

"Who killed Brandi?" he asked in a strained voice.

"I don't know. I don't think it was the guys on the boat where I found her. Her body was transported to the boat by two men who drove up in a van. They would be the main suspects. The boat was just a way of safely disposing of the body."

Sutton seemed to sway for a moment as if he were suddenly light-headed. He blinked and turned, walking toward the couch. In front of the couch was a chunk of granite, rough on the sides, straight and polished on the top, that served as a table. On top of the granite was a bottle of Grey Goose vodka and a half-empty glass.

"You want to join me?" asked Sutton.

"No. Thank you."

Sutton filled his glass and sat on the couch and invited Devlin to sit in the armchair opposite.

"What I don't understand is why on earth you were on the boat in the first place."

"I was following up on something. A lead I'd got on Father Aranha's death."

"What lead?"

"I think Father Aranha was being blackmailed. Gerry, have you ever heard of a place called the November Club?"

Sutton buried his face in his hands and shook his head. He cursed and mumbled, "Oh God," into his palms. Then he came up for air, looked at Devlin gravely, and nodded.

"Yeah, I've heard of it."

"It was on a card that Father Aranha and Brandi Sutton both had in their possession. It links their deaths, so you need to tell me everything you know about it."

"It's a...a gathering. A very, very exclusive gathering. It's incredibly select and incredibly discreet. And it has to be, because of what happens there."

"What happens?"

"Do you really think it's got something to do with Brandi's death?"

"All you need to do is tell me what you know."

Sutton swallowed and took a long, slow breath in. "Escorts and drugs are provided for the enjoyment of the guests. Prostitutes are bussed in from the city, paid a lot of money to entertain the people who get invited."

"And you and Brandi were guests there?"

Sutton took another sip of his drink. He licked his lips and looked down at his hands that were folded into his lap, then back up at Devlin.

"It would help me get through this if I could look on what I say here as a confession. Is that possible, Father?"

"Sure. You can confess anywhere in the presence of a priest; it doesn't have to be in the confessional."

Sutton seemed encouraged by this and nodded, and his hands clasped together as if in prayer.

"That's good to know. Especially because of what I'm about to tell you. You see, the awful thing is...I was invited to the club, and I brought Brandi along with me. I know, I know, it's shameful. I feel so shamed by it. You have to understand that I was under tremendous pressure... Work was not going well, our portfolio was tanking, and..." Sutton glanced at Devlin and saw that his sob story was not visibly moving him. He coughed, straightened up, and continued. "In any case, I persuaded Brandi to come with me and, deservedly, I was punished for it. Brandi met someone there—not one of the...the escorts, someone important. Someone she started to see while she was with me."

"Who was it?"

Sutton hesitated. "What I'm about to tell you has to be in complete confidence. You cannot let anyone else know I told you. Is that understood? Do you promise?"

"I promise."

Sutton inhaled deeply and tipped the last of his brandy back. "A man called Oliver Harris, a slimy little creep, owns the house where the club meets. He's a sort of master of ceremonies and keeps everyone happy. But Brandi told me it's not run by him. He's only the face of the club."

"Who runs it?"

"I don't know. And she wouldn't tell me. But I suspect it's whoever she was having an affair with."

"Why?"

"It's just a hunch. But I think it's a good hunch."

"Where are the parties held? What's the address?"

"It's held in a mansion halfway between here and Sag Harbor. A remote house called Sefton House. It's deliberately out of the way to ensure privacy."

Devlin thought for a moment. He studied Sutton, and then his thoughts went inward, and a deep quiet came over him which made Sutton uneasy.

A couple of minutes of silence came and went. Finally, Devlin said, "When's the next gathering?"

Sutton raised his eyebrows conspiratorially and replied, "As it happens, there's one tomorrow night."

"Well, isn't that lucky?" Devlin got up to leave, and Sutton nearly leaped out of his chair.

"Wait...what are you going to do?"

"I think you know, Gerry. I'm going to go to Sefton House tomorrow night."

"You're not going to go to the police, are you?"

"No. You can relax on that score. I'm just interested in Vijay's and Brandi's murderer. I'm not interested in exposing you."

Sutton nodded gratefully. Devlin turned to go, and Sutton called him back.

"Father...? You said this could be treated as a confession. Could you give me absolution?" Sutton asked. "Some sort of penance?"

"No, Gerry. I'm afraid I cannot."

"Why not?"

"Because I am only permitted to give absolution to those I believe have truly repented."

TWENTY-SEVEN

Devlin was up in the morning with the first light. He hit the empty streets and began crisscrossing the town, looking for the girl. In between covering the village center, he did about half a dozen sweeps of the harbor front, but he came up with nothing. Now the boat had been busted, he had no place he knew she would be. And he needed to see her. He felt a duty to her, to not let her drown in a sea full of sharks. And with the fallout from the bust in the *April Rose* and Brandi's murder, things could easily get really nasty for her. But he had no leads, no earthly way of knowing where she might be. He was about to about to abort the search and turn tail and head back to the rectory when inspiration hit. He remembered the library card he'd seen poking out of her wallet and the conversation about Eleanor Roosevelt.

Devlin drove across town and found a parking spot a little way down from John Jermain Memorial Library. He got out of the car and approached the library on foot, circling the building, looking for the one thing he knew with certainty that the girl took everywhere with her. And it didn't take long for him to find it, slotted into a bicycle rack on a path tucked in between the two sections of the library building. In the middle of the rack, standing out from the more conservative step-through bikes with baskets and the midrange bikes, was a gleaming silver Kingdom mountain bike.

THE GIRL HAD COME to the library for sanctuary. To get away from all the confusion, from a world that was suddenly all out of balance and scary. Nobody else was on the top floor of the library apart from her, and were it not for the calamitous news that Harris had relayed to her about the *April Rose*, she would have already sunk into blissful solitude, cross-legged on the floor, losing herself in the pages of the Eleanor Roosevelt biography. Instead, her mind and body buzzed with anxiety. She was gripped by the sense of things going wrong beyond her control and understanding, things that threatened to overwhelm her. Scary adult consequences stretched out into an infinity of fear.

It all had happened so fast. She had only just made the delivery to the *April Rose* when Harris called her and told her to come back "as a matter of the utmost urgency." When she arrived back at the house, Harris was a wreck, all over the place. He launched into a breathless retelling of the ambush on the boat, so overwrought by the events he was describing that he seemed to be in danger of suffocating. He told the girl how the crew of the *April Rose* had been attacked and the cops had impounded the boat. How there was a rumor that a body had been found on the boat. When he got to the end of the account, Harris and the girl stood in dazed silence. The girl didn't know what to say. What to do next. But she knew one thing for certain: she knew it was all over. Her moment in the sun, her glorious stream of income, the home she had made in this dreamlike world of wealth, it was all gone.

Now, in the calm of the library, she suddenly understood what she had to do next. She needed an exit plan.

She closed her book. The sun shot straight beams of gold across the dark wood of the walls and floors. Constellations of dust motes swirled and sailed about the room. If only she could stay in the library forever, make this place her universe. But that couldn't be. Instead, it would have to be a trip back to Brownsville and the misery of a mother and a stepfather who didn't want her back. As the girl looked out through the bright squares of light and watched the treetops tremble outside, she heard heavy footsteps plodding up the stairs. She looked up and saw a large, dark figure at the top of the staircase.

"You need to come with me."

Markham stood, looking down at her.

"What? Why? I was just at the house half an hour ago."

"There's going to be one more event. Tonight. We need you to set up."

"Tonight?"

"Tonight."

"Okay." The girl got to her feet, but she knew something wasn't right. And she knew Markham had guessed she knew. But she played it straight. She straightened herself out and said, "I need to go to the bathroom first."

"Make it quick. I got things to do."

Inside the bathroom, she pushed the door to the cubicle shut, locked it, and pulled out her cell phone. She heard the restroom door creak and suspected it was Markham lingering. She got the napkin with Devlin's number from her pocket and quickly typed out a text. Then she flushed, washed her hands, and went back into the library where Markham was hovering by the restroom door. The girl smiled, looking at Markham with an open and trusting face, and said, "Okay. Let's go."

"Come on," said Markham gruffly, and he turned to go.

"Oh, wait," said the girl, pointing to the Roosevelt biography on the floor. "I should put this back."

Markham scowled while the girl placed the book she'd been reading back on the shelf.

"Okay, all done," said the girl, and they left.

DEVLIN SEARCHED the ground floor of the library, then the second, and finally the third. If he had made straight for the top floor, he'd have run into Markham and the girl coming down. But as it was, their paths failed to cross.

After a thorough circuit of the library, he went back outside and saw the girl's bike was still there. So he went back in and did another circuit, ending up back on the top floor. But she was nowhere to be seen. While he'd been searching for the girl, his cell had buzzed a couple of times and he'd ignored it, thinking it was a news alert or an email. When it buzzed for the third time, he checked it and saw a message from an unknown number. The text said, "Hey granny. All well with me. Hope you too."

For a moment he was completely thrown and was about to write the text off as a wrong number. But the word "granny" stuck in his head. It nagged at him. He stopped still and thought hard. And then it clicked—his mind raced back to the conversation with the girl in the coffee shop. He remembered her talking about the Eleanor Roosevelt biography. His eyes flicked up to the signs hanging from the ceiling. He saw the sign for the nonfiction section and headed toward it. He searched through the shelves and found the Biography section. In the section marked "L – P," he saw one book jutting out a couple of inches from the others. He pulled it out from the shelf and saw it was a thick biography of Eleanor Roosevelt with the dustcover missing. Flicking through, he found a note slipped in between the preface and the first chapter. The note consisted of five words: "I want a way out."

THE GIRL WATCHED the light and shadow play on the back of Markham's shaven head and the scars that cross-hatched his scalp as he drove the silver Continental back out to Suffolk Street. She saw his eyes in the rearview mirror glance at her. He must have sensed the girl's uneasiness because he flipped a switch on his door and all the door locks bolted into place.

"Give me your cell," said Markham,

"Why?"

"Shut up and hand it over."

The girl did as she was told, and Markham scrolled through her texts and calls and then threw it on the passenger seat.

TWENTY-EIGHT

Paladino had come off shift and walked to her Beetle that she'd parked in the precinct lot. She opened the door, got in, and for a minute or so she felt like she was staring into a chasm. She had thought that maybe the Toyota at the impound might tell her something, or at least open up another lead. But it hadn't. It hadn't because that was the nature of detective work, the kind Greg did so well—dead ends were plenty, and live leads were rare. It occurred to Paladino that the only person capable of solving Greg's death was Greg, and she laughed bitterly.

Behind her, she heard the station door open and shut and two voices talking and laughing. She looked in her rearview mirror and saw Maynard and another patrol cop, a guy called Vickers, both coming off shift together. They waved and she waved back. Then she saw Harrigan come out and get into his cruiser. She muttered, "Moron," to herself and went to start her car, but just as she turned the key, she heard something that made her freeze and her heart start to pump a little harder. It was the sound of a car radio. The radio was playing a particular kind of music, an extreme kind of hard-core heavy metal that shook up the parking lot. The singing was guttural and animalistic and competed with shrieking guitars and an incredibly fast drumbeat. It was exactly the same kind of metal she'd heard on the radio in the Toyota.

Paladino cut the engine and turned her head to where the music was coming from. Over her shoulder, she saw Vickers driving his Honda away, but it wasn't coming from his car. Following behind Vickers was Harrigan's Canyon, and the music wasn't coming from there either. It was coming from over in the corner of the lot, from a parked Chevy Silverado with its engine running, and behind the wheel of the Chevy was Maynard. He had his sunglasses on with his sound system up high. Hard electric guitar chords were blasting out of his rolled-down windows. Slowly, as if in a dream, she got out of her car and crossed the parking lot toward the Chevy. She was dimly aware of Harrigan driving past her, but she didn't care about him anymore. She was focused on Maynard.

Maynard had dipped down out of view and was scrabbling about in his glove compartment. When he sat up, Paladino was peering in at him over his lowered window.

"Hey, Paladino? What gives?" asked Maynard breezily.

Paladino looked at Maynard and then at the radio. "That's quite some music you got going on there."

"Yeah, it's extreme, isn't it? Is it too loud?" He leaned over and turned down the car stereo. "I just like to hike it up when I'm out riding about."

"I bet you do. Say, what station is it you're listening to?"

"You into grindcore, Paladino?"

"Just curious is all. What station is it?"

"It's a New Jersey pirate station. Students run it out of the University in South Orange. Only grindcore station you can get out on the island. About two people actually listen to it. Including me." Maynard chuckled at his own joke, and Paladino leaned on the edge of the window so her face was close to

Maynard's. Close enough that she felt she could see every thought that crossed his mind.

"You know the funny thing? I was over at the impound earlier today. I had a look over the car that killed Greg." Paladino saw the corners of Maynard's mouth twitch and his jaw set. "And the last station to play on the radio in the car that killed Greg played the exact same music that you're playing now. Isn't that a coincidence?"

Maynard laughed uneasily. "Yeah, a coincidence...I mean, there are all kinds of extreme metal, and they probably sound the same to most folks."

"Yeah. But as you said yourself, it's pretty rare for someone in Sag Harbor to be listening to a New Jersey student pirate station that plays...what did you call it? Grindcore?"

Paladino's eyes were boring into Maynard's, and he looked deeply uncomfortable. "Yeah, well, like I said, lots of people listen to heavy metal. Even out here. I really have to be going, Paladino."

"Where were you the night Greg died, Maynard?" asked Paladino suddenly.

"What?"

"You heard me. Where were you the night Greg died?"

"Are you suggesting that I killed Greg? Because of a radio station?"

"I'm just asking a simple question."

"Are you out of your mind?"

"Maybe. I am still grieving, that's for sure. So you can just put me asking you a crazy question down to that. I'm crazy with grief and loneliness, and it drives me to do crazy things like ask you where you were when Greg was run over because of a silly radio station."

There was a silence, and it seemed to Paladino that in that silence Maynard was thinking real hard and real fast. Thoughts whizzing back and forth behind his eyes, eyes that were searching for a way out of this encounter.

Finally, Maynard sighed. "I don't remember, Holly. I don't remember. It was a long time ago." He looked at Paladino, who was staring back at him with a stony, unsatisfied expression. He threw his hands up in the air. "What? You gonna officially interview me? You gonna arrest me? Is that what's gonna happen?"

Paladino didn't answer.

"No," said Maynard. "I didn't think so. Look, I'm sorry Greg's dead, and I know it must have torn you apart—"

"Tell me where you were the night Greg was killed, Maynard. Tell me that and I'll leave you alone. Why don't you check your Google Calendar?"

Maynard looked at his watch. "I don't use Google Calendar. I really gotta be somewhere. I don't have time for this crap."

Paladino nodded slowly and walked around the front of the Chevy and got into the passenger seat.

"What the hell?"

"It's okay," said Paladino, buckling up. "You go where you got to go in such a hurry, and while you're getting there, you can have a real hard think and see if you can remember what you were doing the night of September 20. You can look through your cell calls if it helps, your texts, call friends and family. We can check the shift logs. I got all the patience in the world for your answer, Ben Maynard."

Maynard gritted his teeth and pushed down on the gas in frustration. Then, suddenly, his mood changed, and he smiled. "Okay. You want to come along for the ride, that's okay with me."

"Great. Then let's go."

Maynard headed south through the village. As they rode, Paladino found her resolve melting. She had felt brave when she'd gotten into the car with Maynard. Now that bravery had faded a little. If he was the one who killed Greg, then there was no doubt he was dangerous. Out of the corner of her eye, she looked her colleague up and down. He was young and in good shape, tall, and worked out. Physically it was more than likely he could overpower her. Kill her too. But she had to know the answer to her question.

"So, where were you the night Greg was killed?"

"You know," said Maynard casually. "I'm disappointed in you, Paladino. Disappointed you'd even believe that I was anything to do with Greg's death."

"Then tell me where you were and I'll apologize for even thinking it."

Maynard looked around at Paladino, shot her a brief smile, and looked back at the road. "I guess though," he said, his smile getting broader, "if I really tried to remember, maybe something will come back." He pressed his foot down on the gas, and Paladino felt the car suddenly speed up. "Though it feels like a long time ago..." He pressed harder down on the gas, and Paladino began to feel uncomfortable, out of control, and in the hands of her driver.

"Not for me it doesn't," she replied.

They'd left the village and were heading farther south, out into long, tree-lined roads. Away from the village, away from crowded and public places.

"Where are we going?" asked Paladino.

Maynard didn't answer. He just smiled some more, and it occurred to Paladino that his earlier defensiveness had gone and now he was starting to enjoy this little trip.

"You're in luck," Maynard said with a broad grin. "It's just come back to me, where I was that night. Now I think about it, I do remember it—I remember it quite clearly. September the twentieth. As I recall, it was a lovely evening. End of summer but still warm enough to feel like summer, but cool enough to get the benefit of a refreshing breeze every now and then."

With one hand planted on the wheel and an eye on the road, Maynard bent in his seat a little and reached underneath. In one quick motion, he pulled out a Glock, almost with a flourish, and dug the barrel into Paladino's side.

"What are you doing?"

"What am I doing? Exactly what you wanted me to do, Holly. I'm telling you about the night Greg died. Like I said, it's all coming back to me."

Paladino watched Maynard's features set into a satisfied smirk and felt dull pain as the end of his barrel dug into her side.

"I remember," said Maynard, "seeing Greg that night as he stepped up by the harbor wall. A lonely, heroic figure looking out to sea, thinking no one knew he was tailing a drug operation. That he was all under the radar and such a professional goddamn detective. But that was Greg's problem—if anything the poor guy was too focused. He was so obsessed with what he was surveilling that he had no idea I was only a couple of hundred yards away. Waiting. Watching. Well, you know how Greg was more than anyone else. Just so wrapped up in work. I remember revving the car up—it was a stick shift, not like this baby, so I could really get some torque going." As if to prove the point, Maynard pressed even harder down on the gas.

"Stop," said Paladino.

"What?"

"Please, stop."

"Oh, no. You wanted to know where I was that night. You were really very insistent about that, Holly. I'm making sure I tell you and tell you right." Maynard laughed. "Holly, when I let the parking brake off, that stolen Toyota flew out of the starting blocks like a bat out of hell. It ate up the road, and by the time it was bearing down on Greg, I must have been doing sixty at least." More gas. Paladino glanced at the dash and saw the Chevy was roaring along now at nearly ninety miles an hour.

"Your dear, beloved husband slammed off the grill like a frightened deer and his body—"

"Stop! Just stop!"

Maynard's chuckle was nearly drowned out by the rising growl of the engine.

"Why? Why did you kill him?"

"For money. That's all. Just money. But, boy, it was a hell of a lot of money. Drug money, of course."

"Where are we going?"

"Oh, somewhere private."

TWENTY-NINE

Night brought a silky breeze that took the edge off the Sag Harbor summer heat. In the grounds of Sefton House, cars had begun to arrive. Tires crackled along the long, graveled driveway that had been transformed into a golden avenue illuminated by lit candles standing on either side. High-performance engines thrummed quietly as one by one passengers arrived clad in furs and diamonds and perfectly tailored tuxedos.

The moment the guests' stilettos and handmade leather shoes touched the ground, a frosted flute of chilled champagne was handed to them. The air was so sweet-scented with expensive perfume and cologne that you could easily imagine each breath of it was worth a hundred dollars.

The mansion was uplit by lanterns. Spotlights that had been mounted on the lawn moved across its stone facade. The fountain was floodlit too and surrounded by limos and large, grand 4x4s, all with dark-tinted windows. Two security guards with iPads stood by the entrance to the house greeting people and ticking them off as Sefton House slowly filled with guests and a thrilling sense of expectation.

Even half a mile away, deep in the strip of woods that

surrounded the mansion's thirty-acre grounds, the sound of the night's entertainment moving into gear could be heard by a lone figure moving stealthily through the black woodland.

Dressed in a dark boiler suit, gloves, and boots and carrying a backpack, Devlin moved as lightly as his solid frame would allow, making a path through the trees toward the lights framing the lawn that stretched out behind the mansion. His progress was halted by a high chain-link perimeter fence with barbed wire along the top. The chain-link was small, too small to allow Devlin to get his fingers into and climb, even if he were able to find a way over the barbed wire, so he walked along the fence, searching for a vulnerability. After about a hundred and fifty yards he found it, a rut under the fence that had been dug out by a fox or some other animal. He knelt by the rut and began digging it deeper and wider either side and pulling at the chain-link, widening the aperture until, with some effort and wriggling, he was able to push his backpack under the fence and then drag himself through to the other side.

Devlin stood, brushed off some of the dirt, and moved through the last strip of forest, getting closer to the lawn and the lights of the house. About ten yards from the edge of the forest, he crouched down and began to watch the house intently. Already guests had filed out of the back of the house and spread out over the lawn with glasses in their hands. They stood in scattered groups, and Devlin could hear the light murmur of voices and occasional laughter.

Up to his right, on the side of the lawn nearest to him, was a long swimming pool and a black marble Jacuzzi. Two fire lamps blazed at the bottom corners of the pool. A few guests had already stripped to shorts and bikinis and some to nothing at all and were frolicking about in the luminous blue rectangle. Apart from the guests, there were at least half a dozen waiters who moved unacknowledged among the crowds keeping glasses topped up to the brim. Large french windows across the back of the house had been thrown open to the summer night, letting the light and the sound of a piano within seep out.

Devlin's focus on the party was broken by the sound of buzzing coming from nearby. Squinting through the trees and bushes, he made out a large, square object standing in a small clearing within the forest, and rising from its center was the shape of a cross. Curiosity got the better of him, and he made a detour through the branches and bramble to the mystery object which was about five feet high and six feet long. He pulled out a flashlight. The bar of light illuminated a high stone table that had names chiseled into it, and Devlin realized that he'd come across some kind of mausoleum. It was stained green with moss, and two stone panels had been mounted next to each other on one of the faces of the tomb. But it was incomplete—there was a square hole where a third panel should have been. Inscribed on the two mounted panels were the names Audley Jacob Harris and Shirley Patricia Van-Temple Harris with dates of birth and death and epitaphs. The date of death for Audley Harris was 2003. The date of death for Shirley Harris was recent, 2017. Leaning against the side of the structure was a new stone panel free of moss without any inscription that had yet to be installed.

The buzzing that had first caught Devlin's attention was coming from inside the tomb along with a sour stink of standing water. Devlin pointed his flashlight into the part of the stone mausoleum that was open and saw that every inch of the interior stone walls and lead flashing was covered in flies. He dropped the flashlight lower and illuminated a body lying crooked in a shallow water-filled trench, a naked, male body crawling with insects. Devlin swung the flash around to get a better look and found himself looking at the pale, dead-eyed face of a blond teenaged boy. He immediately recognized the body as belonging to the boy who he'd caught harassing the girl a few days before down on Church Street.

As Devlin crouched low, inspecting the open grave, he heard the crackle of a radio and a brief burst of a muffled voice. A twig snapped and a deep voice came from behind him. "Take it nice and easy, fella. Stand up nice and slow with your hands up in the air."

Devlin did as he was told. He stood and turned to see a security guy, around six foot tall, standing about three yards away and pointing a Glock at him. The security guy was wearing a cheap suit and had a radio unit hung off his belt. He sized up Devlin, then looked down at the black hole in the side of the mausoleum.

"What are you doing here?" said the security guy.

Devlin didn't answer or move a muscle.

"I said, what are you doing here?"

Again, Devlin refused to answer. The security guy muttered a curse and his free hand darted down to unhook his radio. But before he could take the unit off his belt and call it in, Devlin pitched the butt of his flashlight straight at him. The heavy metal handle caught him square on the brow, momentarily stunning him and filling his vision with a field of white. As the security guy reeled back, desperately trying to recenter and re-aim his Glock, Devlin bowled in low, beneath the swinging gun barrel, and took him down onto the soft bracken and dirt, putting half a dozen knuckled digs into his nose and neck until his body stopped jacking and twisting and gave up consciousness.

A kind of quiet returned to the small glade by the tomb. A quiet corrupted by the buzz of carrion flies and guests laughing and talking farther off. Devlin took the radio off the security guy's belt and smashed it against the mausoleum, then recovered the Glock that had fallen to the ground in the struggle.

He slipped his backpack off and unzipped it, taking out a pair of black leather shoes. Then he took off his boiler suit, revealing his clothes underneath: a black tuxedo and bow tie. He put on the shoes, removed the laces from the boots, then stashed them in the backpack which he zipped up and hooked on a low branch of the sycamore he was standing under. With the laces from his boots, he bound the security guy's feet and hands. He ripped off the sleeves of his boiler suit and used them as a gag and blindfold and used the rest of the boiler suit to knot the security guy hard to the trunk of a tree.

Then Devlin took a moment. He smoothed down his hair, straightened out his jacket, and strode out onto the soft, green lawn, zipping up his fly so anyone glancing in his direction would assume he had just answered the call of nature. As he walked, he could feel the reassuring shape of the Glock wedged into the waistband of his dress pants.

Devlin walked with purpose, through the assembled crowds in the garden, up the stone steps, through the central set of french doors, and into a large, softly lit room. Big gold-framed eighteenth- and nineteenth-century oil paintings were hung on high walls: paintings of wooden warships fighting sea battles, of ancient landscapes, and full-length portraits of important dead people. Two crystal-beaded chandeliers hung from the ceiling, and the floor was nearly covered by a vast oriental rug. In the far corner, a man in tails sat at a grand piano playing some kind of jazz melody, and couples danced together across the oriental rug or stood around the outside talking in groups. It was like something out of the Gilded Age.

Devlin cut across the room to the doorway in the opposite corner and came out in a large hallway dominated by two grand staircases sweeping up to the next floor. A waiter glided past and without waiting for Devlin's consent inserted a cold glass of champagne into his hand. This small act almost threw Devlin completely. He was suddenly saddled with a drink and had the overpowering urge to down it in one go. He spotted a table against the wall covered in empty glasses and made a beeline toward it, getting rid of the glass as quickly as he could.

A guy in a blue suit who looked to be in his early fifties was standing alone by the table. He nodded at Devlin and struck up conversation.

"Hey," said the guy.

"Hey," replied Devlin.

"Quite something, ain't it?"

"It certainly is."

"Your first time?"

Devlin nodded and put down his glass. "You can tell?"

"Yeah."

"How?"

"'Cause you look like I feel. It's my first time too." He raised the crystal glass in his hand which was filled with brown liquor. "I better watch this. It may help the nerves but won't help with the fun."

"Yeah," replied Devlin. "You got that right. To be honest, I was only invited a couple of days ago. Happened to be up here on business and got a call."

The other guy looked at Devlin's empty hands and said, "You not drinking?"

"I'm taking a pit stop."

He laughed and took a small sip of his drink. "'Course, there's plenty other stuff to get a buzz on around here." He nodded to a buffet table by the entrance to a room off the hallway which had a line of bowls arranged on it heaped with white powder. Then he sighed and looked around.

"Quite a bunch here. I've seen a guy from NBC, two guys from the Patriots, and one guy I know for sure is on the board of the Federal Reserve." He glanced down at his watch. "I'd say another ten minutes and then the party will really get started. Least that's what I was told."

"What's the game plan?"

The guy in the blue suit looked slightly astonished at Devlin's question. "Wow, you know even less than me."

"What can I say? It was a last-minute invite."

"What's your name?"

"Devlin. Gabe Devlin."

The guy in the blue suit extended a broad hand.

"Name's O'Reilly. Mike O'Reilly."

They shook, and Devlin was momentarily surprised at the ease with which this man introduced himself to a stranger. And then Devlin understood: O'Reilly felt safe here. All of the guests felt safe here, surrounded by their kind and protected in their exclusive and hyper-elite club.

"Now, Gabe," he continued enthusiastically. "Let me tell you everything I know about the November Club entertainments."

"I'm all ears."

THIRTY

"Ah, Oliver. The party going well?"

Harris always got a very peculiar feeling when he came up to the turret room. It was a room that held a great deal of history for him. It had been his father's study when he was a child, a place he'd been forbidden from entering. A sanctuary for his father and his father's hard-drinking associates who would fill the room with smoke and deep voices. If only he had known that the deadly serious business that his father had been immersed in was the almost criminal mismanagement of the family inheritance. When the old man had finally bought the farm, taking his chronic alcoholism, a sclerotic liver, and his delirium tremors with him, Harris Junior had discovered the larder was nearly bare. What little money the old man had managed to leave behind was then sucked up by his mother's medical bills in the last months before she died, in the turret room. The turret room had become his mother's last refuge as she faded away, propped up on pillows, blind and nearly deaf, her food fed to her through straws and her waste taken away in dishes by a team of nurses.

And now someone else had laid claim to the turret room.

"The party is going well, Oliver?" The question came again, in an accent that drifted from the West Coast to the Urals. But Harris knew its real origins—Belarus.

"No, Andrei. No, it's not."

Harris was flustered and not at all his usual genial self. Markham stood to one side of the wood-paneled, octagonal room, his ravaged face blank and stony. In the center of the room, seated behind the low coffee table, reclining on the couch, was Andrei, blond with a handsome, fine-boned face. Angular and Slavic, his sly, pale blue eyes slid back and forth, calculating the world around him like some kind of depraved angel.

Harris knew that both Andrei and Markham had fought together in a distant, hellish corner of the earth before Andrei had got himself into the biotech business. The two men had worked together as mercenaries on the bloody and lucrative errand of a corrupt regime. Andrei was the rich scion of an oligarch family who, after getting a chemistry PhD under his belt from the University of London and seeking to defy his father, embarked on a career in the Belarus army. It was here he had met Markham, a common soldier with uncommon physical strength and courage. Rumor had it they had run a mercenary outfit for a few years scraping a fat profit out of the confused carnage of the Middle East. And it was in this chapter of their lives they had formed a formidable loyalty, based, Harris speculated, on the many terrible secrets they had come to share. But as to why Markham had come back from foreign wars nearly mutilated, yet Andrei had remained perfectly preserved, Harris had no clue.

Andrei was dressed in a crisp white shirt open to the chest and gray suit pants. Lank, lean, and long-legged, he sprawled on the couch, his limbs spread out, like a spider in the center of a web. Laid out in front of him on the coffee table were five thick, long lines of white powder. He pulled out a bill from his

THE SALVATION MAN 191

pocket, leaned forward, and in five consecutive swoops snorted the whole lot up, wiping the tabletop with his hand and licking his palm clean. Harris found Andrei's appetite for narcotics and sex almost as astonishing as his extraordinary constitution which left him completely undepleted by their effects.

There were two smaller rooms on each side of the turret room, and Harris's eyes momentarily glanced sideways to the door on the left which was locked. The last time Andrei had departed, Harris had come up to snoop around and found that the lock on the door had been changed and he was unable to get in. Though he desperately wanted to know what was in the locked room, he hadn't had the guts to ask. In some matters, Harris all too easily accepted his own cowardice.

Two luggage cases were standing by the door, and a suit had been hung up on the wall, ready to wear. Usually, Andrei brought a whole wardrobe with him. Harris surmised that on this visit his guest did not appear to be planning to stay for long.

"The business with the boat being raided by the police... Brandi's body being found there... It's a nightmare...the whole thing is a nightmare... How on earth did Brandi end up dead in a refrigerator?"

Andrei and Markham exchanged a nearly imperceptible glance. "Oliver, I don't know how Brandi ended up where she did. The people we deal with, they're criminals. You know that, I know that. Maybe Brandi was going straight to them for her own personal use and got out of her depth." Andrei shrugged and threw up his hands. "I really can't say. But what I can say is that we're already cutting ties with that operation and, most importantly, it's not your problem. It's my problem."

"I see... Well, what is my problem is that the whole night has been thrown into chaos by my girl not turning up. She hasn't called me; she hasn't replied to my call..."

"The Hispanic? She didn't do much anyway if you ask me," said Markham blankly.

"Didn't do much? She was our silver service—she made sure the right people were given VIP treatment. She made damned sure the people you expressly asked me to especially look after were especially looked after. I don't think you've ever had any complaints...have you? And she's not Hispanic, by the way—her mother is from Brazil, actually."

"Whatever. I got one of our guys filling in for her," said Markham matter-of-factly. "They're making sure everyone gets to fill their snouts at the trough."

"Get to fill their what? At the what? For God's sake, this isn't a crack den, this is the Hamptons—"

Andrei raised a hand. "Oliver, Oliver, calm down. It doesn't matter anyway. I have some news I need to tell you..."

"What news?"

"Two bits of news, actually. First, I'm going to be putting a little extra into your bank account this month. A special reward. To reward you for bringing our special guest here tonight. I know it took some doing to coax him out here, and I couldn't be more grateful."

Harris blushed. "Well, once I told him about the entertainment here, wild horses wouldn't have held him back. He was already a frequent visitor to most of the fleshpots of DC. In fact, I ran into him at—"

"Well done, Oliver. Whatever you did it worked. Can we make sure this guest gets the most special kind of treatment tonight?"

"Of course. What was the other news?"

"Ah, yes, the other bit of news..."

Andrei's body seemed to expand even further, his arms stretching out of their cuffs, his white-socked feet sliding across the carpeted floor. He smiled, a big, pearly white-teeth smile, and said, "I have made a decision, Oliver. It's not great news, I'm afraid. This is to be our last party of the season. For good, in fact."

Harris managed to splutter a "What...?" His puffy, shiny eyelids receded in surprise, and his eyes became comically large. "You mean, that's it? It's all over?"

"Yes. It is."

"But...but it's only July. Our parties go on till Labor Day. Surely we could carry on for this summer..."

"I'm afraid work commitments mean we won't be able to stay in Sag Harbor. And I don't plan on returning here again."

"Well...that's all right. I mean...I could hold the parties by myself."

Andrei and Markham exchanged doubting looks.

"I could..." Harris insisted. "I practically run them anyway."

"I don't think so, Oliver. There is so much to arrange with the other business here." Andrei licked the tip of his index finger with the tip of his tongue. "The special extras."

"Just leave me your contacts and I'll do all of that."

"Oliver, Oliver," said Andrei sympathetically. "I wish it were that easy. But, as today surely proved to you, it's not. The people who send the cocaine and the heroin and the pills, and the boys and girls, the people who deal with the more delicate end of the business here are bad people, and Markham needs to deal with them, and I need Markham with me. And Markham told me about the mess with the kid you invited here the other night." Harris flushed red with embarrassment. Andrei sat forward and said sympathetically, "The people we do business with won't do business with people they don't know. Anyone they don't have a relationship with, Oliver. It's nothing personal."

"And what about the payments?" asked Harris anxiously. "Do they stop too?"

"It was always an ad hoc arrangement. You knew that from the start."

"But...but how am I to manage? To run the house? Pay the staff? Pay for the maintenance? The bills? Markham could introduce me to the contacts," Harris protested feebly. "Assure them that I am trustworthy. Please don't leave halfway through the summer, Andrei... This...the parties...the people...it's my life, Andrei. It is not a word of a lie to say these wonderful evenings have become my life."

Andrei had stopped smiling. His pearly teeth had disappeared. His mouth twitched to give one last brief half-smile. "I don't think so. We have reached the end here."

Harris took a step forward and clasped Andrei's hands. "You made me, Andrei. You took a bereft has-been, a lonely old man living by himself, and showed me such a world. Made me the center of that world. I am begging you...*begging* you, please don't take the parties away from me."

Harris's legs had crooked as if he might actually go down on his knees, but Andrei pulled away and waved a hand at him.

"Oliver, please, don't embarrass yourself. Have you forgotten your dignity?"

Harris had in truth forgotten every last ounce of his dignity and was only thinking of his survival. But Andrei had become visibly stern and annoyed, and something about this room and its history made Harris feel small and ashamed and unable to fight on.

"It's certain, then?" said Harris hoarsely. "This is the last night?"

"As certain as anything could be. Thank you for everything, Oliver. It's been a ball." Andrei glanced at his watch. "Shouldn't you be downstairs, Oliver?"

Harris checked his watch and sprang to attention like the Mad Hatter and began backing toward the door.

"God, you're right," he said. "I'm behind schedule... Oh, and Andrei..."

"Yes, Oliver?"

"Did you want me to bring something up for you?"

"No, Oliver. No boys or girls for me tonight."

"Are you sure? There's some wonderful..."

"I'm sure. I'm being a good boy for now." The pearly teeth appeared again, and Harris smiled. Then Harris scooted out of the door and back down to the house below.

Andrei looked at Markham.

"We'll wrap this up tonight, won't we?"

"Yes," replied Markham.

"Good. I'm tired of having to pander to these people, to Harris, to the mayor—he's the one we had to kill Brandi for, to protect him in order to protect us." Andrei tutted. "I wish we'd found the Harris family tomb a day earlier—we could have dumped the Sutton woman there too. In any case, it doesn't really matter now because we'll be out of here by the small hours of the morning. And then there will no more discussions with Mayor Boyd or all the other the corrupt official of Sag Harbor, or the little fat man."

THIRTY-ONE

Maynard swung the Chevy down Town Line Road. It was dark now, and the few houses that had been dotted along the roadside disappeared from view as they drove farther away from civilization.

Paladino was waiting for Maynard to pull over into some deserted stretch of dark road. Waiting for the inevitable. But the inevitable didn't happen. Instead, he slowed, looking for a turning. When he found it, he turned the Chevy off the road, and, to Paladino's surprise, she saw a white gate and two security guards on either side of it. The guards acknowledge Maynard, and the gate slid open, revealing a wide driveway, lit up with candles, that led up through acres of green lawn the size of a football field to a glittering fountain and a large mansion. Lined up in front of the house were long limos and luxury SUVs.

"This is Oliver Harris's place," said Paladino. "Why are we here?"

"Shut up."

THIRTY-TWO

Mike O'Reilly had been talking for a while, out of nervousness and adrenaline mainly. While he spoke to Devlin, giving him the evening's schedule, his eyes wandered around the room, eagerly checking out the other people standing around them and for a sign the action was going to begin.

First, he had told Devlin how the festivities would start. It would begin, he said excitedly, with a gong. When the gong went, all the talent, as O'Reilly put it, would parade out so as they could be ogled at, to get appetites properly whetted. And then the talent would mingle with the crowd, and the matching up would begin. Couples, threesomes, foursomes, and upward would quickly form and start drifting up to the many bedrooms on the four main floors of the house. And that's where the real business would take place.

"But we gotta wait for the gongs. And the MC, Oliver Harris—he owns the place and runs the parties."

"Harris is the main guy?"

"Yep. I wouldn't be here if it wasn't for him."

"Oh, why's that?"

"Ran into him in a strip joint in DC. Completely by chance.

We got talking, and he said, 'Hey, you'd fit right into one of my events I run,' and gave me his card. He's a top-drawer gent, that guy."

O'Reilly continued to ramble, the booze and his nerves working his tongue looser than it otherwise might have been. He complained about the journey down to the Hamptons and then about traveling in general. He was, he said, mostly in New York and DC on business.

"I spend my goddamn entire life traveling. Packing bags, standing in line waiting to be scanned, eating crappy little airline meals. New York to DC to LA back to New York."

"What is it you do?" asked Devlin.

"I work in diplomacy," O'Reilly replied vaguely. "You?"

"Aerospace."

"What about your domestic arrangements? You married?" asked O'Reilly, raising an eyebrow conspiratorially.

"Divorced. You?"

O'Reilly swigged down the last gulp of liquor in his glass and shook it, rattling the ice cubes around. "I'm a free agent tonight, my friend. What do you do in aerospace?"

"Consultancy. Mix of private and military..." But Devlin didn't get any further. He and the rest of the crowd around him were silenced by the sound of a gong being hit three times.

THIRTY-THREE

With a careful eye on Paladino and the gun still lodged in her side, Maynard had driven to the top of the drive and turned the Chevy right, navigating around the perimeter of the house and through a temporary parking lot filled with more high-end cars. After that, they drove through another temporary lot where people, mostly young, scantily clad women, were disembarking from coaches. These visitors were heavily made up and swinging designer handbags and did not belong to the same privileged class as the owners of the vehicles out front.

So, this was where all the limos had been heading all the nights. What the hell, wondered Paladino, did Harris have going on here?

Paladino had seen Oliver Harris a couple of times, in the local paper and around town. All she had really known about him was that he had lived most of his life in the shadow of his parents. His dad, so rumor had it, was a drunken, bullying failure who'd squandered the family fortune, a fortune amassed by his father and grandfather in the late nineteenth and early twentieth century. Like the rest of the details about the Harris family, Paladino only knew a snippet, that their fortune had been amassed selling soap. Harris's mother had been known around town as an overbearing and deeply unhappy woman who, like her husband, took her cruelty out on their only son. But she had died only a few years earlier, and what money was left, along with the family mansion, had been left to Oliver Harris.

And what a mansion it was. Not like the mid-century and minimalist creations belonging to most of the Hamptons elite. It was grand and stately, almost noble in its restraint.

"What's going on here tonight?" asked Paladino, but Maynard didn't answer. Instead, he kept on driving, following a path wide enough for one car that took them behind the house and into the enormous grounds behind.

As they drove, Paladino could see small groups of people outside in the garden, but most of the party seemed to be happening inside.

Maynard kept driving, past a swimming pool, tennis courts, and a helicopter parked on a helipad. He approached a line of trees that formed the edge of the mansion's grounds and came to a stop. He switched the gun into his other hand and put the selector into park and the handbrake on.

"Give me your cell."

Paladino pulled out her cell and handed it to Maynard, who slipped it into his jacket pocket.

"If you're going to kill me, just do it," said Paladino. "It won't be your first time."

"Anyone would think you wanted to die."

It was a casual comment, but Paladino found herself thinking about what Maynard had said. A week ago, it would have been true. But not now. It had been true for a long year that she really didn't care whether she lived or died. At times she'd wanted to die. Yearned to die.

But not now and not anymore,

She saw that Maynard was gathering his resolve to kill her but that something was stopping him. Maybe, she thought, it was harder this time, face-to-face with your victim. Harder and much more intimate than just pointing a car at someone and pressing a pedal.

But before Maynard could finish his business with Paladino, he was interrupted by the buzzing of his cell phone. He pulled the phone out of his pocket and answered whilst keeping the Glock pointed at Paladino.

"Yeah, I'm here..." said Maynard into his cell. "Sure. I'm coming." He ended the call, and Maynard suddenly seemed preoccupied and less self-assured.

"Stay here," he said. "I'll be back."

Then he got out of the door and locked the car externally. Paladino watched him walk across the lawn to two men who were standing in the shadow of the helicopter.

"You're late," growled Markham.

Markham and Mosley were standing by the helicopter looking annoyed and edgy. Maynard thought about mentioning the cop he had locked in his car but then decided to delay that particular announcement until he'd softened the two stooges up a little.

"Hey, guys, what's the problem?" he said breezily.

"You know what the problem is," said Markham. "You were supposed to be keeping an eye on the shipments. Letting us know if there was any problems. We had a problem."

"There was nothing I could do about it. Apparently, there was some priest snooping around. How could I have known about that? The police and harbor officers, sure, I can keep an eye on those guys for you. But a random priest that turns up out of the blue? That wasn't on the list of things I was supposed to be watching out for."

"There was no list," said Mosley.

"Well, you know what I mean."

"The boss isn't happy. You got a lot of money."

"And I worked hard for you guys." Maynard hunched his shoulders and pleaded, "I offed another cop for crying out loud. I did you a big favor. Maybe I can talk to the boss, smooth it out. Can I talk to him? Can I see him?"

Mosley and Markham looked at each other, and then Markham nodded. "You can come up and see him in a bit. He's busy right now."

"Okay. Great. Great. So, boys, what's on the menu tonight? Got some treats for old Maynard here?"

Mosley smiled. "Yeah, it's pretty special tonight." He stepped forward and put a comradely hand on Maynard's shoulder. "Think you're gonna like what's going on. Did you see the girls getting off the bus?"

"Damn right, I did."

"Plenty of grade A coke and girls for you, my friend."

Maynard laughed. "Just the shot in the arm I need." He indicated back toward the car and said, "Listen, I got a situation with..."

But Maynard didn't get to the end of his sentence about the cop he had in the car. Instead, he felt his knees go weak and warmth spread around his belly. He looked at Mosley, his eyes round and white in the dark. Then he looked down at the blade in Mosley's hand that was covered in blood—his blood.

Maynard said, "What did you do that for?" It was a dumb and embarrassing thing to say, but he meant it. It was such a crappy thing to do, to stab him in the guts when he was supposed to be his friend. But Maynard knew, with an unbearable feeling of sadness, that there wasn't going to be any reply. Or any more words. Ever.

Mosley did it again, dug the blade into Maynard, and this time he turned the knife around so that Maynard felt his guts rotate like wet clothes in a washing machine. Blood began to pour out like a tap was on inside of him.

Maynard fell onto the concrete, and, lying on his wet stomach, he heard the last words he ever would hear, about how his body was to be disposed of.

"Damn it, got blood on me. Gonna have to change."

"Get his keys. Get him in the car and drive him over to the family tomb," said Markham. "What a piece of luck we found it. Couldn't have worked out better."

AS THE SCENE between the three men played out, Paladino had become more and more terrified. She had squeezed herself down between the front and back seat and watched the last minutes of Maynard's life come and go in the rearview mirror.

The two men in suits were now carrying Maynard's body toward the car. She tried to make herself as small as possible, tried to breathe as quietly as she could. Hoping, praying that Maynard hadn't told them he had brought another cop with him. She heard the trunk being opened and what she guessed was Maynard's soft, lifeless body being bundled in. Then one of them, the skinny one, unlocked the car, slid into the driver's seat cursing and muttering, and started the car up. It didn't even seem to occur to him that someone else might be in the car which confirmed to Paladino that Maynard couldn't have told them about her before he was killed.

Paladino felt the car being turned around and driven back in the direction of the mansion. Then it came to a halt and the skinny guy got out, opened the trunk, and pulled Maynard out. Paladino heard Maynard's body being dragged along the grass, and then she heard some rustling, more cursing, and then silence. She waited for what seemed like hours but was, in reality, only about five minutes and then popped her head up. The car was parked by a row of trees on the edge of the lawn, and the skinny guy was nowhere to be seen. Paladino guessed he must have taken the body into the woods that lined the edge of the grounds, using the parked car to shield him from the view of anyone in the house.

Tentatively, she reached over and pulled at the door handle. The locks snicked and the door came free. Keeping low, she sidled out of the door and stepped onto the lawn. Over at the rear of the mansion, there were a few scattered people on the stone patios and in the pool. Paladino looked about, in case Mosley had reappeared from behind the trees, and seeing the coast was clear, she walked across the lawn toward the house, feeling a little more confident, a little less terrified, and a lot more alive with every step.

THIRTY-FOUR

O'Reilly was not cut from the same cloth as most of the other guests. He wasn't born to privilege; he'd had to work damn hard to get where he was, a senior official in the State Department. But he was keenly aware that he was a little rough at the edges. He lacked the social graces of some of his colleagues and nearly all of his superiors. But he was nothing if not ambitious, and here, in this fancy country house in the Hamptons, with fancy, well-heeled folk, was a chance to get into a loftier orbit.

He'd already seen another senior member of the State Department in the ballroom, a guy called Jason Barker, who was a rung up from O'Reilly and worked a different division. He was sure that Barker had recognized him but had chosen not to acknowledge him. No matter, thought O'Reilly. Maybe the fact that he had seen him and knew he had been admitted to such an event might count for something. It might keep O'Reilly in Barker's mind, lead to his name being mentioned in other equally rarified circles. And in any case, that would be the icing on the cake tonight. Because right now Mike O'Reilly was ready to burst with anticipation.

The sound of the gong had had a Pavlovian effect. It had

brought guests swarming into the hallway and the rooms adjacent to it, craning up to see their host, Oliver Harris, the funny little man that O'Reilly had bumped into in DC, take up position on the first-floor balcony. Harris beamed, looking down munificently on his people gathered below as if he were about to give a sermon from a pulpit. He cleared his throat, leaned forward, his hands grasping the wooden railings, and began to speak in a musical, theatrical voice, basking in the role of master of ceremonies and the limelight it cast upon him.

"My esteemed ladies and gentlemen," he began, his chest puffed and his eyes darting from side to side. "Thank you for gracing us with your presence tonight. I promise you, it will be richly rewarded."

A wave of appreciative whoops and whistles gave Harris great pleasure that he could not hide.

"For those of you who haven't attended our soirees before, in a moment I will beckon down from the heavens such beautiful specimens, such delicious young girls and boys as you have ever seen. They will come amongst you—"

Harris was interrupted by a surge of suggestive cheers and shouts.

"—and mingle with you. And if any of our girls and boys particularly please you and if you would like to enjoy some privacy with them, then we have four floors of guest bedrooms to avail yourselves of."

There was another, louder and more boisterous round of whoops and whistles from the guests who had been waiting for nearly an hour and a half for the main event. The mood was becoming rowdy, the sense of expectation in danger of spilling over into frustration. But Harris was expert at judging the moment when the genie should be released from the bottle, pinpointing the moment when the anticipation became most intense, almost feverish. He clicked his fingers, and the gong sounded again. Then, slowly and almost coyly, lines of young men and women began to appear from the wings of the house and descend down the two wide staircases toward the hordes of guests who were practically panting with anticipation.

O'Reilly's mouth was dry, and his body trembled as he watched these young lithe people dressed in tight and revealing clothes step out into the hallway and begin to mix with the guests, who were all at least two decades older.

Though he felt he should make a move, push himself forward before all of the talent was taken, he found himself rooted to the spot, frozen by indecision and shyness. He could see the girls and boys who had descended into the hallway had been quickly surrounded by a sea of gray heads, and he began to quietly panic. What if there was no one left for him? What if he was left alone downstairs as the rest of the people in the house paired up and went up to the bedrooms. Had he come all this way for nothing?

Just as he was contemplating the most miserable outcome, the most miraculous thing occurred. Two kids, a boy and a girl of around eighteen or nineteen, certainly no more than twenty, made eye contact with O'Reilly as they arrived at the bottom of the staircase. The two youngsters blatantly ignored the approaches of other guests who tried to get their attention and made a direct line toward O'Reilly. Without any encouragement, they each took his arm and kissed him on his neck. The feeling was electric, and his excitement became euphoria when he found himself being gently led back toward the stairs and up to the bedrooms above.

THIRTY-FIVE

Having seen Harris's performance, Devlin had very quickly come to a conclusion about the host of the evening. Harris, he guessed, might be the showman, but he wasn't running the place. Someone like Harris couldn't run narcotics and pimp out kids, at least not by himself. To do that you needed someone with muscle and no conscience, someone prepared to do all the really bad things that needed doing from time to time to secure your supply chain.

Devlin watched O'Reilly climb the stairs, lust struck between two teenagers. Couples and groups coalesced around the strange threesome and followed them up to the bedroom floors. In the mix and swirl of old and young, guests and hosts, Devlin too went up the staircase into the higher reaches of the house, remembering Gerry Sutton's words as he climbed the staircases. Sutton had said that there was a place at the top of the house, a place forbidden to most guests, but which Brandi was able to get into.

The sound of excited gossip and laughter echoed along the hallways. One by one, doors open and closed, the bedrooms filled up on each floor, and by the time Devlin had reached the fourth floor, that too was beginning to fill up to capacity. Devlin could see that the fourth floor was the last of the floors that spread out across both wings of the house, but it was not the highest story. There was a further curved staircase, a narrow wooden one, old, worn, and much less loved than the rest of the house, that led up from the fourth-floor hallway.

Standing at the foot of the last staircase was a tall, slim, cadaverous-looking guy in a suit with a heavy shadow of stubble. Like the guy Devlin had encountered in the woods outside the house, he had a radio hanging from his belt. His job was to make sure no one made the mistake of trying to climb the last set of stairs, gently shepherding guests away, back along the hall to the bedrooms.

Devlin mixed in with the partygoers scampering back and forth and was able to make a couple of passes by the staircase and the man guarding it. As he was sizing up the situation, a woman in her fifties wearing a silver cocktail dress came teetering and swaying up the stairs with a half-empty glass in her hand. She was clearly hammered and in danger of falling over. The security guy watched her precarious progress and started to get concerned. He stepped forward and prepared to intervene. Before she got to the top of the steps, she lost her footing and reeled back, using her free hand to grab the railing. Her glass arced in the air, sending a rain of champagne over other guests coming up the stairs. There were curses and shouts of disapproval, and the security guy felt compelled to leave his station and go sort the drunk lady out.

Devlin saw the opportunity present itself to him, an opening of only a couple of seconds while the security guy's focus was taken up with lifting the woman up onto her feet and getting her to the landing. He slid up the single staircase as quickly and as deftly as he could. Leaving the laughter, chatter, and chaos behind, he climbed the unvarnished wooden steps, up a dark cylindrical stairwell, the light from the lower floors fading as he went higher.

The stairwell opened up at the very top onto a small landing. High up on one side of the landing was a large oval window through which the faintest of blue-white glows shone, and on the other side of the landing was a wood-paneled door. The door was old and marked. The carpet on the landing was faded and frayed at the edges. Devlin approached the door, wrapped his hand around the handle, and twisted. The handle gave in his palm, and the bolt switched out of the jamb. With a gentle push, the door swung open to reveal an octagon wood-paneled room with an oval window in the opposite wall, smaller than its twin on the stairwell but shedding the same faint moon and star shine. Below the window were a desk and chair. In the center of the room, a couple of leather easy chairs and a couch had been arranged around a long, low table. In front of the table lay a large, rectangle Persian rug that was spread out on top of a thick red carpet. Mahogany cabinets lined the angled wood walls. Sconces were positioned on the walls, giving an even but low light.

Devlin crossed the room and sat in one of the easy chairs. He leaned forward over the long table. It was made of pine and had been fitted with slim drawers. He pulled out one of the drawers which held a small silver box. He took the box out, placed it on the table, and opened the lid. Inside the silver box were compartments holding a variety of powders and pills. He dipped his finger into one of the compartments that contained white powder and tasted it. The substance had a sharp tang, and his gums and the tip of his tongue started to go pleasantly numb. He dipped his finger into another compartment filled with yellow powder and got a vinegary, harsh hit off it. Cocaine definitely and most likely heroin too. He put the silver box back and opened the next drawer along which was filled with jewelry.

Lying on top was a familiar silver necklace. Gently, he scooped it out and brought it close enough to his face so that he could see the design on the pendant that hung from it by the low room light. It was the necklace the girl had worn with the etching of the tree with a serpent wrapped around it. He placed the necklace back in the drawer and scanned his surroundings.

Aside from the main entrance, there were two main doors leading off either side. One of the doors was halfway open. Devlin walked over and looked inside. Behind the door was a large bedroom dominated by a big four-poster bed. He crossed the room to the door opposite and tried the handle. It was locked, but it was a simple pin tumbler lock. Devlin went over to the desk under the oval window and pulled open a drawer. Inside were pens and notepaper, and scattered about were paper clips. He took a clip and straightened it out and used it to manipulate the small keyhole in the handle of the door. After a minute or so of feeling his way along the pins and coaxing them into alignment the cylinder turned, and the door clicked open. But before he could push the door open and look inside, the main lights came on and Devlin swung around to see three men —the security guy from the staircase, a larger man with a misshapen skull, and beside them, holding a gun, a slim, tall blond man with pale green eyes. Devlin's hand twitched instinctively in readiness to pull out his Glock.

"Don't move an inch," said Andrei. "Or I'll kill you." His accent was American but with an Eastern European flavor to it. "I'm afraid you're trespassing on private property. But you knew that, didn't you, Father Devlin?"

Markham pushed the door shut.

Andrei looked at Devlin. Then he turned to the thug standing next to him and said quietly, "Search him, Markham."

Markham crossed the room, pushed Devlin up against the paneled wall, and reached round to the small of his back and pulled out the Glock. Up close the thug smelled of sweat and earth. Markham looked Devlin in the eye and socked him hard in the mouth. Then he patted Devlin down and rooted out the content of his pockets, throwing them onto the low table.

Andrei watched as Devlin's belongings were taken from him and discarded on the table. One particular object, the silver pillbox, piqued his interest, and he picked it up and studied it, shaking his head and tutting. Markham took hold of the crucifix around Devlin's neck and pulled at it, snapping the chain free. He was about to throw it onto the table with the rest of the items when the tall, unshaven guy spoke.

"I'll have that," he said shiftily. "Looks expensive."

Markham grunted, "You scavenger, Mosley," and threw the crucifix and chain across the room. Mosley snatched it from midair and grinned.

Andrei smiled briefly at Devlin, twirled the pillbox between his finger and thumb, and said, "Take a seat, Father Devlin. The night is already half-done, and there is so much we need to discuss."

THIRTY-SIX

She'd been down to the basement before and knew what a warren it was. But she hadn't been in this remote part of it before. The room she was imprisoned in was deep in the stonewalled corridors that ran under the mansion. There was no source of light here save for the skinny lines of yellow coming through the edges of the doorframe from a light bulb outside.

From glimpses of the room she'd had when Mosley opened the door, she knew that the floor was laid with large irregular slabs of flagstone and that there were big metal pipes lined up vertically against the back wall that looked like they were once part of a heating system. A big rack on rollers had been pushed back against the pipe, leaving the room clear. The stone surfaces felt cold and had a damp sheen. The walls were low and vaulted, constructed a long time ago from large gray blocks of brick. It was a dark, long, narrow room with one door. In the corner, a mattress had been laid out for her, and she made that her base.

But that was all she knew. She didn't know where the rats came from that skittered across the floor from time to time squealing. She didn't know how long she would be kept here, she didn't know if she would be hurt, and she didn't know whether or for how long she would be kept alive.

The girl heard steps approaching from a little way off. They were light, cocky steps, made by a man who enjoyed his own laid-back attitude and bearing a little too much. The girl loathed Markham, but she despised Mosley even more. For an ugly, skinny man, he had a ridiculously high opinion of his own physical attractiveness.

The footsteps stopped outside the door, and the girl put up her hand, preparing to protect her eyes. Then the door swung open, letting in a tide of brightness that overwhelmed her light-starved sight. Gradually the light stopped hurting, and she could see Mosley watching her. Watching her in a way that made her afraid, disgusted, and angry all at once. But most of all angry. Whereas Markham was an unfeeling, desensitized thug, Mosley was an altogether more unpredictable cocktail of insecurity and spite.

"Get up. Comfort-break time," he said with a snarky tone.

She did as Mosley said, and he followed her along the corridor to the nearest restroom, a tiny cubicle next to the old servants' quarters that housed an ancient, chipped, gray porcelain toilet bowl. She shut the door and jammed her foot against it while she sat on the bowl and relieved herself. She flushed and opened the door. Mosley was slouched against the wall opposite with his hands in his pocket.

"All done, Duchess?" he said and chuckled.

"Duchess" was what he called her, and he thought it was as funny as hell.

The girl nodded. "I need some water."

"Not a problem, Duchess."

"I'm hungry too."

"Okay. I'll get you a sandwich."

"How long am I going to be here?"

"Can't answer that."

"If you're gonna kill me, get it over with."

Mosley pushed himself off the wall and loafed over to the girl. "You don't need to worry." He put a hand on her face, let it rest for a moment, and then his fingers began to toy with her hair.

In the midst of her revulsion and fear, she noticed a silver chain around Mosley's neck, and something familiar slipped out from under his jacket. A pearl crucifix.

"Where did you get that cross?"

Mosley looked confused, then glanced down at his chest as if he'd forgotten he was even wearing it.

"Nice, ain't it? Got a guy upstairs in the turret room. The one who busted the boat. Some priest, would you believe it. We're gonna see to him first. So you got some time to think over how you might make things better."

She felt his hand snake around the back of her head.

"'Cause there is one way you can make all this better," purred Mosley. "Be nice to me and I'll be nice to you."

"Get off me," said the girl, her voice full and hard with anger and hatred.

"I'm just being nice."

"I said, get off me."

His features tightened, and his hand turned into a fist that tugged her hair violently to the side.

"You need to be nice back to me, Duchess."

"Get lost, get lost, get lost..." The girl hissed the words out like a spell for protection. And it worked. Sort of. She heard another set of footsteps coming toward them, plodding down the stairs. Heavier, more solid steps than Mosley's, signaling a much bigger man.

Mosley let go of the girl and stepped back, back to be being the louche, cool jerk he mostly was.

"What's going on?" Markham's high, wide shoulders and oddly shaped head loomed down the corridor toward them, seeming to throw everything into shadow.

"She was taking a pee," replied Mosley. "I'm taking her back to the room."

"I'm thirsty and hungry," said the girl.

"We'll get you something," Markham replied.

"What are you going to do with me?"

Markham didn't give an answer and turned to Mosley. "Take her back to the room."

Mosley nodded and pushed the girl down the corridor, following her back to the room and locking the door behind her. Then he walked back to where Markham was waiting.

"What's the plan? We can't keep her here forever," said Mosley.

"Walk with me," said Markham

The two men, the skinny one and the vast one, set off side by side back along the corridor to the staircase up to the house.

"We have to hold on to her for the time being," said Markham. "The boss doesn't want to have another body to dispose of right now. So no doping and dumping."

"She's a real pain in the ass. I'm not some goddamn babysitter. That's not what I'm paid for."

"It's for one more night. Then we move on."

"We move on?"

"Yeah. Our work here is pretty much done. Just one more night is all we need to wrap things up."

THE GIRL WAS BACK in the dark, sitting against the dank wall with only the squeak and shuffle of passing rats punctuating the silence. She felt as if she were being buried alive. After all, she was underground and alone. What was this pace if not a large, stone coffin? And they had Devlin too. The one person in the whole world who had promised to help her. The one person she had come to believe could save her.

The girl was about to sink into a profound depression when a voice from the back of her head came alive and asked one question that offered a faint ray of hope.

THIRTY-SEVEN

Andrei sat on a wooden chair he'd dragged into the center of the room and studied the man opposite him, holding the silver pillbox between his thumb and forefinger. On the low table by his knee lay the Glock that Devlin had taken from the security guy outside. Devlin was handcuffed in a wooden chair opposite. Andrei's gaze switched from the pillbox to Devlin.

"How did you get this?"

"I pulled it off a corrupt, rich man's dead body. I guess he was a member of the November Club too."

"Yes, he was." Andrei smiled and shook his head. "You know, it was just a joke at first, the name 'November Club,' the serpent and the tree. It was a secret code for a very rich man's club. Just another country or golf club but seriously exclusive. So exclusive you only knew it existed if you were a member. These"—Andrei lifted the pillbox—"were an inside joke. If you were at a meeting or a social event and you recognized another member, you'd flash your necklace, cufflinks, or whatever that had been specially commissioned with the serpent on. But then the club grew and became something else. It became what it is tonight."

"You killed my friend, Father Aranha, didn't you?"

"I ordered his death, Markham carried it out. You see, I deal in many things, but at heart, I deal with secrets. And Father Aranha had so many secrets. He took confessionals from some of the wealthiest, most powerful people in the Hamptons. So we used his own secret, what he got up to here, at my parties, as leverage, to get him to tell us the secrets that he had listened to in the confessional. But, alas, he threatened to blow the whistle. Said he'd go to the FBI, CIA, DOJ, you name it, he said he'd go to it, tell everything. So we blew his brains out all over his desk."

Andrei looked at Devlin for the satisfaction of a reaction but didn't get one. So he continued speaking.

"I hoped you'd come. It was hopeful, I know. But I so wanted to meet the man who has caused so much trouble. Who shut down our drug supply and found Brandi Sutton's body. Especially when I found out he was, of all things, a priest. So I got Gerry Sutton to lure you in. And he did it. He did it because he owes me many times over. Eighteen million times over to be exact. In fact, really, I own that man, body and soul. It's why he felt compelled to share his wife with me when I asked him to, why he let the mayor have her too. It's why he didn't even make a squeak of protest when I said I would have to kill her to stop her making so much fuss. He really is the most abject man on the planet, I think. And he did what I told him to without hesitation. And I told him to tell you about the November Club. To entice you to come here. Are you surprised?"

"No. I'm not surprised. But then I know I'm not here because of Gerry Sutton or you. I'm here because I was meant to be here. I was led to Sag Harbor by fate and faith. And I'm here now to bring an almighty judgment down on your head."

Andrei chuckled and shook his head. "You are deluded, you do know that? But, my friend, tonight your delusion ends in this room."

"I will undo you completely," replied Devlin. "Demolish you. Punish you for the murders and the evil you do in this house."

"Evil? In this house? Consenting adults having sex? Taking recreational drugs? Really, how very Old Testament of you."

"What happens here is so much more. The real evil you intend is beyond sex and drugs." Devlin's eyes flickered toward the locked door, and Andrei's eyes followed suit.

"I know the real purpose of this house."

"So you've worked it out, what we do here. Whoopee. Well done, Father." Andrei sat back in his chair and looked quizzically at Devlin, then smiled. "You know, it strikes me that you don't even really know who I am. How rude of me. Allow me to introduce myself. I am Andrei Gromyko, CEO of BioGenesis, philanthropist, environmentalist. I think it's only courteous that you know who the man is who is going to be responsible for ending your life."

Andrei stood and crossed the room, placing himself directly in front of Devlin. He studied Devlin close up, then glanced down at Devlin's left hand. He kneeled in front of Devlin, grabbed his hand, and pulled it toward him, inspecting the palm, eyeing the red-stained scar in the middle. With his index finger, he gently traced the outline of the scar, the rough edges. Then, suddenly and with real viciousness, he pushed the nail of his thumb hard into the healed-over wound and kept digging until the knitted skin began to rebreak. He kept on digging and pressing his finger deeper, reopening the old wound, causing bolts of pain to shoot through Devlin's hand, arm, and whole left side.

Andrei watched the pain registering on Devlin's face with deep satisfaction. Finally, he stopped digging and pressing and dropped Devlin's dripping hand. He studied his own thumb, the end of which was thick with bright red blood.

"You know," said Andrei proudly, "I've always had a talent, Father. A talent for taking things from people. When I befriend people, do business with people, sleep with people, I always take a little something away from them, and it always makes them a little weaker and me a little stronger." Andrei brought his thumb up to eye level and admired the blood that had begun to ooze down it, running over his hand and wrist, staining his white shirt cuff. Very slowly and deliberately, he placed his thumb in his mouth and sucked it clean.

"And I think it's going to be the same with you."

Devlin looked Andrei in the eye, and the two men's iron wills came up against each other.

"But is that what's really happening, Andrei? Have you taken from me, or have I taken from you? Maybe right now, my blood is inside your body, coursing through your blood. Both of us entwined forever."

There was a knock at the door. Markham entered and stood in the doorway.

"What is it, Markham?"

"We're ready."

Andrei grinned, his pearly white teeth dark with blood.

"Wonderful."

THIRTY-EIGHT

Paladino stood at the top of a set of steep, narrow stone steps that led down to a door, a side service entrance to the house. The door was ajar, and there were lights on inside. But there was no sound within. She hesitated, wondering whether she should leave with what she had found out and get to a phone to call the cops. Then again, maybe she should see what else was going on in Oliver Harris's mansion. And while she was scoping the place out, she could find a phone inside.

Tentatively, she descended the steps. Peering through the crack in the door, she was able to make out a large tiled kitchen with a long wooden table in the middle. It was old-fashioned, like a kitchen in an old English country house. She gently eased the door back and saw that the kitchen was, as she had suspected, empty. There was evidence of recent activity, heat from the oven, and the smell of alcohol and cooked food. But the table in the center of the kitchen and the slate countertops around the side had been cleared and wiped down. She could hear scattered voices, voices that reached her from a few rooms away. They were party voices, a low, conversational sound with occasional laughter. It sounded like a party that was no longer in full swing, that was simmering down.

Paladino passed through the kitchen and a large doorway at the other end that led into an oak-paneled hallway. Light from glass sconces gave a low glow to the hallway and to the various oil portraits hung on the wall. The portraits were all of old, bald corpulent men in period dress who seemed to stare down disapprovingly at Paladino. She could see in a couple of the portraits a passing likeness to Oliver Harris. At the end of the hallway was a staircase leading down to what looked like the cellar, and to her right was a doorway onto a parallel hallway. Paladino stepped into the parallel hallway which was much better lit and more modern with a very neutral off-white decor. She was about to head down the hall to the rest of the house when something stopped her dead. A metal click came from behind, and a small hard object dug into her head.

"Now just where the hell do you think you're going?" The voice was deep and slow and calm.

Paladino froze.

"You're not a guest. What are you doing here?"

"I work in the kitchens. I was just leaving," Paladino lied.

"I know all the girls that work the kitchens and the maids too. You don't work the kitchen."

She felt his hand fish around in her black pants and pulled out her wallet. Her wallet that had her NYPD ID card. He heard him open up the wallet.

"What? You're a cop? Okay. You're coming with me. Outside."

But before she had a chance to turn around, there was the sound of a sharp crack. The guy with the gun let out a cry and then there was another louder crack. Paladino stepped back and turned to see the guy, young and in his twenties in a suit, on his knees clutching his head. Behind him stood a teenage girl with dark hair, dirt all over her face and clothes, holding a heavy brass pan in her hands. With one final blow, she hammered the pan across the guy's head, and he went down like a sack of potatoes.

The girl and Paladino stared at each other.

"You're the cop that Father Devlin was talking to," said the girl, still clutching the pan. "I saw you together at the Grindstone coffeehouse."

"Who are you?"

"I'm the one who just saved your ass."

"What the hell is going on in this house?"

"Everything."

"Why are you covered in dirt?"

"These are a lot of questions, lady." The girl picked up Paladino's wallet and handed it back to her. "You're a cop, right?"

"Yeah. I am."

"Good. I was kidnapped. They were keeping me locked up downstairs in the basement. There were rats getting in the room where I was being held, so I figured there had to be a way out. And there was. But the bad news was it was through a pile of rat- and roach-infested rotting firewood. Which is why I look like this. We need to get out of here."

"Yeah," said Paladino, looking at the guy out cold on the floor. She picked her badge and the security guy's gun off the floor. "We can go back through the kitchen."

Paladino set off down the oak-paneled hall, but the girl grabbed her arm.

"Wait. Hold on a second. We can't just leave."

"Why not?"

"They've got Devlin."

THIRTY-NINE

O'Reilly awoke with a start from a short and extraordinarily deep sleep. He woke up really fast, in a snap, like he was being pulled up from the bottom of the sea. One moment he was on the ocean floor, the next he was heaving and blinking in the hot sun and the salty sea wind. And all because something in the room had changed. The room. Where he had done such depraved things, things beyond his well-worn fantasies. Unbelievable things. All the lights were off, and it was dark, real dark, and he was alone and naked in the bed.

"Hello?"

His voice came out weak and weirdly high-pitched. There was no reply. The girls and boys who had obliged him, ravished him, had disappeared. The immense rush of drugs and booze had curdled into a sickening hangover. O'Reilly guessed it must be somewhere in the small hours before dawn. He was about to raise his hand and look at his watch when someone, somewhere in the shadows of the room, spoke.

"I trust you had a very enjoyable evening, Assistant Secretary O'Reilly." The voice was smooth with a slight foreign accent and sailed out of the darkness. O'Reilly squinted and made out a figure who was sitting by the bed. Before he could reply, O'Reilly was blinded by a bright bulb that blazed in his face. As the initial glare faded, he was able to make out two figures behind the dazzling light. A slim man with collar-length hair by the bed and a bulkier man sat across the room, looking at him.

"But the thing is," continued the smooth, accented voice, "I don't need to trust you had an enjoyable evening. I know you did."

O'Reilly heard noises coming from across the room. Grunts and moans, like an animal, that grew louder. His eyes were now managing to adjust better to the light, and in the corner of the room, a large television screen had been placed in front of the fireplace. On the screen, he could see bodies writhing and grunting. The pit of O'Reilly's stomach lit up with recognition and flamed with the most abject shame. He was the central figure on the screen.

"Turn it off. Please," he whispered.

"I don't think so, Michael. Not yet."

His interrogator continued to speak over the moans and sighs as the film kept playing.

"Now, I don't need to remind you that you're a happily married man, Michael, with three wonderful kids and a four-year-old German shepherd." His interrogator turned to a shadow sitting behind him. "It is a German shepherd, isn't it?" Whoever he was speaking to seemed to confirm this fact, and he turned back to O'Reilly. "And I'm afraid to say your predicament only deepens, as I cannot guarantee to you that the females and males whose company you so thoroughly and explicitly enjoyed this evening are old enough to consent to sexual acts in the State of New York."

O'Reilly's pudgy body deflated with a deep sigh of despair. The groans from the TV continued, escalating, growing more intense. O'Reilly felt he was in hell. The worst kind of hell. A hell of his own making.

"And we live in such an extraordinary age that anything can make its way out into the public realm in the time it takes to press a button. Within seconds things can be posted, retweeted, favorited, liked, unliked, spreading faster than the most contagious virus, spreading at a speed only limited by human curiosity and data bandwidth." His tormentor gestured to the figures on the screen. "Should this film, for instance, be allowed out into the world wide web, it would be devastating for you and everyone you love, and who loves you."

"What do you want?"

"Ah, good, straight to the point. Not for nothing are you an executive at the Bureau of Intelligence and Research, Michael O'Reilly. Actually, this is the part where I give you the good news. I want very little from you, Mike. Only one very simple and straightforward thing. I want you to tell me all about something very dear to my heart. I want you to tell me about project Salvation Man."

"How...? How did you know...?"

"What we know and how we know is not important. But what you can tell us is very important and could save your career and family."

A tear ran down O'Reilly's cheek, and he let out a faint whimper.

"Okay. Okay...but please, for the love of God, turn it off."

The interrogator turned to the shadow behind him, one of three in the room O'Reilly now realized, and nodded. Finally, the groans ended.

"Now. Let me tell you what I know. Project Salvation Man is a foreign asset carrying research and intelligence about advanced genetics. Genetics that are rumored to be nearly a decade ahead of current published and classified research. But that's all I know. So now you, Mike, are going to fill in the gaps."

O'Reilly, staring back at his captors like a cornered animal, sighed and cleared his throat. "Salvation Man is Professor Feng Zhou, head of genetics and microbiology at the Xinjiang Technical Institute in Urumqi, China. He recently turned up at the US Consulate in Almaty, seeking asylum in return for everything he's been working on for the last twenty years, research that's most likely involved unethical experimentation on political prisoners in detention camps. And that's pretty much it."

"That's it?"

"Yeah. That's all we know."

"What is his research focused on?"

"We don't know. He has promised to tell us when he's safely touched down and assured of asylum and protection."

"No, no, no. That's not good enough."

"It's all I know, I swear."

"But you must know when he's due to fly in. The details of his flight."

"Yes. I do."

"Then tell me, and if I have to prompt you again for details, my threats will be no longer be threats."

FORTY

When Andrei had left Devlin in the octagon room, one of his men, Mosley, the slim, tall, cocky one, had taken his place. Devlin saw that Mosley was wearing his crucifix and that the front of his jacket and pants were covered with patches of dried, dark red blood.

On his way out of the room, Andrei had whispered an instruction in Mosley's ear. Devlin had a pretty good idea what the instruction was, and his guess was confirmed when Mosley stood opposite him and pulled a Glock out of his holster that hung from his belt. Eyeing Devlin, he seemed to relish the moment and the weight of the gun as it rested in his hand. Then he smiled and aimed it at Devlin's head.

"Right between the eyes, Mosley," said Devlin matter-of-factly. "Don't mess it up."

"Oh, I won't mess this up. But I might want a bit of a starter course before I get to the main meal. Maybe I'll shoot you a few times in the legs first, watch you wriggle about before I put one in your head. I've had a lot of practice at this kind of thing."

"How much practice do you need to have to kill a guy sitting in a chair six feet away?"

"Enough practice to be able to kill him without giving it a second thought."

"You enjoy shooting sitting ducks?"

"I enjoy shooting losers like you."

Devlin could see Mosley's finger curl around the trigger, but he didn't look away; he kept looking him in the eye. Challenging him to shoot. Keep the link going, thought Devlin, keep the interaction happening. Every second is a victory, every second is another possibility.

"You want more than my death. You want my fear, but I'm not going to give it to you. I do not fear you. I do not fear those who kill the body but cannot kill the soul. I rather fear him who can destroy both soul and body in hell."

"I don't believe in hell."

"Then why are you wearing my crucifix?"

Mosley's frowned, glanced down at the cross on his chest, and said, "Because it's expensive."

"You sure that's the only reason?"

There was a moment of hesitation before Mosley replied. A moment in which, Devlin suspected, Mosley might not be completely sure if there was another reason for wearing the cross, in which he felt a dim flicker of conscience. Then Mosley switched out of whatever thought had caught hold of him and smiled again.

"I really am going to enjoy this, fear or no fear."

Mosley's knuckle began to whiten as he put pressure on the trigger. Devlin looked right into the black hole of the barrel and heard an almighty bang.

FORTY-ONE

"Six thirty? You're sure about that?"

"Yes."

"Because if what you're telling me is wrong, your daughter will be watching that film of you through her tears by breakfast time."

"It's six thirty. I'm telling you, that's the time."

"Where is it coming in? Which airfield?"

"Joint Base Andrews."

Andrei checked his watch, swiveled in his chair, and looked back at Markham. "Too far, even by helicopter." Markham nodded. He turned back to O'Reilly. "Get them to change their route."

O'Reilly looked astounded by this request. "Change the route...? I can't..."

"Why not?"

"It's completely...unorthodox... We would never ask a mission like this to change route... All the security protocols..."

"I know you have the seniority and the clearance to make this change, Michael."

"It might look suspicious..."

"Do it. Or I destroy your life." Andrei turned to Markham, who pressed the remote control and the screen flashed into life. "Okay... Okay... Stop... Please turn it off."

"Then get on your cell and order the flight to alter its route. Tell them it was a preplanned change only known by those with the very highest clearance."

O'Reilly nodded, memorizing and mouthing the words he'd been given.

Andrei turned to Markham again. "There's an airfield near Westhampton. Francis S. Gabreski. Even with an earlier ETA, we'll still get there in time. Get the coordinates ready."

Markham nodded and left the room. Andrei turned back to O'Reilly and leaned over him. "Now all you need to do is tell your team exactly what I tell you to say. And if for one moment you find yourself lacking in...motivation, just think of your daughter's eyes tearing up as she sees her old man in a pit of human depravity."

O'Reilly clutched his cell to his chest and nodded slowly and obediently back at Andrei.

FORTY-TWO

The party had decamped from the first floor and the outside grounds to the rooms above, and Harris found himself alone and bereft, wandering among the empty downstairs rooms. Not only was this to be the last party he was also without his girl Friday, his angel, his Tinky, to administer to him and send his blues away.

What, he wondered, was to become of him? He had no actual monetary means to keep this beast of a house going without Andrei's regular contributions. Within two months he would be struggling to keep his head above water and pay the huge bills that a house like his accumulated. He'd have to fire all the staff tomorrow. That was a grim certainty.

"Dear God," he muttered, and his heart sank at his much-reduced prospects. "I'm done for."

He headed to the back of the house, first to his study where he picked up the leather case that Tinky had used to make her room visits, and then through the oak-paneled hall lined with his predecessors, and into the kitchen.

He sat in the old flea-bitten armchair and opened the

leather case on his lap. Then he rolled back his cuff and shot himself in the arm with the good stuff. Immediately the world and all its mundane concerns began to recede, and he let out a sigh of profound relief. The sweetest and most intense feeling flamed throughout his body and mind, creating a humming joy and bliss.

"Oh... Oh, yes."

Harris's head tipped back, and his jaw dropped open.

Time passed and when he opened his eyes again, he could smell gasoline. He looked up to see the great bulk of Markham, that gargoyle of a man, standing in front of him.

"Markham, everything all right?" he asked sweetly.

Markham replied with a shake of the head and raised a gun. Harris thought he heard Markham mumble something like "time for your special reward," and then there was a flash, a smell of gunpowder, and finally, like the sea falling back from the shore, the world and all its mundane concerns receded from Harris forever.

MARKHAM PUT the gun back in its shoulder holster and with a foot slid the two cans of gasoline he'd been carrying under the kitchen table. Then he crouched and picked the old man up, slinging him over his shoulder.

He took Harris's limp body out to the woods that lined the grounds, found the family tomb, and slung Harris's body into the dark square hole. He stayed crouching for a minute, peering into the buzzing darkness, alive with flies and filled with death.

"Sorry, old man. It's gonna be a bit crowded in there."

He took a small black case that'd been left on top of the tomb and opened it, taking out a drill and a Ziplock containing long screws. One by one he drilled screws into the slab, setting it firmly into place.

Then he placed the case back on the tomb and walked back toward the mansion.

FORTY-THREE

Mosley's gun was aimed at Devlin, but his focus was on the door that had been flung open, slamming against the paneled wall. Standing in the open doorway looking defiantly back at them was the girl and Paladino.

Devlin heard Mosley spit out the word "bitch," and in his peripheral vision he could see Mosley's barrel swinging in an arc toward the door. Bound hard by rope against the chair, Devlin's ability to move was minimal, but with one rock he was able to tip himself forward onto the balls of his feet and get momentum enough to charge into a distracted Mosley's side. Devlin's charge sent Mosley crashing down before he could take a shot. But there, on the floor, lying crooked and immobilized by rope, Devlin's options evaporated, and Mosley was already getting back on his feet.

Except now Paladino was in on him. She had a pistol in her hand and gave Mosley an almighty smack around the temple with the butt. His body seemed to reverberate and shudder under the blow of the gun, and his own pistol left his grasp, tumbling to the floor where it was instantly gathered up by the girl.

Mosley lay curled on the carpet, cradling his head, moaning and concussed.

"Thanks," said Devlin, lying on his side on the floor. "Now. Please, could one of you get me out of this damned chair?"

FORTY-FOUR

O'Reilly was pale and red-eyed with fear.

"They won't comply. They're saying my code is expired. They won't take my order without a current operational code."

"Why? Why is the code out of date?" shrieked Andrei.

"They change it randomly. All the time."

"Why can't you get another?"

"Because I'd need my laptop. I'd need to be plugged into the secure DOJ network. I can't do that with my cell. There's nothing I can do. I swear. Please..."

Andrei pushed his hands through his hair and interlinked them behind his head. He leaned back in his chair and looked at the ceiling. In the low light, O'Reilly could see the other men, suited, square-shouldered, almost interchangeable. Then he saw Andrei was looking at him and smiling.

"Michael, Michael, Michael," he said and sighed. "You aren't getting out of here without giving me something of use. That's not how this sort of thing works."

"But what can I give you?"

"What you know."

"I've told you, I don't know anything other than where the plane is landing."

Andrei looked at O'Reilly intently. To O'Reilly it seemed as if Andrei's pale eyes were stripping his outer layers away, making him even more naked than he already was. Then Andrei frowned as if he were deeply puzzled by something.

"This Professor Zhou. Why has he chosen political asylum now? It's so high risk for him. What's in it for Zhou, Mike?"

O'Reilly's eyes flitted around the room nervously, and Andrei leaned forward.

"Oh, Mike. Please don't tell me you're holding something back from me, because that would be disastrous for you." Andrei turned and nodded to one of his men, who flicked a remote control.

"Okay, Okay. Please... Stop it..."

Andrei nodded again, and the film stopped. Then he fixed his stare on O'Reilly.

"So...? What's the secret, Michael?"

O'Reilly licked his lips and spoke slowly and hoarsely. "He's coming back to see his estranged wife and daughter."

Andrei clapped his hands and laughed. "Of course!"

"They were given asylum and new identities five years ago. His wife made contact at an international conference Zhou was attending. Sent a note to one of our diplomatic staff there. She said she wanted out for her and her daughter. She didn't want her husband to come with them. Said their marriage had collapsed. We figured it was money in the bank for us, a bargaining coin for the future. So we arranged a snatch at the next conference in Madrid. Five years later, he gets in touch. Says he'll exchange his research for political asylum and one meeting with his wife and daughter. Turns out it was money in the bank."

"Do the wife and daughter know?"

"Not yet."

"Delicious." Andrei leaned forward and took O'Reilly's hands in his own.

"You know the next part, Mike. What you must tell me... Where do they live?"

FORTY-FIVE

Paladino and Devlin stood over a prone Mosley. Devlin reached down and ripped the crucifix off his neck. "You're not fit to wear this." He tucked the cross into his pocket and turned to the girl, who was standing in the middle of the room, staring at Devlin accusingly.

"You were supposed to help me," she said indignantly. "You said. You promised."

"I'm sorry. I guess I'll just have to eat my words and say thank you for rescuing me. I was getting around to it, I promise. I just got delayed by this guy." Devlin indicated toward Mosley. "I'd better take that." Devlin held out a hand, and the girl handed over Mosley's gun, and Devlin tucked it into the waistband of his pants.

"And you, Paladino. How did you end up here?"

"I found out it was another officer, Maynard, who murdered Mike. Maynard took me here to make sure I didn't talk. But before he could deal with me, he got shot by this guy." Paladino kicked Mosley, who shuffled about pathetically. "What the hell is this place?"

"It's an old-fashioned honey trap," said Devlin. "They lure

people here, well-connected people, to supposedly discreet parties and blackmail the guests. Oliver Harris is only the front, the fall guy. They blackmailed Vijay for confessional information and had him killed when he threatened to go to the police. I guess Maynard was on the payroll and killed Greg to protect the drug operation for the guy who runs this place, Andrei. He's from somewhere in Eastern Europe, I think…"

"Wait," said Paladino. "Andrei? Andrei Gromyko? A tall guy, right? Blond hair?"

"Yeah."

"I was called out to his research labs a few days ago. BioGenesis. For a reported break-in."

"What did they take?"

"Nothing. At least, nothing was reported stolen. It was part of a spate of break-ins, including up at the senator's place. They didn't take anything there either."

Devlin's hands clenched into fists, and his face darkened. For a moment he didn't speak and became still, his attention focused on some private thought.

"What? What is it?"

"What if those break-ins were a distraction? Staged. Designed to get the cops to focus their patrols away from the harbor? Away from where all the action was?"

"I guess. With the sheriff's office on strike, it would have been a smart strategy. To keep the harbor clear and the drug supply open which I guess was headed here to keep the guests happy." Paladino frowned. "You said that they blackmailed the people here. How did they do that?"

Devlin turned to the locked door. "I think the answer's in there."

FORTY-SIX

The oak door gave with an almighty crack, and Devlin squinted into a dark and silent room, his eyes unable to make out the objects within it. Behind him stood the girl and Paladino with a gun trained on a cowering Mosley, still holding his head in pain, still sitting on the floor.

Devlin hit the light switch, and the room revealed itself. A whole bank of television monitors arranged in rows were hung on along the far wall. Each monitor had a label stuck to it with two numbers scribbled on the label in black ink. Below the monitors was a long desk lined with laptops and headphones. Stacked at one end of the room were square metal units, servers for the information gathered here to be stored on. And everything was off. Dead.

Paladino, still with a gun on Mosley, craned to get a line of sight into the room.

"What is it? What's in there?"

Before Devlin could answer, he heard a thud and the sound of furniture crashing. He turned to see Paladino ducking a chair that had narrowly missed her and then the flash of a gun.

Devlin rushed out into the turret room and saw that Mosley had gone and Paladino was almost out the door after him.

"Wait..." yelled Devlin. "Let him go. He's not worth the chase."

"Son of a bitch," said Paladino sourly. "Shouldn't have taken my eye off the ball."

"It doesn't matter. He's no use to us. You still rescued my ass, right? That's what counts."

"What's in the room?" asked the girl, lingering at the entrance to the side room. Paladino and Devlin joined her, and they stared at the array of monitors.

"It's CCTV," said Paladino

"Yeah," replied Devlin. "This is where they record what goes on in the rooms. This is the sting. But Andrei, the guy who runs this operation, he's not interested in money. He's interested in kompromat." Devlin ran his eyes across the rows of monitors and stopped at one monitor in particular. Whereas the other monitors were all disconnected, a small red light was still glowing on this one. Devlin placed his hand on the screen; it was warm to the touch. He pressed the power button, and a picture flashed up. The feed on the monitor came from a bedroom. The camera had been placed looking down on a bed so it could be seen in its entirety. On the bed was the inert body of a man. His neck had been slashed open, and the bed linen was soaked in blood.

The girl moaned, and Devlin suddenly realized how young she was. She put her hands to her eyes and pressed her head into Devlin's side. Devlin instinctively put a protective arm around her.

"Who is it?" asked Paladino.

"His name's O'Reilly," said Devlin. "He was one of the guests tonight. I met him downstairs." He shut off the monitor. "We need to find that room." Devlin pulled the label off the screen which had the numbers 4 and 7 written on it in blue ink.

"What do you think the numbers mean?" asked Paladino.

"The floor and room number at a guess. This must be a room on the fourth floor, the one directly below us." Devlin turned to the girl. "You should go, now."

"I want to stay with you two."

"It's too dangerous."

"But I have nowhere to go. This place was my home."

Devlin took out his crucifix and placed it in the girl's hand. "I promise you that I will make sure you are okay. That you are looked after. I owe you my life, and I will do everything to make good on that. Take this crucifix as proof of my promise, my duty to you."

The girl took the cross. "You promise?"

"I promise."

They went out into the turret room, but instead of heading for the door to the main house, the girl headed toward the other door, that one that led to the bedroom.

"Where are you going?" asked Paladino.

"Secret exit," she said, grinning with pride.

"What secret exit?"

"When Harris's old lady was sick, she was laid up here. She insisted on it, and Harris, who was terrified of her, practically had a hospital set up here. So they had to figure out a way to get her in and out. Follow me." The girl took Devlin and Paladino into the bedroom and then through another internal door into a large bathroom decorated with marble tiles and gold fittings. In the corner of the bathroom was a wooden cubicle with two brass buttons. She pressed one of the buttons which set off the sounds of pulleys whirring into action. Then, when the whirring had stopped, she pulled the wooden door back to reveal a waiting elevator and stepped in.

"I'll be seeing you," she said and waved.

"You will," said Devlin.

"Promise?"

"Promise."

The girl pulled the door shut, and the pulleys sounded again.

Devlin turned to Paladino. "Let's go take a look downstairs."

FORTY-SEVEN

Markham stood at the top of the staircase on the third floor and checked his watch. By his feet were the two jerry cans. He was about to unscrew them when a man in his fifties with pomaded silver hair and wearing only briefs and gold jewelry wandered up to him.

"Hey there," said the man. "Is there any red wine about? Something not too fruity like a Côtes du Rhône. Fetch something from the cellar for me."

"Room service is over, buddy."

The man in the briefs scowled at Markham.

"Hey, I'm not your buddy, and you're just the waitstaff. Now..."

Markham knelt and pulled up a pant leg.

"What the hell are you doing...? Stand up and get me some wine," barked the man, who was standing over Markham now, glaring down at him.

Markham stood and without answering made a jabbing motion that was quick, expert, and almost dainty. The man in the briefs took in a whoosh of breath and placed his hands on Markham's trunk-like arms to steady himself. Then Markham made another quick motion, like a miniature genuflection, and the man's guts began to seep out.

Markham withdrew his small silver push dagger, and with a large hand around the man's neck, he lifted up his victim and threw him over the balcony.

Then he knelt once more, pulled up his pant leg, and placed his push dagger back into its ankle holster. He stood and tutted.

"Come on."

A minute passed and Andrei and his consort of suited guards appeared, marching along the hall toward him.

"All done?" asked Markham.

"All done," replied Andrei. "Where's that moron Mosley?"

"No idea."

"Well, screw him. Let's start the exit plan."

Andrei and the men descended the stairs quickly. Markham didn't follow; instead, he began unscrewing the lids off the jerry cans, but the sound of feet coming down the stairs toward him caused him to stop what he was doing and reach for his push dagger again. He was bracing himself for an encounter with another guest when he saw who the footsteps belonged to. Mosley was sprinting toward him with a fresh cut on his forehead.

"Mosley, where you been?"

"I got held up. But it's okay now. Let's get this done fast."

"Here, take this. You do one side, and I'll do the other."

Markham handed a can to Mosley.

The two men splashed the gasoline down each of the staircases. When they got to the hall on the first floor, Markham pulled out a metal cigarette lighter, flicked it open, and lit it up. Mosley stepped back and watched as Markham threw the flickering lighter onto the floor. The fire took hold instantly, spreading like anger in seconds, and consuming the staircase and then the landing above. Alarms went off and sprinklers were triggered, but they were going to be too late and too little.

Markham turned to Mosley and grinned, more than satisfied with the effects of their work. Then the two men headed out of the mansion.

As they left the building, in the floors up above, doors started to open and guests began to flock out of the bedroom. They saw the thick black smoke coming toward them, filling the hallway so that they couldn't see or even breathe easily. Mass panic took hold as fast as the fire had.

Outside, in the twilight, a group of six men ran to the waiting helicopter, its blades already rotating at speed. They boarded, and in moments the chopper took off, affording Andrei and his company the best seats in the house as they watched windows shatter and smoke begin to billow out of the upper floors, as Sefton House and all of its inglorious past began to burn to the ground.

FORTY-EIGHT

As Devlin and Paladino descended the narrow staircase from the turret room to the rest of the house, the sense of something being badly wrong started to grow. First came the ring of the fire alarms, then the smell of smoke, and then the sounds of stampeding feet and screams of panic. Then they felt the heat.

Devlin and Paladino came out onto the landing on the fourth floor to see people fleeing the bedrooms and pushing their way down the stairs past the raging fire whose hold on the house was growing by the second. Some guests chose to run and tumble down the stairs and through the flames; others were climbing over the balconies and dropping onto the landing below with varying degrees of success.

Paladino watched in horror as hordes of rich people ran around like headless chickens. It was like watching the deck of the *Titanic* as it sunk. And then the strangest thing happened. The crowds parted, and standing in front of her in nothing but briefs was Curtis Harrigan, his oversized, overfed, underused body looking pathetic and repulsive. On seeing Paladino he had frozen, his panic momentarily overtaken by shock. He was lost for words. But Paladino wasn't. Over the cries and shrieks, through the smoke and heat, she bellowed.

"I see you, Curtis. I see you for who you are, and it's over for you. I know why you're here, and I'm gonna make sure the whole world knows too."

The color had drained from Harrigan's face. And his white-as-a-sheet face and obese, naked body disappeared behind a crowd of people rushing between them in a new wave of panic. And when the crowd had passed, Paladino could no longer see Harrigan. And she realized that someone else was yelling at her.

Over the bedlam, Devlin, who had moved far enough along the hall not to have seen Harrigan, was screaming over the heads of the guests at Paladino to follow him.

She took after Devlin, who headed down the east wing of the house, against the flow of fleeing guests. Farther along the hall, the smoke was still thin and more bearable. Devlin counted off the bedrooms till he got to number seven. The door was wide open, and the bed was empty.

"Wrong room."

They backtracked across the landing, again weaving through the panicking crowds, the harsh smoke causing them to choke and cough. They got to number seven. The room was locked, and Devlin shouldered it open. Inside they found O'Reilly's body, pale and drained of blood, spread out on wet, dark, wine-red sheets. On the television screen in the corner of the room was a frozen image of O'Reilly naked and surrounded by other, younger naked bodies.

Paladino shut the door to keep the smoke at bay. "Who was he?"

"I met him downstairs. He said he was someone senior with the diplomatic service. Andrei wanted something from him."

"What?"

"No idea. But whatever it was, I think they got it."

"Then we're at a dead end. We got nothing."

Devlin ran his fingers through his hair and sighed.

"There has to be something. Some thread somewhere we can pull on."

The screams and shouts outside were getting louder, and Paladino could feel the heat rising higher. Smoke was building all the time.

"Well, whatever, we really need to get out of here or we're toast."

Devlin didn't answer. Instead, he sat in the armchair by the bed and seemed to slip into deep thought.

"Devlin? What the hell are you doing...? We have to get out before the fumes kill us..."

Devlin remained silent, impervious to the fire and chaos outside and Paladino's remonstrations. After about thirty seconds, he looked up at Paladino, his eyes bright and intense.

"The night of the break-in at Andrei's. You said you went to the senator's too. There was a break-in there?"

"Yeah."

"What's the senator's name?"

"Lawton. Helen Lawton."

"What did they take?"

"What?"

"The night of the break-in, what did they take?"

"Nothing. They didn't take anything there either."

Devlin's eyes lit up. "Nothing?"

"Yeah, nothing."

"Then that may be the thread."

"How?"

"Because maybe something was taken, but there's a reason why it wasn't reported. Let's get out of here."

"About damn time. We should use the back way."

Devlin went into the bathroom and ran two washcloths

under the faucet and handed one to Paladino. They placed them over their noses and mouths and ran through the now empty hallway, nearly choking on the smoke, dropping onto all fours and crawling under the thick fog, then finding their way back up to the turret room where the air was still breathable. They took the small elevator like the girl had done before and came out in Harris's study. The elevator shaft was at the back of the house and still untouched by the fire that had progressed up the main, front staircases. From there they went out the back way, through the kitchen, and out into the cool night where people were flooding out of the house in various states of undress, black and charred with smoke. In the distance came the sound of sirens.

"Follow me," said Devlin. "I know a quick way out of here. I've got the truck parked half a mile away."

"Where are we going?"

"To speak to the senator."

FORTY-NINE

When the bell rang, Senator Helen Lawton was already wide-awake despite it being just a shade before five in the morning. She was simultaneously indignant and fearful about who it was who had the impertinence to call on her so early. She put on a robe and went to the front door—and nearly slammed it shut right away.

Standing on the porch was a very odd couple: a tall, burly man in a black tuxedo with fresh cuts and bruises on his face and a smaller blonde woman of around forty. Both had smudges of black on their faces and necks and over their clothes. It was only because she half recognized the woman, though from where she couldn't immediately recall, that Lawton didn't shut the door.

"I'm so sorry to call on you so early," said the woman, "but it's incredibly urgent we speak to you. I'm Officer Holly Paladino from Sag Harbor Police. I was here a few days ago with Detective Harrigan...the night you had a break-in."

Lawton nodded as she recalled that night, which, in truth, had never really left her. A cold shiver ran down her back. A feeling of inevitability. She had known there would be consequences.

In a dazed, sleep-deprived state she muttered, "Come in," not even inquiring who the man standing beside the police officer was.

The three walked through the hall and into a cozy living room with a deep, soft couch, armchairs, and an old marble fireplace with an antique fire grate. The senator took the armchair, and Paladino and the man took the couch.

"This is Father Devlin, Senator. He's been helping me with the matter that I'm investigating."

"What matter is that?"

"An extremely serious one. That a man called Andrei Gromyko has been blackmailing members of the government to gain intelligence that's valuable to him."

The senator stiffened in her chair, and her eyebrows arched. "It's Officer Paladino, isn't it?"

"That's right."

"Officer Paladino, this isn't a matter for the police and certainly not an officer. This is for the FBI to look into."

"Yes. And they will. But the reason I'm here is that I believe the break-in at your house that I attended was related to these crimes."

"How?"

"What did they take?" asked Devlin.

Lawton turned to the man sitting beside Paladino. He had a strange gravity and an intensity that had an almost physical effect on her which Lawton dismissed as a product of her extreme fatigue and the early hour.

"They..." She faltered and then said quietly, "Nothing. They didn't take anything."

"Senator," said Devlin. "I believe they did take something.

Something important. Something so important that maybe you might not want to admit that it's been stolen."

Lawton took a breath and said as firmly as she could, "Nothing was taken. I think you need to leave."

"We'll leave," said Devlin. "Sure. But if we do, Officer Paladino will need to escalate this, as you say, to the FBI and the DOJ, and that may not be something you would want to happen."

Lawton stood. "I think you've said enough. You need to leave now..."

Devlin stayed sitting, and Paladino didn't move either.

"I think Andrei Gromyko ordered the break-in here," said Devlin. "They were after something. Something sensitive. Something that I think you haven't admitted was taken. And if you don't give us that information yourself, then we'll go through the FBI to make sure we uncover it that way. Which I think could be much more painful for you."

Lawton felt her knees weaken and her head swirl as if walls were closing in on her.

"We believe," continued Devlin, "that Andrei and his people have intelligence that they are moving on. They have already murdered three people that we know of, Senator. But we can stop him. He's headed somewhere—he left Sag Harbor in a helicopter an hour ago. Whatever he's after, I think it's going down right now, so it's really important you tell us what you know."

A carriage clock on the mantelpiece ticked through the silence, and outside the next day was coming fast. Devlin and Paladino waited for the senator to reply. For what seemed like a long time, Lawton looked out the windows into the twilight and then back down at her clasped hands. Privately, she was weighing up the risks, the very personal risks to her. In her mind she saw a future filled with headlines, news reports, and Senate inquiries. Images of her in front of a line of her peers speaking into a microphone.

"Okay..." she said finally in a hushed whisper. "You're right, they did take something. A classified file that I had taken home from the Bureau of Intelligence. It was hugely sensitive, and I should never have taken out of the bounds of my office. But I was hellishly busy and thought I could take a shortcut to get more done. So I took it with me. And then, when it was stolen, I should have raised the alarm. But I was a coward. I stayed silent. And now...Dear God..." She looked at Devlin and Paladino in anguish. "People have been murdered?"

Paladino nodded. "Including a senior DOJ official."

Lawton buried her head in her hands and felt the crushing weight of guilt.

"We can put this right, Senator," said Devlin.

"We? Who even are you? You're not even a cop..."

"After we're gone," said Devlin, "I want you to do a couple of things..."

"What...? You want me to...?"

"I want you to call a very senior man in Homeland Security. His name's George Brennan."

"George Brennan? I know George."

"I worked with George in Special Investigations in the Air Force. Ask him about me. The answer he gives will tell you everything you need to know about who I am and why you should trust me. If you don't like what you hear, call the FBI. But I have a feeling that won't be necessary."

"What was in the file, Senator?" asked Paladino.

Lawton looked back and forth between Paladino and Devlin. For the second time, she thought about the headlines, the news reports, the special Senate hearings. She thought about the three murders.

"Oh, God..." With a step of blind faith, she took the chance being offered to her, doing it chiefly out of self-preservation. "It was an intelligence briefing that outlines a proposal for the political asylum of a Chinese scientist, Professor Feng Zhou. We had strong reason to believe that his research is of huge importance. In the last few days, we've received fresh intelligence about his research, and if this new information is accurate, then Zhou's work could profoundly change genetics. Zhou has been smuggled out of China and across Europe in defiance of the Chinese authorities. What wasn't in the papers, because it hadn't yet been planned, is the time and location of his arrival on US soil. Joint Base Andrews tonight at 2100 hours."

"What's he researching?" asked Devlin.

"Genetic editing. His work is far ahead of anyone else in the field."

"What kind of genetic editing?"

"That's what we're gonna find out when he lands, Father."

Paladino turned to Devlin. "They must be heading to Stratton."

Devlin frowned, then shook his head. "I know Stratton. It doesn't make sense. It's too fortified. They wouldn't stand a chance getting in and out. I don't think they can be headed there."

"Then what are they up to?"

"They must know something else. Something we don't." Devlin looked at Senator Lawton. "There's something else, isn't there? Something that wasn't in the papers."

"No. Nothing else. Nothing I can think of... Except..." Suddenly Lawton's eyes, as tired and sore as they were, lit up. "The other reason he decided to escape from China and come here. His family."

Devlin leaned forward. "Tell us about his family, Senator."

"His wife...estranged wife and his daughter. They

emigrated shortly after Zhou and his wife separated and haven't seen each other since. She works as an ER doctor."

"We'll need her address."

"I can't give you that."

"Okay. Fine." Devlin pulled out his cell, unlocked the screen, and handed it to the senator. "Then call the FBI and have them go after Zhou. But time is running out fast."

"It's us or the FBI, Senator. But make the decision quick."

There was a silence, and drops of light rain pitter-pattered against the window.

"Why are you so intent on doing this yourself? What's in it for you?"

"This is very personal to me," replied Paladino. "Andrei Gromyko killed my husband. A detective in Sag Harbor."

"Of course." Suddenly the penny dropped, and Lawton connected up the name with the news reports from a year ago. "You're Greg Paladino's wife...I should have realized when you were here before, when you told me your husband had died. I'm so sorry. I guess I was so caught up in my own problems I just didn't put it together. What happened to him was dreadful...evil."

"All I want is to make sure Andrei Gromyko pays for what he took from me."

"Where does Zhou's wife live?" asked Devlin.

"Trenton..." replied the senator, her eyes still fixed on Paladino. "Trenton, New Jersey. I'll get the exact address from my laptop."

After they had the address of Zhou's wife, they hardly bothered with goodbyes. But as Devlin left, the senator called out to him.

"Father, wait... You said there was a second thing you wanted me to do..."

"Yeah, there is. The second thing I'll tell you about when this is all over."

FIFTY

Could this be the Salvation Man? This fragile-looking individual? He was so slight that the next gust of wind might knock him over and so pale too.

Sergeant Cody was waiting on the sidewalk, watching Professor Feng Zhou as he said goodbye to his estranged wife and teenage daughter. Whatever had been said between them while they were in the house, it had ended in floods of tears.

Professor Zhou turned his back on his sobbing family and walked toward the marine. In Zhou's hand and clutched firmly by his side was the compact aluminum case he hadn't let out of his sight since he landed and what must, Sergeant Cody concluded, contain the great secrets that he had been smuggled into the US for.

"All done, sir?"

"Yes, Sergeant Cody. All done. You can take me to the debrief."

"If you don't mind my asking, what did you say to your wife and daughter?"

"I don't mind you asking. But I'd rather not say."

That was Professor Zhou all over, unfailingly polite and even-tempered. Cody had been looking after him for one day and couldn't help liking the old guy. The two of them returned to the vehicle where two other marines were waiting. Cody and Zhou got in the back, Zhou placing his aluminum case in his lap, and Cody gave the instruction to the privates in front to roll.

"So, what's on my itinerary now, Sergeant?"

"First, you'll do a debrief with various agencies: the State Department, Homeland, the CIA. To establish the nature and scope of your intelligence..."

"How long will that take?"

"That all depends on how much you know..." Cody stopped talking. He squinted across the professor and out of the window. Then he went nearly as pale as Zhou and muttered, "What the hell?"

Sudden bright blinding lights exploded onto the car. Then came the sound of an engine revving hard, and barely a second later a massive blow shuddered through the car, slamming it off the road. The car shunted violently against something solid like a tree or a wall and came to a crunching stop.

Carnage began to fill the car. The driver's head had been smashed against the wheel, and he slumped to the side, his head covered in blood. The engine revved again, and the bright lights retreated. Cody frantically tried to open the door when the window splintered, and he recoiled back into Zhou's lap, a black hole in his forehead. The back door was wrenched open, and Zhou was pulled out.

Zhou staggered out into the road, his side burning with pain but the aluminum case still clutched to his chest. He could stand and nothing felt definitely broken, but he was weak and unsteady on his feet. The warm, close night smelled of gunpowder, and he could see two figures silhouetted by headlights: a large square man with a bald head that looked like it had had a small bite taken out of it, and a slim man with fine hair that hung down to just above his collar. They were standing in front of a truck with fat tires and gleaming bull bars fitted to the front. A row of blazing bright halogen lamps had been added to the truck which, along with the truck's headlights, dazzled Zhou.

"Professor Zhou. You cannot imagine how honored I am to meet you at last."

"Who are you?" said Zhou, peering into the white wall of light.

"Oh, don't worry. I don't expect someone like you to know someone like me."

The larger of the two men came toward him. Zhou took a step back, and agonizing pain shot up his leg and his right side. The man grabbed him and pulled him across the street toward the truck. Zhou screamed as his body sent out pain alarms from multiple points. He was slung into the back seat and, imprisoned by invisible ropes of pain, felt the case being pried from his arms.

The door shut, locks snapped into place, and the engine started. Zhou's eyes were clamped shut, and his teeth gritted tight, letting only the occasional moan creep out. He heard a voice coming to him from the front of the car. Addressing him. But even if he was minded to reply, he wasn't able to.

In the front, Markham was at the wheel and Andrei was sitting beside him, holding the case on his lap.

"I'm looking forward to you telling us all about the work you've been doing," said Andrei. "The rumors we've heard about your research are mind-blowing. You should have a Nobel Prize and millions in the bank by now, Zhou. But I guess you were working for the people and the state, not for the glory."

Andrei gazed down at the aluminum case.

"Boy, I cannot wait to get this thing opened and have my best people look at it." Then he tilted the case on his lap to inspect it more closely. "A fingerprint scanner." Andrei turned to Markham. "Bad news, my friend. You won't need to torture the combination out of the professor."

FIFTY-ONE

When Paladino had to drive fast, she really drove, with fierce focus and controlled aggression. They went around the bottom of Brooklyn, through Staten Island and south on the 95, making it into Trenton in just over three hours. They pulled up outside the modest brick duplex and saw a light was still on downstairs. Devlin and Paladino both took a good up and down the street.

"What do you think?" asked Paladino. "Has Andrei been already?"

"With a head start and a chopper, I'd say that's pretty certain."

They headed up to the front door, and Devlin rang the bell. A moment passed in which there was no audible movement inside, as if whoever was at home was deciding whether to answer, and then the hall light came on followed by quick, socked footsteps on carpet. The door opened and a small woman appeared looking angry and anxious.

"I'm so sorry to disturb you, ma'am," said Paladino, flashing her badge. "We're trying to locate your husband, Professor Feng Zhou. We understand he may already have visited you?"

The woman's eyes darted back and forth between the two strangers.

"Yes," she said hesitantly. "He was here."

"When?" asked Paladino.

"Why are you looking for him?"

"We believe he may be in some danger. That there may be people trying to locate him for intelligence purposes."

"But he was with a soldier. He had protection."

"Ma'am," said Devlin. "The soldier with him may well have not known about this specific threat."

"That's why we're here," said Paladino. "When did he leave your house?"

"Not long...about twenty minutes ago."

"Do you know where they were going? What direction they headed off in?"

"No. No. I don't. What danger is he in?"

"As long as we find him, no danger," said Paladino. "And we're gonna find him."

Back in the car, Paladino sat silently at the wheel, and Devlin was pensive beside her.

"Where the hell would they have gone? We have no trail."

"No. We don't. So we're gonna have to take it one step at a time. This is a one-way street, right? Let's ride a block."

"Baby steps, I guess."

"Baby steps."

They rode to the end of a block and stopped.

"Now what?" said Paladino, scanning the empty street.

"I don't mean to be impolite, but I need some silence. Just let me think a minute."

"Right. It's the silent thing again. Like during the fire at the mansion."

Devlin clamped his hands on his lap and stared straight ahead, out of the windshield and like he was looking through the buildings that surrounded them with X-ray eyes. Time passed, and Paladino got edgy and impatient and was about to break the spell of silence when Devlin raised a hand and said, "Listen."

Paladino cocked her head a little and listened. There was a dog bark, the sounds of kids shouting.

"What?" she whispered

"Can you hear it?"

"What?"

"The siren."

Paladino listened harder and realized that Devlin was right. Dimly in the background, she could hear a faint whine of a cruiser.

"This is New Jersey. There's probably always a siren somewhere."

"It's all we've got. Drive toward it." Devlin pointed to the next junction ahead. "Take the next right turn."

Paladino did as Devlin instructed, following his occasional directions. As they drove, the priest's head was bowed in intense concentration, picking out the siren's sound and navigating them to the source like the noise was whale song and he was Captain Ahab himself. They drove for half a dozen blocks, zigzagging according to Devlin's guidance. The siren grew louder as they got closer, and then it stopped.

"What now?" said Paladino.

"What's that?"

Devlin was looking straight ahead, squinting into the distance, Paladino followed his gaze, and right at the end of the street she saw the glow of blue lights. She drove toward the lights, and as they got closer, she could see a group of uniformed police behind a tape stretching across the road.

"It looks like a crash."

"Drive up to the tape. Close as you can."

Paladino eased forward and came to a halt by a cop standing a few yards in front of the tape. The cop approached, and Paladino cracked open her window.

"You need to turn around, ma'am. No traffic allowed through."

"Sure, Officer. Will do. Sorry, professional curiosity got the better of me. I'm NYPD too." She showed her badge. "Been on vacation and heading back. Is it a traffic accident?"

"I wish," said the cop, letting his official demeanor slip a little now he knew he was in the company of another cop. "It's worse than that. It's a bloodbath. One car T-boned another car, and then they shot one of the occupants, a marine, and drove off."

"Jeez."

"Yeah. Damn mess."

"They found the guys who did it?"

"Got every unit out looking. Eyewitnesses say they headed toward East Trenton."

"Terrible. I hope you catch the sons of bitches."

"Me too... Me too."

"I'll keep an eye out."

"Thanks."

There was a shout from one of the cops by the crumpled vehicle, and the officer signaled for Paladino to turn it around. She complied and then headed back the way they had come.

"Well, I guess we better head out to East Trenton, then. But it all feels like one hell of a Hail Mary pass. Then again, I guess Hail Mary passes are your specialty."

FIFTY-TWO

Halfway along a deserted road lined with business parks and warehouses, Markham stopped the truck, a GMC Canyon, turned off the headlights, and jumped out. He jogged over to a chain-link fence that marked out the perimeter of a large brick warehouse and unlocked the gates, swinging them open to let Andrei drive the truck through. Then he shut the gates and followed the truck up to a wide steel door entrance. Sirens sounded nearby, and he hastily set about unlocking the steel door. There was a box on the wall which he opened with a key to reveal a keypad and another keyhole. Markham typed in a code, plugged in another key, and turned it, triggering the steel door to slide open. The truck drove into the warehouse, and Markham slipped in behind it. Then the door slid shut.

Inside, Andrei switched on the truck's headlights so Markham could find the light switches and turn them on. Banks of fluorescent lights hanging from a network of white metal struts crisscrossing the corrugated roof buzzed into life, illuminating a vast space filled with tall aisles of shelves stacked high with medical supplies.

Andrei killed the truck lights and ordered Zhou out of the

vehicle. Zhou staggered out onto the floor of the warehouse, looking washed-out and gaunt with dark circles around his eyes. Andrei told Markham to fetch three chairs. Markham got the chairs and placed them in the space between the parked truck and where the lines of shelves began. He pushed Zhou down into one of the chairs, handcuffed him to the chair leg, and he and Andrei sat in the other two chairs facing Zhou.

"Who are you?" asked Zhou.

"I'm Andrei Gromyko. CEO of BioGenesis. In fact"— Andrei spread out his arms—"this is one of our warehouse units. And I want what you've been working on, Professor Zhou. I want to know what it is our intelligence community wants so badly."

Andrei had been sitting with the aluminum case in his lap. Now he picked it up and held it in his hands like it was the Holy Grail. He stood and approached Zhou, and with the case in one hand, he grabbed Zhou's index finger and pressed it against the fingerprint lock. Lights embedded in the fingerprint scanner lit up with a UV glow, and the locks on the case unlatched. Andrei retreated to his chair and inspected the contents, unable to disguise his joy. Inside, the case was inlaid with blue velvet, and there were different bespoke compartments individually filled with half a dozen syringes, sealed vials containing a clear liquid, and rows of black capsules. The instruments inside the case were pristine, unmarked and unblemished, and glittered in the unnatural light.

"Now you will tell me everything. You will tell me the significance of what is in your case."

Zhou looked blankly back at Andrei and shook his head. "Never."

Markham rose and loomed over Zhou. He swung the side of his hand against Zhou's face, knocking him and his chair onto the floor.

"Get up," said Markham. "Get back in the chair."

With lights flashing in his eyes and the room spinning, Zhou got himself to his feet and pulled himself back into the chair. Markham sat down.

"You will tell me everything, Zhou," said Andrei.

"I don't care what your monster does to me. I won't tell you anything. Not a word."

"Oh, but you will. Because if you don't, I'll go back to Grand Street, take your wife and daughter to this warehouse, and torture them and kill them in front of you."

Andrei watched Zhou's face drop and the last flicker of defiance die. It was a moment to cherish, a moment of victory, but it was strangely soured by a shiver that went right through Andrei's body like he'd caught a sudden fever. And then his mouth filled with a bitter metallic flavor that turned his stomach and which he recognized immediately. It was the taste of the priest's blood.

FIFTY-THREE

Devlin held his left hand. Without any reason, his old wound had begun to ache like the devil. He tried to block out the throbbing pain and scanned the buildings on each side of the road as Paladino drove, but it was getting worse.

"I think we're lost, Devlin. We're just driving about blindly."

The priest didn't answer; he was staring down at his hand. The wound in the center of his palm had broken open, and drops of blood had risen to the surface. He wiped away the spots of fresh blood on his pants and examined his palm again. The bleeding seemed to subside, and the pain began to fade.

He looked out at the street they were driving through. It was a nothing street in a nothing neighborhood. They were passing a big warehouse that was part of an industrial estate. It was part of a long corridor of big anonymous buildings, low-rise and commercial with haulage trucks and vans parked outside. Occasionally the pattern was broken by an isolated block of apartments.

"You okay?" asked Paladino.

Devlin fisted his hand up. "Yeah. I'm fine."

THE SALVATION MAN   273

"I'll ride on to the top of this street and then back around."

It was midnight and warm. They were almost out of East Trenton now, heading toward the borough of Ewing.

"I'm gonna swing around and go back," said Paladino, pulling over. "Do another sweep."

She did a three-point turn and set off back the way they'd come, but both Paladino and Devlin were thinking the same thing: there was no trail, and they were on a fool's errand.

They traveled back through the same flat, forgettable landscape of small run-down industrial constructions. Paladino was getting increasingly twitchy and impatient, and frustration ate at Devlin too. And to make matters worse, his hand started to ache badly again. With his right hand, he grabbed his aching left hand and massaged it to alleviate the discomfort and realized the wound had begun to bleed again. Devlin looked out of the window and the building they were passing, a long brick warehouse, and had an extraordinary thought. This was where his wound had played up before, right on this stretch of road. As they carried on, the pain in his hand dulled and weakened.

"Stop," said Devlin.

"What?"

"Stop. Pull over. Now. We passed a warehouse. Andrei's in there."

"We passed a hundred warehouses."

"Drive back... Drive back the way we came..."

"But—"

"Please."

Paladino did what Devlin asked and turned and drove. She felt incredibly tense, and Devlin's whole vibe was spooking her. He was holding his wrist and scrutinizing the buildings they passed with an almost crazed intensity. She had never seen him like this, so possessed, so dark.

"Here," said Devlin. "Pull over here." He took out Mosley's gun from the glove compartment.

Paladino stopped the car, and before she could kill the engine, Devlin had jumped out and was walking away with the gun in his right hand and his left hand bunched into a fist. She got out of the car and followed him.

"Hey? What's going on?"

Devlin was a few yards in front of her. "He's in here. I know it. I can feel it."

He turned and put a finger against his lips, then carried on walking toward a warehouse surrounded by a chain-link fence. As he walked, the ache in his hand got worse and blood had started oozing out of his wound. But this time he understood why.

Devlin looked at the building he was standing in front of. It was a long rectangle, two stories high. On one side of it was a much smaller building with a sign on it advertising welding supplies, and on the other was a square vacant lot overgrown with shrubs. The building had no windows, but through the crack between the big steel doors and the concrete, he saw a thin strip of light bleeding out. He inspected the wide steel doors.

"Andrei is in there. I know he's in there. You have to trust me."

If it had been anyone other than Devlin, Paladino would have told them to take a running jump. But, after all they had been through, she had little trouble trusting Devlin. "Okay. What do we do now?"

"We don't knock on the front door, that's for sure. We find another way in. You go one way, I go the other. Let's meet round the back."

As Devlin answered he was already walking away from Paladino, skirting and checking the perimeter of the building. Paladino laid a hand on the reassuring bulk of her gun hanging by her side, the one she'd taken off the security guy in Sefton House which was slotted into a spare holster she'd had in her car. Then she set off in the opposite direction from Devlin, checking the warehouse for entry points.

Around the back of the building, Devlin found stacks of wooden pallets pushed up against the rear wall. He pulled the smallest stack, about a dozen pallets high, up against a taller stack. He climbed up onto the smaller stack and, using the top ledge of a window to get a footing, managed to push himself up onto the higher stack. There, standing a good thirty feet above the ground, he was face-to-face with one of the first-floor windows. It was a single-pane slider with an internal clasp. Devlin placed his hands on the glass and jiggled the window in its frame so the clasp on the inside moved up and down. At first, he could only move it fractionally, but as he moved the pane more firmly, the clasp began to slip out of place. Eventually, the clasp unlocked and the pane of glass came away from the frame. Devlin placed the glass by his feet and slipped in through the opening.

He found himself on a narrow steel gallery that was high up and ran around the inside of the warehouse. It was a couple of feet wide with steel tube railings and only a few feet below the lights that hung from the roof. He was level with the top of rows of high shelving units crammed with packaged supplies. And there were voices, the sound of men talking, coming from somewhere down below. He crept along the gallery toward the voices and saw three men seated in a triangle by the main entrance. Andrei and Markham were facing an older Asian man who Devlin knew must be Zhou. Devlin crouched low and listened.

FIFTY-FOUR

"First you will tell me all about your research," said Andrei. "Then after, we stay in the warehouse for the night. Tomorrow, when the heat has died down, we'll move you somewhere else."

"Where?"

"Somewhere remote, isolated. Where you and I can really spend some quality time together. Where we can reap the fruits of your work. I cannot wait. So, Professor, tell us what you have in your case...?"

Andrei paused. A wave of nausea passed over him again. Exactly the same as before, accompanied by a metallic tang in his mouth. The taste of blood.

"Are you okay?" Markham had noticed the color fade from his boss's face.

Andrei had suddenly become jumpy and anxious. He stood and looked around the warehouse and shouted, "Is someone there?"

Silence. No reply came. Instead, a gunshot rang out, and Andrei felt a breath of air touch his cheek. He even thought he heard the whizz of a bullet pass his ear.

From somewhere in the shadows that lay between the high, packed shelves came a voice.

"If you were a cat, you would have just lost a whisker."

Andrei touched his cheek in amazement. Both he and Markham, who had drawn his gun, peered anxiously into the gloomy aisles, looking for movement.

The voice, a woman's, came again, echoing around the high walls and vast space. "Put the gun down."

Markham looked at Andrei, and this time he felt a breath of air against his cheek as another gunshot rang out.

"Drop the gun. Now."

Andrei nodded at Markham, and the gun fell to the floor.

"Good boys. Now take five steps back."

Andrei and Markham did as they were ordered, backing up against the hood of their parked truck, and out of the shadows emerged Paladino holding a gun.

"You're the cop from Sag Harbor. What do you want?" asked Andrei.

"I'm here for the professor."

UP IN THE GALLERY, Devlin found a metal staircase that led down to a middle gallery and then to the floor of the warehouse. He raced down to join Paladino, who was holding Andrei and Markham at gunpoint. Paladino ordered Andrei to throw over the keys to Zhou's cuffs. He slung them over and smiled at Devlin.

"Of course, the priest. How the hell did you find us?"

Devlin held up his bloodied palm. "Because of you, Andrei. I think I was right; you and I are connected."

Before Andrei could reply, the steel door began to shake and slide open, revealing the night. Devlin and Paladino swung around toward the opening slab of steel to see who was coming.

Andrei used the distraction to reach into his pocket and thumb the remote key fob for his truck. Devlin and Paladino were momentarily blinded by the sudden glare of the truck's halogen lights flashing on. Seconds later came a deafening burst of automatic gunfire that exploded just above head height against the aisles' metal uprights and the plastic packaging along the shelves.

Andrei, Markham, Paladino, and Devlin flung themselves on the floor as rounds of gunfire peppered the inside of the warehouse, hitting concrete, steel, shattering plastic packaging and crates.

Devlin had gotten down on one knee and was partly protected by the angle of the truck, so had a much better position than the others. Through the dust and chaos, he could make out that the bullets were coming from one gun being fired from the parking lot, and it was coming closer. As the shooter neared, Devlin saw it was Mosley, firing an automatic rifle and grinning his lopsided grin.

Under the rain of bullets, Andrei had grabbed the metal case and got into the truck.

"Paladino!" Devlin yelled. "Look after Zhou."

Paladino, also pinned down by Mosley's fire, acknowledged Devlin's order but could do little to heed it. Devlin crawled forward to get to the truck.

The truck, driven by Andrei, backed up, and Mosley had stopped firing and was piling into the back seat. Markham chased the truck as it turned, but just as he got a hand on the door handle, he felt a sting of hard pain in his calf and stumbled and fell. Down on the ground, Markham saw that his calf had been nicked by a bullet.

"Son of a bitch..." he snarled and saw Devlin advancing toward him, gun in hand.

"Get up," shouted Devlin, his gun aimed at Markham's

disfigured head. But before he could force Markham to get up, the truck came squealing back. Andrei was at the wheel and driving it right at Devlin, bright headlights glaring and bull bars gleaming.

Devlin reeled back, sprawling onto the concrete floor, his gun flying into the shadows of the warehouse. Markham stumbled onto his good foot and made for the truck again.

"Stop, you son of a bitch," screamed Paladino, and she let off a shot.

Undeterred, Markham ran after the truck as it reversed again. But Devlin was determined to stop him. Even if Andrei and Mosley got away, he'd catch Vijay's killer. He lunged at Markham, throwing him onto the ground. The truck carried on reversing, and Paladino kept firing at it, forcing Andrei to keep backing up until he gave in, turned the truck away from Paladino's fire, and squealed off into the night, making his and Andrei's escape.

Paladino had run out of ammo and had no other cartridges. Zhou was still slumped and by the looks of things unconscious, cuffed to the same chair he'd been in since he'd arrived.

Paladino's loyalties were split between Devlin and Zhou out cold in the chair. But those things had to be put aside for the one thing she cared about: avenging her husband's death. She ran out of the warehouse and got into her car and, seeing the truck in the distance, headed off after it.

Devlin and Markham stood face-to-face, framed by the open warehouse door.

"You murdered my friend," said Devlin. "Now I'm going to make that right."

"Be my guest," Markham rasped.

The two men moved toward each other and then circled. Markham was the first to make a move, a step forward and swipe that Devlin ducked. Under the arc of Markham's swing,

Devlin landed a punch right in Markham's gut. The bigger man, winded and stung, wheeled back, his temper breaking into a fury, and came down on Devlin with fists like two moons. The first strike sent Devlin sprawling sideways, barely managing to keep his balance. The second flattened him. Markham stood over Devlin's prostrate body and planted his boot, splattered in rivulets of blood from his flesh wound, into Devlin's stomach. Devlin's whole body convulsed with the force of the blow, and he grabbed at Markham's leg like it was a spear in his stomach. Markham leaned down, grabbed Devlin's hair, and yanked the priest's face up to force him to behold his tormentor.

"You are nothing to me," bellowed Markham. "I killed your pervert friend, and now I'm gonna kill you."

He removed his foot from Devlin's midriff and lifted the priest up by the collar virtually one-handed, holding Devlin eye to eye.

Markham snorted. "This is too goddamn easy..."

Then the priest smiled.

"Why are you smiling, you fool?"

Markham's words trailed off, his legs weakened, and his energy started to seep away. His stomach was suddenly warm. A peculiarly sharp trickle of pain started to bleed up and down his body, like a crack in his being was opening up. Devlin pried himself out of Markham's weakening grip, and Markham looked down to see the thing he'd feared. His push dagger had been removed from its ankle strap and was planted in his chest, Devlin's hand still wrapped around the handle.

Quietly, almost prayerfully, Markham whispered, "No..." He collapsed in one movement as first gravity and then death claimed him.

FIFTY-FIVE

Devlin surveyed the carnage and looked over at Zhou, who was slumped in the chair with his chin resting on his chest. He spotted the keys to the handcuffs, lying where Andrei had thrown them, picked them up, and went over to uncuff the professor.

"Professor? Professor Zhou?"

Zhou looked at Devlin with wide eyes, then looked around the warehouse wearily. "Get me out of here." He stood with some effort. "Take me somewhere else. Somewhere safe. Before the authorities arrive. I need just a little time. Just a little time."

"What about the case? The case that contained your research?"

Zhou laughed. "The case isn't my research."

"Then what...?" Suddenly Devlin understood. "You're the research, aren't you? You really are the Salvation Man."

Zhou nodded and put a hand on Devlin's shoulder. "Let's go. And I'll tell you everything you need to know. And what I need from you."

FIFTY-SIX

Paladino managed to close in on Andrei's truck. Her heartbeat was racing faster than the car engine, and with Andrei's truck in her sights, she decided her next move would be to get up alongside it. To ram it. To do whatever it took to take the man who was responsible for her husband's murder off the road. But that all changed when she saw, a mile or so up ahead, a halo of blue and heard the scream of sirens coming the other way.

Andrei's truck began to slow as he realized the way ahead was impassable. The wall of cop cars was coming closer and growing larger.

He was trapped. Cop cars in front, Paladino behind.

The truck came to a stop.

The sirens grew louder.

Paladino stopped about three hundred yards behind Andrei, grabbed a magazine from her glove compartment, and got out of her car.

Then she heard Andrei's engine start up, and he swung his truck around, facing away from the police cars and toward Paladino, and he began to pick up speed. Calmly and methodically Paladino unholstered her gun, loaded it, and leveled it at the oncoming truck.

In the distance, some way behind the truck, what seemed like a hundred cop cars were descending at speed.

The truck was getting close now. Paladino could see Andrei's face behind the wheel and Mosley beside him. They were heading right for her, the revs of the engine climbing.

"This time I saw you coming," whispered Paladino. "This time I'm gonna stop you. This is for my husband." With only forty yards between her and the looming truck and with a supernatural calm, she let off all the rounds in her cartridge, putting them all into the cab of the truck.

With ten yards to go, the truck suddenly lost control, swerving and tipping, then rolling and sliding till it came to a rest five yards in front of Paladino.

Then the cop cars arrived.

FIFTY-SEVEN

Devlin and Zhou walked for three or four blocks, away from the commercial low-rise buildings, and found an all-night diner. As they walked, Zhou asked Devlin questions. Who he was and what he did. When he found out that Devlin was a priest, Zhou smiled broadly and looked deeply satisfied. It seemed to comfort him. The professor still looked wan and ill, but his spirits had revived somewhat.

Inside the diner, it was quiet with what looked like few truckers and shift workers separately dotted around the tables. The two men were seated quickly and handed cups of coffee by the waitress. Through the blinds Devlin saw it had started to rain lightly, pebbling the windows and distorting the car head-lights that passed outside.

"The risk you took leaving your country, coming halfway across the world with stolen secrets... It was all to see your family?"

The professor looked at his untouched coffee and then gazed out onto the highway. He thought for a moment and then stared with an unsettling directness at Devlin.

"Yes. But there are other factors too. And to explain fully, I need to tell you something about me. Who I am and what I have done and how those two things have become one. I have spent the last twenty years working in the field of genetic editing. Editing the human chromosome using pioneering CRISPR technology. During the last five years, I perfected a technique for modifying a particular aspect of the human genome. The ability to fight disease. Shamefully, I was made to perform trials on humans: political prisoners, people accused of spying, and who were kept in a detention center not far from the lab. But I could not stomach it or live with what I was doing. So I began to administer placebos to the inmates and the real trials to myself. I faked all the results except for my own. And the results of the experiments on myself were incredibly promising. To the point that I had achieved what I had set out to accomplish, astonishing results."

"What was the aim of the research?"

"To make the human genome immune to Nidovirales."

"I'm afraid the medical training I had was a while ago."

"Nidovirales is an order of viruses that infects animal and human hosts. It includes SARS, MERS, and coronavirus. I've genetically edited some of my white blood cells to create potent antibodies and T-cells that are able to fight this order of pathogen."

Devlin put his mug down and stared at Zhou in astonishment. "You're immune to it?"

Zhou nodded.

"That's incredible. That would mean an end to the threat of all flu pandemics, the search for new vaccines every year. It would save millions of lives. That's a historic achievement."

Zhou looked down at the table, almost embarrassed.

"Yes, it would. But, alas, there's one small drawback with the research I did on myself."

"What?"

"It's killing me."

There was a moment of silence. The rain continued to patter on the glass, and a truck whooshed by outside.

"That is a drawback," said Devlin.

Zhou smiled. "My genome, or at least the section I edited, is unstable. I am dying. Fast. There is still value to be had from my research. Once I'm dead, a team of suitably brilliant scientists will be able to study my body and try to improve on what I have done. To maybe find a way of doing what I've done without the fatal side effects. So all is not lost by any means. But I needed to get out of my country before I died. To see my family, as you said, and to make sure my discovery was shared with the world. And, I think, to meet you too."

"Me? Why?"

Zhou's answer was cut off by a sudden coughing attack. The convulsions shook his body, and when they finally stopped, he wiped away a small drop of blood from his lip. He studied the red mark on the back of his hand and shivered.

"How long do you have?" asked Devlin.

"Hours. Maybe less."

"Hours?"

"The aluminum case that Andrei took from me was actually very important but only to me. It was the medication to keep me alive. It wouldn't have lasted much longer anyway. It was only meant to sustain me for a short amount of time. I didn't tell the US authorities about the...flaw in my research because I feared it might weaken my potential bargaining power. But now my life support is gone, I don't mind so much. I don't mind because I've found you."

Zhou looked at his image in the rain-swept window.

"I'm dying," he said. "It's close now. So close I feel I am not in this world really anymore." Zhou looked back at Devlin. "You know, I didn't use to believe in ghosts, but perhaps I misunderstood what the word could mean. Because I believe that I am like a ghost." He paused again as if searching for a thought that had escaped him; then he seemed to find it and continued. "The last five years of my life, my body became my own scientific experiment. Something I took apart and put back together again, that I meddled and tinkered with. When the US government finally gets to me, I'll be dead and they'll want to investigate my body again, for the last time. Dissect me and scrutinize me. I'm tired of being a laboratory rat. I feel like I've erased my own humanity, my soul. And now I'm about to cross the great border, from this world to the next, I want someone...I need someone...someone with the gift of spirituality and belief to carry me over. That person is you. You are my ferryman. Please stay with me. Be with me when I die. Please, Father."

"Of course."

As they drank their coffees and talked, Devlin could see Zhou getting weaker. The burst of energy he'd had when they were at the warehouse had gone completely. Eventually, Zhou clasped Devlin's hand.

"It's near. I can feel it. Can we walk? Go outside? I want to be outside. In the air. Beneath the stars."

They left the diner. Zhou now needed Devlin's assistance to move. He leaned into him, putting his weight onto Devlin's frame, and they walked slowly into a small concrete lot next to the diner. Bolted to the railing at the entrance was a sign for a flea market, and inside the enclosure were run-down empty stalls. Devlin and Zhou found a bench farther back from the road where they could sit and watch the traffic.

Zhou was deteriorating fast. His face was haggard, and his breaths were labored. So it surprised Devlin when the professor turned to him and smiled.

"We were meant to meet," said Zhou. "I believe it is destiny.

So that you could help me travel from this world to the next... and I could give you something in return."

"What?"

Zhou's eyes seemed to glitter, and despite his worsening condition, he smiled. "Freedom." His eyes had become wide and intense, focused on Devlin to the exclusion of everything else. "I think you're looking for some kind of freedom, and you will get it. Not now. Not tonight, I'm afraid." Zhou placed a hand on Devlin's sleeve. "But I have a certain feeling that someday you will find someone who will know how to free you."

Devlin felt a hope burst back into life in his chest that he hadn't even known he'd lost. "Thank you."

The rain had stopped, and the cloud cover had broken up so that the two men could see the universe above.

Zhou held Devlin's hand. His breaths were so weak it made Devlin think each one might be his last.

"Would you like me to give you last rites?" asked Devlin.

"Yes."

Devlin obliged, and after rites were administered, Zhou said, "Should I be scared?"

"No," replied Devlin. "You shouldn't. But you will be anyway."

Zhou smiled. "Where will I be going?"

"To a peace you will have never known of before or imagined possible."

"Will you do me one more favor?"

"Of course."

"Visit my wife and daughter. Let them know I was thinking of them and only them when I went."

"I will."

"Thank you. You have given me the thing I needed. A safe passage."

That was the last thing Zhou said. He lived on for a few

more minutes, and his head lolled a little and Devlin put his arm around him. He let the professor's slight body sink into his embrace, and with great effort, Zhou glanced up at the stars for one last time. Seconds later he gave a weak cough, and his chest stopped rising and falling.

Suddenly it was peaceful. More peaceful than Devlin had ever remembered the world being.

Devlin sat for a while holding Zhou, thinking about his wife, about the man who murdered her, about the path he had bound himself to, and he noticed a peculiar thing—the pain in his left palm had disappeared, and Devlin saw that the red wound had gone, completely healed over.

The sky lightened and the sun peeped over the horizon, and Devlin's cell buzzed. It was Paladino.

"You okay?" asked Devlin.

"I'm fine. Andrei and his goon are dead. Where are you?"

"I'm with Professor Zhou at a diner called the Wayside. It's about fifteen minutes from Andrei's warehouse." Devlin looked up into the sky and saw three helicopters approaching. "And I think we've got company," said Devlin.

"Yeah. I think you'll find you're gonna have every law enforcement agency in the land coming to join you."

EPILOGUE

"The Second Thing"

TWO WEEKS after the girl went back to live with her mom and stepdad in Brownsville, it started to turn bad. She always knew it would be a matter of days before her mom couldn't take it anymore and would throw her out. To be fair to her mom, she was just stuck in the middle. The girl hated her stepdad, and her stepdad hated her. The girl didn't really blame her mom for having to choose. She was forced to.

Then the letter arrived.

It was from a lawyer's office in Manhattan that had about seven names in its title. It was typed on fancy paper with a fancy heading. The letter said she had been selected for an endowment by an educational charity set up by a senator called Helen Lawton. The letter said she was to arrange a time to attend the lawyer's office at her own convenience. The girl didn't know how they knew where she was living, but in her experience, rich people, especially lawyers, always knew how to track poor people down. Especially if they were owed money.

So, one bright day in early August, she went to the office and had a big fancy meeting with big fancy lawyers. She was given a cup of coffee she didn't touch but took because it was free. She was treated very courteously and told that she had been selected by Senator Helen Lawton as the recipient for a bursary to cover her education up to any level she wished. She would also receive, as long as she was in education, all rent, living expenses, and medical care within reason.

They asked if she had any questions.

She did, but she said no anyway.

She was told that if she did have questions, she had been allocated a lawyer at the firm who would look after her endowment and be available free of charge for any advice she needed.

She thanked the lawyers and left.

On the steps of the law firm's building, she saw it was a beautiful day.

And then, across the road, sitting on the bench, she saw the priest.

She crossed the road and approached him.

She said, "Are you following me?"

AFTERWORD

If you've enjoyed The Salvation Man please subscribe to my
newsletter for latest news and updates...

http://eepurl.com/gdVyyX

There's a third in the series coming soon!

Best,

James.